PRICE FROZE IN MIDSTRIDE, TURNING TO FACE BROGNOLA

"One look at you," he said, "and something tells me we have major problems."

The mission controller nodded. "The A-team of microbiologists from the CDC was flown to Ford Detrick to analyze the contents of the cylinder. I didn't tell you earlier, since I was holding out some hope."

"The Center for Disease Control?" the big Fed said, and was almost afraid to push any further for an explanation.

"I just received a full report from sources of mine at the CDC and Detrick." She stared Brognola dead in the eye. "Hal, this is something beyond worst-case scenario. In fact, I wish what they had found on the *Napoleon* was as simple as suitcase nukes."

Brognola felt his stomach churn. Fanatics had access to bioweapons—and the perfect delivery system.

DON PENDLETON'S

STONY

AMERICA'S ULTRA-COVERT INTELLIGENCE AGENCY

MAN®

AXIS OF
CONFLICT

the
TERROR
file
Book 1

®

A GOLD EAGLE BOOK FROM
WORLDWIDE®

TORONTO • NEW YORK • LONDON
AMSTERDAM • PARIS • SYDNEY • HAMBURG
STOCKHOLM • ATHENS • TOKYO • MILAN
MADRID • WARSAW • BUDAPEST • AUCKLAND

First edition August 2003

ISBN 0-373-61950-2

AXIS OF CONFLICT

Special thanks and acknowledgment to
Dan Schmidt for his contribution to this work.

AXIS OF CONFLICT

CHAPTER ONE

The end was coming, and he knew it was coming soon. Call it bringing justice to jihad killers, but one way or another, Ben Colder suspected someone wouldn't live out the next few hours. That was fine by him, as along as the right—or wrong people— were eighty-sixed to join in hell their brothers-in-blood who had long since been pounded to pulp in Afghanistan. For years the jihad bastards who perpetrated unspeakable and cowardly acts of mass murder had seized the upper hand, holding the reins of terror simply because intelligence gathering was once viewed by too many in Washington as just this side of Gestapo tactics, performed by overzealous operatives with more bloodlust than good sense or the first degree of concern for diplomatic relations.

Yesterday no longer existed. In some sad and sorry way that suited him, but it was a shame nonetheless that it had taken the deaths of countless innocents to land the good guys on a level playing field. It was a brave new world out there, he knew, where the guardians of freedom and democracy could act out the bloodiest revenge fantasies of outraged Americans.

Funny how times changed. For instance, after years of being handcuffed by budget restraints and hand-wringing politicians, HUMINT, COMINT and SIG-INT, from the CIA, FBI, and NSA on through to Interpol, were working overtime three days after the attack on New York a couple of years ago. Backed by tragedy, the wrathful masses and a ballsy Oval Office, the full weight of American military and intelligence operatives, covert and overt, was rolling over adversarial and fanatical Islam, a tidal wave of retribution that would see no end in sight until the scourge was obliterated off the face of the earth, down to the last AK-47-toting jihad fanatic hiding in the jungles of Indonesia. The gloves were off, and there was nowhere left on the planet for the butchers of the innocent to hide, no cave deep enough, no jungle thick enough.

It should have been this way years ago, he thought. The good guys were long since overdue to stick it to the stickers, deliver rough swift justice to the unjust.

Through the one-way glass panes, fixed by adhesive tabs to the window of the Company safehouse, a suite in the Hotel Drjic, he should have felt secure enough from watching eyes, all but invisible to their quarry. Only he had worked deep cover long enough for the CIA to trust bad instincts when they began flaring from scalp to toe like a string of firecrackers. Right then, every combat sense honed under fire from Somalia to Manila warned him the watchers were made, the pack of terrorist hyenas lurking somewhere, prepared to pounce.

No problem; this black op from the Company's new Special Tracking and Investigation Division— STID—had a job to do, and do it he would, especially since a few months back the jackals had provided him motivation in the form of vengeance for those comrades captured and tortured to death in Sudan. Not only butchered them, he recalled, but the murdering bastards had recorded the sessions on video and left the tapes behind, as if tickled to brag about their ghoulish feat to the infidels.

He would find the rotten SOBs and return the favor in bloody spades.

So he watched the drab white block-shaped buildings, specifically eyeballing the curtained third-story window of the apartment in question. It was a good day, he thought, to stalk and slay, the weather alone providing ample cover to creep up on some bad guy's six. The sprawling village of Drjic and the forested hills beyond were hunkered beneath an umbrella of fog while being slicked by freezing drizzle. Not much by way of traffic, either vehicular or human. By now villagers and tourists alike were all but driven by Mother Nature to shelter in a dozen or so *kavanas*— cafés—where the party crowds whiled away the afternoon over brandy and cognac.

The world could play, but Colder had deadly serious work to do. Unfortunately, they were on the time clock of Tiger Force 12, with Colder waiting for word at Camp Bulldog along the Bosnian border. If something didn't break soon, he and his partner would have to suit up in rain slickers, lugging cameras and camcorders and notebooks around the village proper and beyond, keeping up the ruse as photojournalists for *National Geographic*.

Colder sat, watching and waiting, hoping the targets would head out for whatever their final destination. Whatever the rendezvous was all about, it was believed by the head shed a deal was on the table involving a massive weapons cache in the countryside—only initial and sketchy intel from spooks above him hinted at some special cargo in the neighborhood, smuggled in with a little help from known war criminals. He assessed the numbers, the situation as well he understood it. Known Taliban and al-Qaeda goons, four in all, had been pinned down by American intelligence and tracked here to Drjic.

The group was headed up by a mullah known as Haroon Kanbar, top lieutenant and personal hangman for the one-eyed mullah of Kandahar infamy. HUMINT, AWACS and other eyes in the sky had monitored their boat ride from Egypt, four days earlier, where they sailed to an Adriatic island before a fishing trawler dumped them off in the port city of Split. From there, it grew even more sordid and ominous, with Colder, his partner and the hunter-killer team whisked in-country before the targets came ashore. But he knew ahead of time he was being marched into a part of the world where the brutal and the criminal still ruled. He'd been around too long to be surprised by much. Still, the truth was, the name of this country alone conjured up a host of bizarre and savage images, among flights of fancy that wormed into his thoughts the longer he rode out this surveillance and boredom settled in.

Croatia.

The small country, shaped like a boomerang with a rugged, foreboding interior, was a known refuge for Serb and Croatian war criminals in hiding from The Hague. Forty-odd war criminals still traipsed around Bosnia and Croatia, often seen by the FBI sipping cognac and cozying up to the Russian Mafia in Zagreb and Belgrade, with another thirty-plus sealed indictments The Hague didn't seem too anxious to deliver. Two of those Serb butchers had seen fit to accommodate four Muslims they hadn't that long ago attempted to rid their land of. Colder knew. He'd seen them pull up in their Mercedes limo, not twenty minutes after the terror foursome arrived and began chattering over their sat phone.

Aware this was a land rife with ages-old ethnic hatreds, religious intolerance for the other guy, knowing they were still finding mass graves, he drew his thoughts back to the task at hand. He felt his hand inching up toward the shoulder-holstered SIG-Sauer, a clip of nine .45 ACP rounds in hollowpoint up the snout, good to go to blast gaping fatal holes in the opposition, war criminal or Muslim scumbag, it was a coin flip as far as he was concerned. Once again, his mind began to wander back to those videos, when his partner spoke.

"Hear that? They keep switching from Arabic to Pakhtun…"

He turned in his chair, found Jack Weller hunched

over the trio of consoles in the shadowy cavern of the suite. He looked at the near childlike glee in the eyes behind the glasses. The balding, scrubby-pink-clean Weller, on loan from the NSA, was alternately tapping the three sets of keyboards. He struck Colder as more suited to a desk job than the shadow world of spookdom, where guns blazed and treachery and betrayal were the rule and not the exception. The man loved his high-tech toys, no doubt, glued to the monitors for hours on end, addicted, it seemed, making Colder wish to God the head shed had glued to his hip a little rougher breed of op. But the state-of-the-art Omni Tracker, squirreled away in a floor vault before their arrival, was, Colder had to admit, something to marvel at. The triangulation of listening, tracking and deciphering was hooked in to an NRO satellite parked over this part of the world, which, in turn, fed intel at light speed to a roving AWACS, three-way intel pinging back and forth to keep all hands in the hunt, bouncing data to the CIA station chief in Belgrade, back to Langley. Parabolic laser sensors from the AWACS could even penetrate walls, or so Weller claimed. So far, Colder hadn't seen it, and the only time they had intercepted conversations was courtesy of Omni cutting into cell and sat phone transmissions.

Weller was grinning, he saw, all lit up, Santa in cyberspace. "These guys think they're slick."

"Yeah, tell me about it. Assholes can shave off their beards, throw away the turbans, grease some Pakistani flunkies and have some Doctor Frankenstein change their faces, but they're stuffed and buffed in about three shakes.''

Colder saw Weller throw him a curious look, then the NSA loaner nodded. He didn't get it, but Colder let him play Super Spy. ''You're right, they're no match for a supercomputer that's as close to God as I've ever seen... Hold on...I have the same one on the sat phone again. I'm tracking the transmission...voiceprint reading now. Come on, baby,'' Weller urged the monitor, headset on, staring as the words scrolled at light speed, screen winking when language was converted to English. ''Give me...'' Weller froze, twisting in his chair, said, ''It's a match, one hundred percent verification. It's Kanbar. They say they're leaving in five minutes.''

Colder was up and moving, Weller looking alarmed as he grabbed a camera and camcorder. ''Shut it down, my friend. We're out of here.''

''Wait a second. The order was to alert—''

''Hey!'' Colder stepped up to Weller, shoving the props at the NSA man, who reluctantly took them. ''This is my show. When I know where they're going I'll call it in. And don't make me repeat myself.''

''I don't understand....''

Colder let the guy bleat on about chain of command, standing orders, bucking protocol, but he was grabbing up his large duffel bag, the one with the MP-5 subgun, complete with spare clips, grenades, delivered courtesy of diplomatic pouch from Belgrade. The Duane Dieter CQB blade was already sheathed in an ankle holster, and Colder had been fantasizing for several days about using it on one of the targets. "You don't have to understand, Weller. You don't even have to like it, just do it."

"But, I should at least stow this—"

"Stuff that noise. No time to pack it up." When Weller hesitated, Colder pinned him with an angry stare. "Do I need to remind you what these bastards did? Do I need to tell you that Culler and Baldwin were not only men I worked with, but were the best damn friends a man could ever have, and who left behind wives and children and who were lied to about the circumstances they died under, just to spare them the horror?"

Now Weller got it. "I've seen the videos...."

"Right out of Scarface, pal. You ever see that movie?"

"I don't believe so."

"They strung them up in chains, Weller, buck naked. The big rat bastard, remember, offscreen, chuckling."

"The so-called Sword of Islam."

"Bragging about the big events to come in the name of Allah while they used a blowtorch on two stand-up Americans fighting to defend their country. Burned off their nads for starters."

"Please, you needn't—"

"Stuff your please. They used bolt cutters to snip off their toes next, then took a chain saw, working their way up from their feet, using torniquets, ice-water showers and morphine to keep them alive while they dissected them. I see I have your attention. I see you understand now.''

"This can't be about vengeance."

"The hell you say."

"We need them alive for interrogation. We need to know why four Muslim extremists are suddenly in Croatia, given a guided tour by Serbian war criminals.''

Colder flew back to the window, cursed when he saw two of the four terror mongers standing beside their BMW, throwing around paranoid looks, ready to bail. "That's exactly what we'll do." He whirled, on the move, nodded at the camcorder in Weller's hand. "We'll even film the Q and A, Scarface Part Two. If you don't have the stomach for that kind of action, you can stay but I'll shoot up your precious Omni first."

Weller shook his head. "Sounds like I don't—"

"Right, you don't have a choice. Here," he barked, snatching the second nylon bag off the floor and tossing it at Weller. "This one's for you."

BELOC ZHARJIC WAS in the process of making certain he never saw The Hague. Rumor had floated his way the past month, thanks to his Russian comrades, that a sealed indictment was going to be dumped in his lap any day now by some UN Peacekeeper. They may or not hang Slobodan, but Zharjic had no intention of finding himself in the hangman's noose simply because he had followed orders, filling up mass graves with thousands of Muslim and Croat bodies before the Americans began bombing Belgrade off the Balkan map. The fact that his soldiers had raped, pillaged and burned entire villages had never caused him to lose sleep, since he knew Bosnian Muslims had proved over the years they could have given marauding Turks a lesson in barbarity. An eye for an eye, he believed, only worked if two eyes were plucked out. However, he was aware his new comrades knew the sins of his past, and that gave him cause for concern. Thing was, they were on the run, in hiding, and looking to carry on personal agendas as much as he was, not to mention money talked and grudges walked. The world these days, he thought, was making for strange bedfellows all over the globe. Everyone wanted more weapons, bigger weapons to seize the upper hand of Armageddon, and he faulted, like the Arabs, one country for that. He chalked up this new alliance to one simple fact, all hearts pumping in rhythm to a dance of hate and vengeance. They both despised the Americans. Just as the Arabs wished to see the infidels driven out of their respective countries, he was longing for the day when he could return from exile—wherever he was going—and claim the Balkans as his kingdom.

The problem now was slipping out of the country, in tow with four of the world's most infamous faces, while being dogged by the CIA. The road out was paved already, the scheme erected during many deals cut in the shadows from Belgrade to the Sudan to Moscow, and it was too late to ponder failure. He didn't need to know all the facts; he just needed to run.

Sitting on the divan, Zharjic sipped his cognac while the two standing Arabs zipped about the living room, the mullah, his man of the hour, on the sat phone again with cronies already slipped in-country by homegrown Croatian and Bosnian brothers in jihad. Two of the mullah's brothers had already bolted out the door, in flight now with standing orders. It was the man with the American Army camouflage jacket who concerned him the most. Tajib had vanished with a duffel bag into the bathroom for fifteen minutes when they had first entered. He had returned, sans bag, but bulked up beneath the jacket as if a magic massive dose of steroids had transformed him into some Arab Arnold Schwarzenegger. The new Tajib made sense, actually, Zharjic knowing how the Arabs performed when the American sharks were circling, blood in their nose. He was grateful, just the same, that Burprija and Vojvod, executioners once under his command, were stuck to his side, ready to go to the mat if something went wrong. Beneath all three of their black leather trench coats they had Russian machine pistols stowed in special shoulder rigging.

Ah, but there would be trouble soon before the light shone again. It seemed to the former Serb colonel that he had been down this dark and lonely road before. A hunted animal, but again like the Arabs, if he was cornered, he would go out with a roar, die on his feet.

He scanned the angry and once notorious but now

transformed face as the mullah reached for the pager fixed to his belt. No beeping, it was a vibrating signal, alerting him the American operatives were on the move. The plastic surgeon, Zharjic noted, pouring one last glass of cognac, had done a remarkable job on the mullah, now a major operative for the Omani, who was the so-called Sword of Islam. Nose job, chin implants, colored eye contacts, no beard, hair closely cropped—Zharjic knew the drill personally. He had been under the knife himself, shaving his head finally while sprouting a goatee.

"It is time," Kanbar announced. "Your man at the desk came through," he said, dropping the trench coat back in place.

"Was there ever any doubt?"

Kanbar grunted. "If there was, you would be the first to know. One matter I need to address, as I sense you are having reservations."

"I heard. You intend to take one of them alive. I suppose my objection would fall on deaf ears."

"You have been paid to aid and assist, here and beyond. Trust me, you will be protected until my men can deliver you safely inside Russia, as God is my witness and my savior."

"If what I believe you have in mind will happen, you will need more than God to save you."

Zharjic rose, killing his drink, jerked his head for his bodyguards to move out, then saw the dark look shadowing the mullah's face.

Kanbar smiled then his expression hardened. "We have come this far together…keep the faith."

THE MOMENT FELT all screwed up, a ticking hand grenade in his belly warning him it was about to hit the fan, a hurricane of feces set to blow him all the way across the River Styx. First, the two Arabs had vanished out front. Colder checked the street, no sign of terrorist life, though, heightening his alert for coming doom and gloom. Mystery number one.

Nearly as nervous now as Weller, who looked set to grow cold feet and race back for the safety of Omni, visions of the swarthy deskman leaped to his mind's eye. Briefly he recalled the curt nod, the hinky look in the eyes, the forced grin, as the lobby jockey watched them vacate the hotel over the top of his newspaper. Number two puzzle, the guy hoarding secret knowledge of a setup in the works?

Too late to return to the warm cocoon of their room now, Colder was striking out on his own, bulling ahead, sure he was destined for a major dressing down by the head shed, just the same. If he could pull off a snatch, say, grab up one prisoner, he was certain his sin of insubordination would be forgiven in light of success. Better still, if he could snap up the mullah, threaten to hoist his severed head on a pike, he was sure the cleric would squeal, point the way to their vaunted leader, this Sword of Islam.

At least that was the plan.

He plunged into the fog, hood up, as the drizzle gathered sudden strength, slashing off his face, forcing his gaze to a narrow slit. The mist was so thick that he couldn't see more than four feet in any direction, the redbrick buildings towering above him making him feel pinned in the narrow alley. He checked the rear, wondering if that was a shadow in the fog, then heard Weller bleating, distracting him.

"This isn't good. I have to ask you reconsider...."

Colder was facing front, baring his teeth as Weller reached their Volkswagen van first, when one of his two worst fears was realized.

The first round plowed into the nylon hood, flinging Weller face first into the shotgun door with such force the van rocked, the NSA man wilting like vaporized metal, leaving no doubt he was rubber-bag material. Colder pivoted, cursing the fact he was zipped up, clawing to tug down the zipper when shots two and three cracked, splitting the mist, invisible lances of doom. He lost track next of how many more rounds tore into him, since he was down and thrashing, on fire from head to toe, feeling the warm stickiness flowing down his legs. As he watched the dark wraiths rolling his way out of the fog, he became aware they had shot to cripple.

Worst fear number two slapped him next. They wanted a prisoner.

Colder would be damned before that happened, willing his ruined arm somehow to try to pull the commando blade, but he was in too much pain and way too slow. The boot shot out of nowhere, clocked him in the jaw and doused the lights.

DEAN HARKER DIDN'T know what to make of Colder not checking in as ordered. Waiting for the sat phone to ring, the CIA special op found himself scowling at the bank of monitors in the command and control center of Camp Bulldog, a belly full of AFU—All Fouled Up—churning away. He knew the mullah had made the rendezvous, same apartment that two other known al-Qaeda operatives had visited with the Serb war criminal three months back. A wish list of ''should haves'' ground the anger deeper into his gut. Croatia seemed to have become a layover point for those al-Qaeda and Taliban goons who had long since fled Afghanistan, leaving him to ponder why a Serb war criminal with known ties to the Russian Mafia was sleeping with the kind of people he had once done his damnedest to eradicate through ethnic cleansing. Should have grabbed up the two terrorists when they were first sighted, he thought, snatch Beloc the Butcher, too, and strung him up by his testicles until the answers came squealing forth. Should have gone in right away with the black ops of Tiger Force two hours ago, damn the standing order to get to the bottom of this bizarre alliance, follow the scumbags to whatever their rainbow at the end of the line. Should have—

Stow it. Whatever was happening, if anything, could only be proved if he was out there in the field. Silence from his surveillance duo only wanted to inflame his imagination with all manner of dire scenarios, expanding the wish list of should haves.

He glared at the sat link, considered raising his surveillance team, then found himself staring at someone's idea of black humor. There was a wallboard of computer printouts, posters of twenty of the world's most-wanted terrorists looking him back. Some comedian had planted a dartboard above the usual suspects, a dart with an American flag stuck in the number one terrorist's nose. It was Mullah Kanbar, though, who was the bad guy of the month. What the world at large didn't know, he thought, was that the shattered remnants of the Taliban and al-Qaeda had regrouped, some forming a new organization, al-Amin, with a whole lot help from the brothers in Hamas, Hezbollah and terror groups as far away as the Philippines. A bunch of questions about al-Amin's sudden interest in Croatia as a new front to plot attacks needed answering, but the head shed, in compliance with the administration's latest Executive Order about engagement, left him wondering if Tiger Force 12 even cared about intelligence gathering, or bagging the mullah alive and kicking.

Recalling what had happened to two CIA agents recently, and he could appreciate any simmering hunger for ultimate justice. Ugly enough they had been murdered, but those videos…

He shook off the images, believing they would find and bring to justice, in some way, shape or form, the perpetrators.

Somewhere in the world, in hiding, was al-Amin's mastermind, the dreaded Nawir Wahjihab, dubbed the Sword of Islam. It was a long shot that the murdering mullah knew where the Omani was, but he had to try to take the cleric alive, find out for himself where and what Wahjihab had lurking in the wings, if he could.

Harker was about to go in search of the black-ops

commander when he saw the big as a grizzly buzz cut leader, known to him only as Colonel Joe, sweep through the doorway.

"Saddle up," Colonel Joe said, M-16/M-203 combo slung across a shoulder. "Time to rock and roll."

"Let me try and raise my guy first, Colonel."

"They had their chance to phone home. The choppers leave in two minutes and ticking. We've got a fix from the AWACS on the mullah and the Serbs, and they're moving. You onboard, or do you want to stay and play with yourself?"

Quickly Harker slipped on the shoulder rigging with the Beretta 92-F, hauling up the intel packet on the suspected destination of their targets. It was often a shaky alliance these days, CIA intel ops working together with hunter-killer teams who itched to shoot first before all the *I*'s were dotted. Before he could voice any more concern, he found the commander of Tiger Force 12 was out of sight.

THE INTERROGATION session was more gruesome than even Zharjic anticipated, or could stomach.

The village of Cdin was a bombed-out abandoned ruin, thanks to his own personal savaging, and a fair amount of torture had been performed by Zharjic's soldiers right there in the distant past. A number of ghosts from yesteryear wanted to howl to mind as he grimaced and watched the Arab take the edge of the CIA man's own commando dagger and add to his agony with impromptu surgery. The blade was heated by a lighter, then the Arab rested the edge on exposed flesh before he sliced long and deep over the stomach. Kanbar was firing off questions, while the bound CIA man choked back a scream, the camcorder set up beside the mullah. Zharjic had put enough Bosnian Muslims and Croats under similar interrogation to know he was going nowhere fast. The CIA man would take any secrets with him to the grave. A check of his watch, twenty-four minutes, and he knew time was wasting on this nonsense.

"What do you know about us? How many Americans are in Croatia? How did you know we were here? Speak, damn you, or I will make your suffering last until you beg to die!"

To the CIA man's credit, knowing he was gone either way, he actually laughed through his agony, cursed the mullah for the son of a whore and donkey droppings that he was. Zharjic was frankly amazed.

He turned away, the crumbled slabs of the stone hovel trapping the stink of singed flesh and running blood despite the cold air seeping through fissures where Serb artillery had rained down long ago.

"We must go," he growled over his shoulder. "He is going to tell you nothing."

"I will decide when it is finished."

Zharjic left it at that. A group of ten Croat Muslims had met them at the ruins, he recalled, all of them armed with AK-47s, a smattering of RPGs, and he wondered coming in how many relatives of this ragtag rebel band he had slain in the past. Either way, it was time to flee for the uncertain future. How the mullah planned to smuggle them all out of Croatia was anybody's guess, but he just wanted to melt into the complex of caves in the Velebit Mountains where he understood some precious package was waiting for Kanbar. Now this. A freak show underway in a sprawling stone graveyard, stalling the bailout.

He muttered a curse on the way out the door, his bodyguards falling in, machine pistols out and ready. Zharjic fired up a smoke, watching the Arabs milling about the motor pool. A check of the wooded hills next, a blanket of dense fog smothering the higher peaks, hearing the screams of the CIA man under the knife, and he shuddered, but not out of pity for the poor slob inside the ruins. In those woods were mass graves where his soldiers had machine-gunned hundreds of men, women and children, some UN idiots claiming to this day they were still finding thousands of skeletons with his name stamped to them. No, recalling the slaughter didn't bother him in the least.

It was the young Serb Lieutenant Vadin who slithered into his recall, a skeletal hand, he imagined, reaching out from the grave. Even to this day, it disgusted him to remember Vadin, standing over the mass grave, silent tears rolling down his cheeks. At first, he wasn't sure what the lieutenant was saying, or if the horrors of war had rendered him insane, thus useless. As the bodies piled up and Vadin's weapon remained silent, Zharjic had walked closer, anger rising over this pitiful unprofessional display. The lips had been moving, but Zharjic wasn't sure what he had been hearing. He had crept closer, the sound of autofire ringing out, muting pleas of mothers for mercy for their children. And then he made out the words.

Vadin had been praying. The lieutenant had looked up to the sky, and in a pathetic childlike voice that still enraged Zharjic to remember to this day, the kid had cried out, "Where is God? Where are you God?"

As if, Zharjic recalled, God cared, if He even existed. He had flown into a rage, slapping the young lieutenant, cursing him up and down the edge of the trench for the yellow-bellied coward that he was. The young lieutenant had casually dropped his weapon, and a slow change had shadowed his expression. What had it been? Zharjic wondered, balking. Defiance? An inner peace welling up from inside, a light of righteous wrath flaring in the eyes, as if to tell his commanding officer this was wrong, and there would be an answer? It had been a first, and a last, but Zharjic saw in his mind's eye his pistol leaping out. One bullet to the brain, and Vadin had toppled into the sea of bodies.

"You pray for them, you can die with them."

The triple crack of pistol shots rang out, Zharjic hoping the mullah came to his senses, ending it. But it was the squawking of the two-way radio, an Arab speaking into the unit near a van, a sudden flurry of activity and an air of tension that told Zharjic that all was suddenly not well.

"What is it?" he barked at the radioman, rolling up the side of the motor pool. "Talk!"

Instead of answering, the defiant bastard, he saw,

was hollering at the ruins. Wheeling, Zharjic found the mullah racing outside.

"What?" Zharjic bellowed.

"Our spotters," the mullah said, as if that were supposed to be some kind of answer. He began handing out orders, Zharjic watching as four of the Arabs fell out, began vanishing inside the crumbled shell of another hovel. "We must go!"

Zharjic grabbed the mullah by the shoulder.

"The Americans are on the way. Two attack helicopters!"

Zharjic bit down the bitter chuckle, held on to Kanbar, shook his head, then jabbed a finger into his chest. "If I do not make it out…"

"If we do not move now, none of us will make it out!"

THE APACHE GUNSHIP drubbed the shooters with one Hellfire shoved down their gullets, but Harker began entertaining visions of a debacle on the table for the good guys. Try telling Colonel Joe, however, that the bulk of the enemy was right then hauling ass up the hills, slithering into the cave complex, his transmission from the AWACS lighting up the NAVSTAR OMNI monitor with a hardforce of nearly twenty targets. Try warning the commander of Camp Bulldog that intelligence was next to zero on how the complex was laid out, where it went or how many goons were hunkered down and waiting to blow the roof. Tack on booby traps. The mullah's track record in Afghanistan indicated his soldiers would charge Americans as human bombs, vaporize themselves along with a dozen or so Green Berets or Marines combing the caves.

Pointless to fight it, he thought. It was the colonel's gig, and Harker began thinking the good commander maybe knew something he didn't.

Harker shook his head, wondering how much worse it would get when it did. M-16/M-203 combo in hand, he followed the hunter-killer team off the Black Hawk, the ghost village swarmed by Tiger Force 12, ops whipping this way and that with assault rifles, ready to blast anything that moved. He heard an op holler out from the doorway of some ruins, "In here, Colonel!"

The mop-up never came, the Apache soaring over the ruins, screens searching for live ones, Harker watching as black-clad hunters fanned the rat's nest where the formidable tank killer had left a smoking crater and a few strewed severed limbs. Harker charged inside on the colonel's heels, then he saw it.

A stream of curses poured out of the colonel's mouth as they stood and took in the horror. The colonel snatched the video off the ground, then ordered the late Ben Colder's mutilated and bullet-riddled body taken to the chopper. Rage boiled inside Harker. It was obvious what had happened, the mullah beating them to the punch, another tortured American prisoner to add to the ghoul's hit parade. Harker felt his blood pressure shoot off the monitor, his ears roaring. The longer this covert mission played out, the higher the unanswered questions piled. He began to wonder if even the CIA head shed had an inkling of what the hell was really going on here in Croatia. Or, worse, if they did, he was purposely left out of the loop.

Colonel Joe held his ground, as a soldier's hand-held radio squawked about enemy positions in the foothills. "You'll pardon me for sounding insensitive, Mr. Harker, but this is what happens when guys don't follow orders and strike out on their lonesome. Lone Rangers don't exist in this colonel's world."

Harker nearly exploded when the colonel slapped the video on his chest, then the Tiger Force commander bolted out the door.

Carry on.

The next few minutes seemed a sweeping blur to Harker, aware at some point he'd have to view the horror show, a debriefing in the future for which he didn't have the first stinking answer, knowing there was a missing corpse of another op somewhere in the country. In the chopper, M-16 clenched in his fists, he decided to go along for the ride, shoot if shot at, then round two flared up as he spotted shadows in the mist below where he suspected the maw of the cave had been blasted into the side of the cliff during one of many wars, and jihad troops were down there, ready to go the suicide distance.

The fire and thunder rolled on, as the Black Hawk lowered, Colonel Joe leading the charge out the hatch, the Apache lowering the boom on whatever enemy numbers were clinging to a last stand above. Harker fell in, out the door, climbing the gully when he heard the familiar jihad war cry.

"Blast that son of a bitch!"

The human bomb flew over the ridge, mummied with enough dynamite to blow half the mountainside clear to Romania, screaming, *"Allah akhbar!"*

Harker hit the deck, sliding a foot or two back down the gully, stones tearing at his belly. He was holding back on the trigger of his M-16, stitching the crazy extremist SOB, a twelve volley salute of auto-fire cutting loose and ripping the man apart but not before he set himself off in a thundering ball of fire.

"Looks like we hit the jackpot, sir."

"It does, indeed. The mother lode that makes the global terror machine go round."

"Not so fast, gentlemen."

Harker was feeling like a third wheel on a bad date. He had trouble making out the exchange between the op, the colonel and a new guy who strode up to the mystery cache with a large aluminum suitcase in tow. The guy wore a bomber jacket and had wavy gray hair, and Harker wondered where the new guy had been stashed during the flight. And on grew the riddle, he thought.

His ears ringing from the massive blast, images of bodies flying all over the cliffside fresh in mind, the moment felt hazy, surreal. Incredibly, the suicide bomber had struck out, merely bathing the point men with flying gore. The Apache had paved the way next with a Hellfire rocket, but the initial charge into the cave had been the most dangerous. When the last extremist was waxed and on the way to Paradise, Tiger

Force 12 had moved deeper into the cave, mine sweepers detecting trip and antipersonnel mines. It was hard, slow going, Harker having trailed the hunter-killers deeper into the cave, trip wires turning up, crates of weapons and explosives uncovered in fissures along the way. No Kanbar or Serb war criminal among the dead, and the way the offshoots of the complex fanned out, winding down to God knew where, Harker suspected the head rats had scurried out of the nest. Unbelievable.

Now they were grouped in a wide circle of black rock. At first, when the ops began cutting open burlap sacks, prying off the lids of wooden crates with commando daggers, he wasn't sure what he was seeing. Plastic-wrapped bundles were pulled out, sliced open to reveal currency from at least a half-dozen countries. He recognized dinars, Euros, old American hundreds that didn't look so old.

"Rubles," Colonel Joe announced. "Look at this, Harker. That's a stack of North Korean wons. Yeah, those are pesos, son."

Pesos? he nearly screamed. "Somebody care to tell me what the hell is going on here?"

Ignored, he watched, the new op settling his briefcase on a crate. As the men threw it open, Harker saw him raise a small digital monitor, sliding out what looked like a microscope. Huffing, he paced, the guy crumpling, rumpling, sniffing, eyeing and snapping various bills before he ran them under the scope, grunting to himself, punching the keypad.

"What?" Harker snarled. "Say something dammit! What is it?"

The gray op turned, slow, as if he held some divine key to the mysteries of the universe, and said, "They're counterfeit."

CHAPTER TWO

"All I want for Christmas is peace on Earth and a girlfriend who looks like Shania Twain. Is that asking for too much, is it?"

"That's it. You're outta here, Pops."

Carl Lyons wasn't feeling so hot, though he was, so to speak, a walking radioactive furnace. Burning, blistered, itching and feverish, thanks to falling asleep in the sand and baking under a Miami sun hotter than the hell, the Able Team leader was sick, tired and generally pissed off at the world. No hot babe on his menu yet—despite having seen every other suit taking a lap dance in the Kitty Kat Klub—having stayed tanked just to kill the ungodly misery of sun poisoning, throwing away more money than King Solomon on his worst hedonistic day since touching down at Miami International, and now this. The last thing he needed now was lip—Pops?—from a twenty-something bartender, the kid looking to him like his toughest day ever was straining for a hard-on after a night of booze and blow, who sported a slicked-back, boofed-up haircut from outer space, and worst of all, was cutting him off when he'd just began hitting his tenth double whiskey with a splash of ginger—or was it the fourteenth?—and while he was maybe about to get lucky, in his mind, with a clone of Shania who was all giggles and smelling like heaven's on fire on the stool next to him. Four days of R and R with his good buddies of Able Team, and the good times looked destined to never begin rolling.

Lyons removed his Blues Brothers shades and slipped them in the pocket of his white sports jacket. When the bartender made his move to snatch his drink away, Lyons leaned up, put on an easy smile and said, "I tell you what, son. You can eighty-six me from this mobbed-up toilet, but you even try to pull that drink away, I'll slam a twenty in the jukebox on the way out and play my favorite three KISS songs fifty times."

"A threat? Is that a threat? You threatening me?"

"No. It's a promise. Fifty KISS songs."

It appeared to Lyons they had reached an understanding. The kid grinned, bobbed his boof, backed off, but there was something in the expression Lyons—a former L.A. cop—didn't trust. The bartender was gone to round up the cavalry, most likely, melting around the corner of the massive marble-and-glass horseshoe-shaped bar, when Lyons felt a silky mitt slip something in his hand. Turning, Shania's twin was all smiles, holding his eye, then Lyons glanced at the slip of paper with her name—Gigi—and phone number before making it vanish in his pants pocket.

"You have all the charm of a crocodile, but for this phony coked-up money-grubbing town it's like a breath of cool air in mid-July, considering what I have to deal with,'' she said.

Lyons put on his best winning smile. ''Something in the way you move makes my little heart go pitter-patter, too.''

''Pull it back, stud. I didn't quite go that far.''

''My mistake.''

''Try not to make another.''

''How come I love the sound of that?''

She paused, measuring Lyons, then said, ''I'm on next, but call me. We can do brunch, say tenish?''

''Be still my foolish heart,'' Lyons said. ''Tenish, it is.''

She tapped a red-nailed finger on Lyons's blistered cheek. ''A tourist.''

''I hate it when I'm obvious.''

''I have a little something that can fix that up when I see you.''

''I'll bet you do.''

''Try and be a good boy and stay out of trouble, at least until tomorrow morning. Toodles.''

Lyons held his arms out by his side. ''Hey, I look like a problem kind of guy to you?''

He was missing her already, knowing he was persona non grata at the Kitty Kat, Shania grinning and waving back over her shoulder. He wanted to watch her slink away, then spotted the two goombahs near the shower stall where a bathing beauty was getting rave reviews from a howling mob.

Lyons panned on, saw three more goons with earpieces link up near the shower stall, all eyes aimed his way. Dark suits, some short-haired or buzz cut or straight out of a hippie peace march, they were all packing. Not good, since, even if he was on vacation, the ex-L.A. detective never left home without his .357 Magnum Colt Python.

He decided to hold his ground, take his sweet time with his last drink, play out the coming drama. He was on vacation, wasn't he? Why was everybody messing with him? Where was Shania when he needed her? Where were his social skills when he needed them most? What the hell, huh, he thought, fighting off a wave of nausea he figured was more sun poisoning than booze.

He kept taking in his surroundings, casual, feeling the heat build, but it wasn't the suits and various celebs of South Beach cheering on fifteen naked beauties. He was getting tired of this joint anyway, he decided, the rock music so loud it cleaved an ax through a brain already jellied and throbbing from around-the-clock boozing, not to mention burning now from the low-grade fever of sun poisoning. The strobing diamond-shaped chandeliers, reflecting light from all points, seemed to hurl out a fire of their own, making him wonder if his colorful flamingo-and-palm-tree aloha shirt was a magnet for light and heat. He looked around a little longer, checked his six. Lo and behold, he found Hermann ''Gadgets'' Schwarz and Rosario Blancanales in a far corner booth. They were a little more reserved, sports jackets and flaming aloha shirts like himself, but they appeared to be having a little more civil and gentlemanly time of it. One blonde, one brunette had the other two members of Able Team boxed in, quietly laughing and conversing when Lyons caught Schwarz's eye, raised his glass, then drew a finger across his throat.

"WHAT'S CARL trying to say, Gadgets?"

"Problems, that's what," Schwarz replied. "About six of them. Oh, Carl, you…"

Men who lived on the edge of hell, by the sword of combat, never knowing when their next breath would be their last, forever stressed and always giving more than they got, had a way of unwinding that could make a pack of hyenas appear civilized, and even hyenas deserved to feast once in a while on the good stuff. Or at least that was the way, Schwarz recalled, their fearless leader had put it to them on the flight down to Miami after the flight attendant had dumped off their fifth round of drinks. This was their fourth night in Miami, and most of their time had been spent trolling gentlemen's clubs. Schwarz was amazed beyond joy and near tears they hadn't been locked up or shot up by Dade County's finest.

That, he saw, was about to change. It was inevitable, he figured. Carl "Ironman" Lyons just had a way about him that seemed to draw trouble. They had already been eighty-sixed from three previous strip joints, though quietly, questioned by Miami's finest during the daylight hours while tooling around in their Mercedes rental car, cops pulling them over, wondering if they were the town's latest cocaine cowboy imports, from the sounds of the Q and A.

Right then, Schwarz figured he could forgive Lyons his overindulgence. In a way, it was sort of his and Blancanales's fault for walking away when Ironman had passed out in his briefs on the beach. It was a big chuckle then, walking away, gone for lunch and a tour of South Beach clubs and the Art Deco District, but it had proved a whopping error in judgment, about to come full vicious circle, unless he missed his guess. Figure a full day where Carl had been laid up in their hotel room, burned to a crisp, sweating and shivering it out, drinking one fifth of whiskey after another just to calm the snarling big guy, and the leader of Able Team was still in some serious pain. The booze wasn't helping anymore either, par for the course, and Schwarz figured Lyons would dole out agony for an army to the first joker who came knocking to clean his clock. In the killing fields it was fine, Schwarz thought, running wild, kicking ass, blowing things up, but when walking around in so-called civilized or polite society…

Shave the stripes off a tiger, and Schwarz knew you still had a tiger. What could he do? Lyons was Lyons, Schwarz concluded, their leader, their buddy, their— what? Hero? Well, he didn't look so heroic from where Schwarz sat, and knew that even Lyons was about to need a little help from his friends.

Schwarz glanced at Blancanales, felt the ladies get uptight, conversation and giggles gone like smoke in the wind, as the Able Team commandos put on their war faces. Schwarz counted six security goons, three each closing from both sides of the bar. Which left, by his earlier guesstimate, another four to six lurking about the sprawling two-tiered arena of fun and games. The crowd partied on, oblivious to the coming storm, and that could prove good, or downright ugly if a full-scale battle erupted. Schwarz was ready to rise when he spotted the dark man in the white suit. He was lean, maybe Italian, but he could have been Arab, hawk nose and neat goatee. He flicked at his ponytail, calm, in control. Something glistened on his earlobe, and Schwarz made out the diamond, probably the size of a golf ball, even at the distance. Schwarz figured him to be the owner, watching him hold his turf on the other side of the bar, sipping his drink, one hand looking to be glued to the string-bikinied derriere of a dancer, Ponytail giving the nod to one of his security goons to make their move.

"Excuse us, ladies," Schwarz said, peeling off a hundred-dollar bill from his R and R wad and flipping it on the table. "That should cover the drinks and the pleasure of your company."

"Later, girls. Duty—sort of—calls," Blancanales said, squeezing past his lady friend, falling in behind Schwarz.

"Oh, this is not good," Schwarz muttered. "Why now, Carl?"

"If Carl starts something, Gadgets… We're all packing like the goon squad."

"I know that. If it hits the fan, we'll just pull out our Justice Department…"

Schwarz froze, thinking ahead, slapping at his pockets.

"What?"

"Check your pockets, Pol."

"I didn't bring mine. I thought you and Carl...."

Schwarz cursed. All of them, he realized, sick to his stomach, had left their bogus Justice Department credentials behind in their hotel room.

"If it goes to hell, Gadgets..."

"I know, I know, you don't have to say it."

Worst-case scenario, Schwarz knew, was cop trouble if a drunken shootout began. All three of them, he thought, hoping against hope they left here in peace, worked as operatives for America's ultracovert Stony Man Farm. But not even their boss, a high-ranking Justice Department official by the name of Hal Brognola, who ran the Farm and was liaison to the President of the United States, could bail them out of this mess if Lyons went apeshit and some rent-a-cop got busted up, or worse.

Schwarz picked up the pace, groaning when he saw one of the goons drop a paw on Ironman's shoulder, which, he knew, was as burned and blistered as if he'd been microwaved. Lyons grimaced, turned on his stool and bared his teeth.

"Oh, shit, I know that look," Blancanales muttered.

"Yeah. Here we go."

"TAKE YOUR HAND off me, friend, and don't do that again."

"Look, you don't want to get froggy, pal."

"I'm finishing my drink, then I'll leave in peace," Lyons told the goon. "The hand?"

Lyons took a rapid head count, knew he was hemmed in, a wall of muscle on both sides. The goon pulled his hand back, Lyons thinking he'd bought a reprieve, then some goof in a suit had to get smart.

"Call it a night, old man. You don't want any trouble. The way it looks, if I put a pin in your face I bet you'd pop like a pimple anyway. And we don't need that kind of mess all over the bar."

Lyons lifted his glass. "Why don't you make yourself useful there, dude, and go clean a toilet."

"That's it, asshole. You're finished now."

Lyons read the menace, full-blown violent intent, saw it coming and let the goon get as far as clamping both hands on his shoulders, lifting him off his stool. Pain, in this instance, was good. Every sunburned inch of screaming flesh, on fire now, was pain and motivation enough. It cleared the boozy sludge and put piston force in the elbow Lyons drove into the goon's stomach.

"He's got a gun!"

Lyons heard one of the goons hollering about his weapon, figured his jacket had fallen open to reveal the big cannon. No time to pull any punches now; Lyons was up and wheeling around. He speared the tip of his shoe into another goon's family jewels, one more goombah falling, squealing and woofing to his knees, grabbing at his sac. Somewhere behind the goon squad, he heard Schwarz bellowing, "United States Justice Department! Lose the gun!"

"Fuck you! I don't see any badge!"

If nothing else, it told Lyons they were thugs and punks, plain and simple, no Miami Vice moonlighting for a second paycheck, or so he hoped. It meant he could ratchet up the punishment, go for broke if a piece swung his way.

He started to feel an overpowering wave of nausea bubble like volcanic lava in his belly, moving up his chest, and silently cursed the ferocious Miami sun that had turned him into some blistered freak show straight out of the *X Files*.

Then a fist like a sledgehammer flew from his blindside and blasted off his jaw. The lights faded, and Lyons feared it was over for him before it even started. He tumbled, facedown into the bar.

THE STAMPEDE STARTED in shrieking and cursing earnest when a goombah from his nine o'clock grabbed the Beretta 92-F. Two, then three shots were triggered into the ceiling as Schwarz danced a jig with the guy, his nose so full of cheap aftershave the Able Team commando thought he'd vomit his steak-and-lobster dinner. One of the glass chandeliers overhead took the brunt of 9 mm subsonic rounds and an avalanche of lethal shards and slivers began pelting patrons, goons and Able Team, cranking up a din that could have wailed from the bowels of hell. Schwarz ended the embrace by lancing a knee into the goon's groin, then connected a jackhammer uppercut to the nose. The guy staggered back, arms windmilling, blood flying, but he slammed into another security guard with a drawn Glock. The collision threw the goon's aim off, a shot cracking out. As luck had it, the round coring into the shoulder of a gun-wielding security guard who was drawing down on Schwarz. Screaming in pain, the would-be shooter grabbed at the crimson hole, hopping around but triggering wild shots. Where they flew was anybody's guess, but one bullet brought down a sheet of mirrored pillar behind the Able Team warrior when a slipstream of hot air breezed past his ear. A bunch of suits took the glass bath, ducking, weaving, howling mad as they shoved and bulled their way clear of the bar brawl, a Robert DeNiro clone blasting a path through another goon in flight, bowling down the goombah, his suit trampled into puddles of spilled beer as other patrons stomped over his thrashing frame.

The wounded security shooter was lining up Schwarz when he saw Blancanales take care of that particular problem. Stool in hand, Blancanales swung, a home run that nearly took the guy's head off at the shoulders. The problem was, two more reflexive rounds shot skyward, shearing off more glass, showering naked females.

Utter chaos raged all around Schwarz, as he waded closer to the bar where two reinforcements, guns drawn, were slamming their way through the fleeing herds of suits, the fun bunch bouncing around like table-tennis balls, toppling all over the place.

So much for Miami sun and fun and cheap thrills, he thought. They'd be lucky if they lived long enough to see the inside of Dade County lockup.

SOME SUIT WITH MORE *cajones* than good sense and who looked like a stunt double in a gangster movie decided Blancanales was a bad guy. The Able Team commando was vaulting over the last row of leathered booths, coming down, when the stunt double rushed him, all snarls and craning roundhouse. Blancanales saw it coming, ducked the blow easily enough, then came up from behind the guy, who had given his all and was floundering ahead, trying to keep his balance.

Hands taloned into the shoulders of his suit, Blancanales wheeled, helped him stand, a marble pillar in sight to his ten o'clock. Bouncing the guy's face off the pillar to a sickening squelch of nose bone, Blancanales silently thanked the clown for trying to Charles Bronson his way into the act as he saw the cavalry coming. Two more goombahs made the foray, a buzz cut Frick and Frack armed with Glocks, looking to draw a bead through the surging mass of flesh. Blancanales hurled his current opponent, his sailing limp sack hammering into the twins.

Strike.

Whether it was the human missile, spilled brew under their feet or both, Frick and Frack dropped like bowling pins.

It was time to bail, Blancanales knew, searching for Schwarz and finding him giving a rising goon a one-two combo that whiplashed his head and sent him reeling into the bar.

Then he spotted Ironman, and Lyons was having some definite problems standing and finding his way back into the brawl. Blancanales was about to wade through the stampede, elbowing a suit here and there, when he balked at what Carl did next.

Carl 'Ironman' Lyons vomited all over the bar.

"POLICE! Freeze, asshole!"

Lyons was too busy spilling his guts all over the bar to hear much else other than the roaring in his skull. All he knew was that some guy had nearly knocked him out with a sucker punch, and that didn't wash with Lyons.

Not in this life.

And all he saw next was the beer pitcher.

It was in his hand before he knew it. Lyons whirled, seeing the buzz cut goon, one of the security thugs, he believed, digging inside his jacket for something. There was a gun in his hand, though, and Lyons simply reacted to the threat. Two steps forward, and the leader of Able Team smashed the pitcher off the goon's skull. The gun dropped, but the goon didn't, so Lyons exploded a left hook into his jaw that launched the guy clear over a row of booths.

Where the hell were Gadgets and Pol? He was searching the stampede, spotted Schwarz doing an impromptu wrestling maneuver as he had some poor goombah by the sac and shoulders, ran him forward and hurled him over the bar. The crash of liquor bottles and the bar mirror coming down jolted Lyons with fresh waves of sense-splitting detonations. He shuffled a step to his side, searching for fresh meat when...

Lo and behold, he found his initial nemesis staggering to his feet, shaking glass out of his hair. Lyons nearly smiled, then fisted up a handful of hair, whipped the guy around and began bouncing his face off the bar top.

"Did I hear something about a pimple popping?" Lyons demanded, one, two more slams off the marble top, then started using the guy's face to mop up his vomit with long driving sweeps. "Kept your mouth shut and I would have been gone! I hear something about not messing up your bar? How's this for messy? All I wanted was to finish my drink! And I was about to get lucky with Shania Twain, you miserable bastard Mafia bootlicker!"

"Police! Freeze!"

Lyons thought he heard it right now, renewed anger and fresh bursts of adrenaline clearing the cobwebs.

"I said freeze! Let go of that man now or I'll shoot!"

He saw the four uniforms, guns drawn, craned his head and spotted five more of Miami's finest pouring across one of the dance floors. He spotted Blancanales putting the finishing touches to a foe, a straight shot to the mouth that sent the guy flying back, then Pol raised his arms, looking at the cops, as innocent as hell.

Schwarz was already hands-up, holding his turf in a bed of glass, running booze and groaning stiffs.

Lyons held up his guy like a trophy, the skinny goon moaning, woozy, then tossed him away. "We're with the United States Department of Justice. Easy, guys. I'm reaching for my credentials."

Lyons was patting down his pockets, frowning, wondering why they were empty, when he heard Schwarz call out, "Forget it, Carl. We left them in the room."

"We're screwed, Carl," Blancanales chimed in, as if he didn't know that.

"That you are," a cop growled.

The cops were closing, tentative, one of them ordering Able Team, "All three of you, assume the position on the bar."

Lyons cursed, saw his adversary struggling to stand, a finger pointing at the Able Team leader.

"This guy, Officers, he started it...."

Lyons slugged him in the jaw and put him down for the count.

"THIS IS DEFINITELY a first, Carl, even for you. A most unique situation."

"I don't feel so unique at the moment, Hal, so let's cut to the chase."

Something like twelve hours had passed before Lyons was allowed his one phone call. He believed the three of them had been transported to downtown Miami, but his memory was hazy. The whole nine yards of fingerprinting, booking, mug shots he did remember, before getting tossed into solitary in a county jumpsuit.

He cradled the phone in his shaking hand as best he could, a uniform close by, scowling him down. The noise of inmates, howling and whooping and demanding to call lawyers and bondsmen down the hall, was carving daggers through his hangover. He was pretty sure Gadgets and Pol were in the same building, but...

Brognola's voice seemed to shoot like cannonfire through the phone, edged with anger so loud and clear, Lyons might have been sitting in his office at the Justice Department.

"If I was there, Carl, I'd personally put a foot square up your ass. In fact, I have a good mind to let you three rot for a few days."

"Hey, come on, Hal, I maybe caused you a little grief—"

"Grief? You want to hear about grief? Let's take a look at the lightweight fare of charges. We've got drunk and disorderly. We've got destruction of private property. We've got inciting mayhem—"

"Inciting what? Hey, wait a second," Lyons snarled. "It was those guys. The goon squad pulled the pieces and began blasting—"

"Here's the heavyweight list," Brognola went on, as if he hadn't heard Lyons. "Assault, assault with intent, assault on a police officer—"

"What cop?"

"Three off-duty Miami police officers and one Vice cop were moonlighting as part of that security detail."

"You're shitting me! That toilet is more mobbed up than Capone's Chicago. They work there, they're dirty."

"Or undercover. Maybe you blew their cover."

"Okay, okay, fair enough. Well, Gadgets and Pol

weren't that toasted, so they couldn't have been charged with drunk and disorderly."

"You getting smart-ass with me?"

"So, what's the story? You post bond, or better still flex a little official muscle so we can walk in a couple of hours. No fuss, no muss, no one ever knows we existed. Miami never seems to turn out the way I picture it in my dreams anyway. Every time I come down here shit happens."

"Bond?" Brognola chuckled, but the sound was mirthless, and Lyons winced. "What, you going to show up for arraignment tomorrow before the judge down there?"

"Hell, no. We just pack up our R and R and blow town."

"You're not going anywhere. You're staying right there in Miami."

"Whoa, Hal, you that pissed at us?"

"Can you think clear enough to remember who and what you are, and who you work for?"

"I'm sure you'll remind me in no uncertain terms when I see you."

"Count on it. All right, listen. I've got some calls to make, damage control that makes me wish I was a Clinton lawyer."

"How long?"

"As long as it takes. I may have to go all the way to the governor."

"Well, he's a stand-up guy, and you can always count on his brother, if worse comes to worst."

Brognola grunted. "Use the time to sober up. Playtime's over. You've got a mission waiting for you right there in South Florida.''

Lyons was about to pursue it, then realized the line might be tapped as Brognola hung up in his ear. A mission, huh? he thought, trying like hell to piece together the previous night, coming up short, but visions of Shania Twain came to mind.

''Let's move.''

Lyons hung up. The seriousness of what he'd done sank home, as he turned and faced the officer. ''I understand I assaulted a police officer.''

''Four of them, you and your pals. One of them's in the hospital with a wired jaw.''

Lyons grimaced. ''Hey, look…I'm sorry. I didn't know. I used to be a cop myself. L.A.''

The officer seemed to consider something, then nodded. ''You'll have plenty of time to think things over.''

Lyons said nothing as the officer took him by the arm and began leading him back to his cell.

CHAPTER THREE

"Tell me why I'm not surprised," Barbara Price said, the expression on her stunningly beautiful face torn between a frown and a smile, as she shook her head, the honey blond mane tied back in a ponytail swaying with the motion. "As bad as it was, it could have been worse if one of them had pulled a trigger."

"Well, it's taken care of, everything from their fingerprints to mug shots to all charges in the process of vanishing, thanks to a couple of my agents who are paying a 'professional courtesy call' to Dade County with orders straight from this office to forgive and forget," Hal Brognola said. "And you can believe I owe some huge favors from here to the governor's mansion in Florida, and if I owe, they owe *me* at least enough to keep this kind of nonsense from ever happening again. You can rest assured I'll have a few choice words for our party animals when I see them."

"When will they be released?"

"When I'm damn good and ready to make one final call down there to give the magistrate the heads up, which means I'm in for one last round of squawking I may have to direct straight to the governor.''

Price smiled at the speakerphone with its secured line to the big Fed's office in downtown Washington. ''If I didn't know better, Hal, I'd say you sound like an angry father.''

''Yeah, me and my three prodigal sons. Enough said, let's get down to business. Where's Striker?''

''He just stepped in,'' Price said.

Mack Bolan walked into the Computer Room, the nerve center of Stony Man Farm. He found the key members of the cyberteam gathered at their various workstations, tapping keyboards, hard at it to jump start whatever his next mission and help keep it online for the duration.

The big man in the wheelchair was Aaron ''the Bear'' Kurtzman, head computer wizard of the intel-gathering juggernaut. Kurtzman, he knew, also made some of the worst coffee on the planet, strong and thick enough to choke a bull elephant, but after nodding at Price, the Farm's mission controller and his sometime lover, then announcing himself to Brognola, Bolan made a move for the pot and poured himself a cup.

The members of the cyberteam were so locked into their various duties at the monitors they didn't acknowledge his presence. He took no offense, aware they were gripped in the magic of their own worlds, paving the way, gathering critical data at light speed, sorting out the players, complete with all pertinent background on the day's bad guys. There was Akira

Tokaido, the Japanese-American computer wizard, sporting the usual blue jeans, denim jacket and rocking in his chair to whatever moved him on his CD player. Huntington ''Hunt'' Wethers, the ex-professor of cybernetics at Berkeley, was glued to a monitor where he appeared to be juxtaposing a variety of faces over one another, altering their features with a click of the mouse, adding beards, removing hair, chin implants and so on. The striking redhead was Carmen Delahunt, formerly of the FBI, but recruited by Brognola to join the best and the brightest there at Stony Man Farm.

Shaved and showered, dressed in black turtleneck and khaki trousers, Bolan had been standing down for two days after his latest mission. He was the Farm's lone wolf operative, but when called upon by Brognola, the Executioner had no problem whatsoever teaming up with Able Team or Phoenix Force, the commando units of the ultracovert agency. Unlike Able Team, Bolan had different ideas about R and R, having used his timely wisely to bone up on the coming mission the past day or so, his only rest and relaxation an hour or so spent alone with Barbara Price. SOP normally dictated a sanction from the President before the warriors of Stony Man were cut loose. Bolan assumed they had a green light from the Oval Office.

He was moving toward Price when he suddenly spotted Yakov Katzenelenbogen in the far corner. The gruff Israeli was watching the VCR's monitor, the former leader of Phoenix force appearing to tremble with barely suppressed rage.

And Bolan could see why. Duty called the Executioner once more, and, as usual, he was geared up to go the distance, do whatever it took to take rough justice to the latest batch of savages. The parameters of the mission needed some defining, but he could be sure that what Katz viewed was a big slice of the action that would eventually be addressed, and woe be unto the butchers who had lately decided capturing and torturing CIA ops wasn't enough, but who got sadistic kicks from filming scenes straight out of hell. Bolan watched the horror show, as, he knew from an earlier briefing, the CIA special op went under the knife of a shadowy figure just off-camera. Bolan clenched his jaw, having some but not all of the particulars about this latest gruesome freak show perpetrated by the terror mongers. Katz slammed his prosthesis on the table, took the remote and blanked the screen.

A somber anger fell over the room, as all eyes turned toward Katz.

"Sons of bitches," Katz muttered, stood and joined Price and Bolan. "I almost wish you hadn't sent me a copy of what those bastards did to another one of ours, Hal. As if I needed incentive, but it's that kind of evil that might put me back out in the field yet. That's three of our guys, shipped home in pieces, while those bastards stand around and chuckle and carve them up like turkeys and proclaim their holy war. I tell you what..."

Bolan could well appreciate Katz's murderous ire, more hungry himself than a moment ago to get out there and dish out some payback. Katz, retired from Phoenix Force, was the Farm's tactical adviser, but he would, Bolan knew, march back out there into the hellgrounds, if called upon. But these days, his skills were needed behind the lines. Not to mention the former Israeli colonel still had invaluable ties to Mossad. If anyone knew who was doing what in the terror world, Mossad did. More than once Katz had used his connections in the Middle East to aid and assist in dismantling a fair number of rats' nests.

Bolan pulled up a rolling wingback chair, settled in. "What do we have?"

"You can get filled in by the others, Striker," Brognola said. "I'm signing off to deal with a few more whopping migraines before I can get our three party animals out of the hole. Stay in touch and stay frosty."

"Will do," Bolan said, and Brognola was gone, the soldier well imagining the big Fed scowling in his office, chomping on his ever present stogie, swilling coffee and downing one pack of antacid tablets after another in a vain attempt to subdue the rumbling volcano in his belly. The monumental hassle that Able Team had caused Brognola was a first, and in a class all by itself, a hedonistic foray and subsequent brawl involving assaults on police officers, though unwittingly, that could have eventually pointed fingers of blame back to Stony Man Farm, exposing all of them. But Bolan understood those guys, just the same—

three commandos, forever living on the edge, stealing what pleasure they could get when they could, since tomorrow might never come. He could forgive Able Team this transgression, and under different circumstances, might have even chuckled it off.

"What we have, Striker," Kurtzman began, clicking on the wall monitor to frame twenty of the world's most infamous terrorist faces, "is a murdering mullah by the name of Haroon Kanbar."

"I'm familiar with the name. Believed to be the architect of a nerve gas booby trap that took out six Marines who were combing the caves in Tora Bora."

"It never made CNN," Katz said, grabbing a chair. "This SOB, Kanbar, one-time top lieutenant to the one-eyed mullah, likes to leave behind videos or mail them to al-Jazeera."

"Slipped out of Afghanistan," Price said, "via Pakistan."

"And the CIA believes another fifty to sixty Taliban and al-Qaeda beauties, maybe more," Kurtzman said, "likewise vanished into thin air while the ISI was tightening the noose in Karachi."

"And what was left of the Taliban and al-Qaeda," Bolan said, "created a sister organization, al-Amin. They recruited heavily from Hamas, Hezbollah and the Abu Sayyaf group."

Kurtzman scowled at the wall monitor. "To name the short list of known terrorist groups. Al-Qaeda and al-Amin, are, however, linked, albeit loosely. They exchange operatives, intel, brainstorm future attacks together. Kanbar is a major player, head viper of operations in the field, but this snake,'' Kurtzman said, highlighting a face, ''has shot to the top of the list of the bad boys club. Nawir Wahjihab, known to us as the Sword of Islam, has been around for years, recruiting, running camps and religious schools, those *madrassas* where young impressionable minds are molded with hate and rage for us infidels to be shipped out as human bombs when they graduate with their PhD in fanaticism. He's been building al-Amin quietly over the past few years, reading the writing on the walls of the Afghanistan caves. He's cut loose his predators on a scale that's growing by the week. More suicide bombers blowing up Tel Aviv than ever, plus the carnage has recently spilled into Germany, Belgium and England, as you know. Night clubs, shopping malls, the jihad turning up the murdering heat, gunning down and blowing up so many chunks of real estate that Europe is becoming an armed camp. This guy's shot to the short list of seeing some ultimate justice. Problem is, no one knows where he's holed up.''

''The elusive ghost,'' Bolan said. ''The general of al-Amin, last seen in Chechnya, Somalia, Sudan, France....''

''And there was even a Wahjihab sighting in Mexico City,'' Price said. ''He's everywhere and he's nowhere.''

''Well, if that's true, he made a guest appearance south of the border,'' Bolan said. ''We know the terrorists have been quietly attempting to slip operatives and weapons through our Mexican backyard. It's no big secret the Mexican authorities will take a few bucks, no matter what or who from, wink and look the other way.''

''And if that's true, we're hoping that you might get to the bottom of it,'' Price said.

Kurtzman went on. ''We'll get to that, Striker. Wahjihab. Born in Yemen, he moved to Oman where his father somehow ingratiated himself to the sultan. The old man became a huge mover and shaker in the banking business. Oman, as you know, produces little more than a smidge of petro compared to Saudi Arabia, but like Bahrain, they've become a major banking industry.''

''Namely OBUs,'' Delahunt commented.

''Offshore Banking Units,'' Price said.

''Laundering money,'' Delahunt added. ''That's been my job—follow the money. Islamic charities, business fronts and so on.''

''Again, we'll get to that in a minute, Carmen,'' Kurtzman said. ''When Daddy Wahjihab kicked off, Nawir inherited a big chunk of change. Some smart investments doubled his pleasure. He's also believed to have fattened his coffers some more through 'investments' in narcotics and arms sales. Hunt, you have the floor.''

''Okay, here we go,'' Wethers said, his mouse hooked into the monitor. He began clicking through a series of facial alterations on Wahjihab and Kanbar, aging them, no hair, short hair, the whole range of plastic surgery.

Bolan watched, Wethers announcing he had personally created this "plastic surgery" program.

"I also did a voiceprint analysis," Wethers stated, "on the Marquis de Sade in question on the videos. Matched to Kanbar on all three, with Wahjihab giving me a hundred percent verification on the first two. I've run the gamut of every conceivable way the top snakes could change their appearance. Try as someone might to hide by looking like someone else, there's something I call the individual factor. I'm not saying anyone should take one of these guys out for dinner and strike up a conversation, but there's a way in which a person carries himself. Certain habits, say cigarettes, nervous mannerisms, a twitch or the way he speaks, certain words, euphemisms and so on, that can reveal who is behind the mask."

"You'll get copies of every way the top twenty could have altered their appearance," Price told Bolan, "and so will Phoenix. But, for now, you're going to Florida."

"Please tell me," Bolan said, "I'm not going down there for baby-sitting detail."

Price grinned at Bolan, as Kurtzman clicked on. "Rahim Baruk. Egyptian. Changed his name to Theodore 'Teddy the Titan' Islip."

"Guess he was shedding his Islamic roots and embracing everything the Koran deems unholy, considering he's been living the 'sinful' Western lifestyle he once might have denounced," Katz chipped in, his eyes lighting up once again with anger.

"Came to this country fifteen years ago on a student visa when such things were easily obtained and glossed over by the INS," Kurtzman said. "Educated at the University of Miami, armed with business and accounting degrees. How he got his money to invest in a series of nightclubs around Miami, we figure it was funneled here by Egyptian fundamentalists. He's a big shot and a bad boy around Miami, and he's the owner of the gentlemen's club our newly dubbed party animals wandered into."

"My starting point," Bolan said.

"One of two," Price told him.

"Carmen?" Kurtzman said.

"Islip—we, the FBI, the CIA and the Treasury Department believe—is a funnel for al-Amin funds." Delahunt took her own clicker and snapped the next frame to a global map where red lines connected stars from Mexico to the Caribbean to Europe and the Middle East to the Philippines. "Money laundering is the third biggest business in the world after petro bucks and foreign exchange. I've managed to track it down—"

"With, don't forget, dear lady, a little help from America's favorite Japanese cybersamurai." Tokaido had the earbuds out, the rock and roll killed. He grinned at Delahunt, who nodded and smiled back.

"With, actually, a lot of help from Akira," she said, "who hacked into the mainframes of the Financial Crimes Enforcement Network in Virginia. Islip has three clubs, two restaurants, a car dealership and a trucking business. We believe the vehicles, shades of the French Connection, are how he moves whatever contraband around the country. He imports all makes of European vehicles from René Puchain of Marseilles underworld notoriety. I've connected the dots to an Islamic charity in Texas, to Islip accounts in Mexico City, OBUs in a dozen other countries, but a lot of cash seems to go through a Puchain account in Marseilles."

"Puchain," Katz said, "is the problem Phoenix will tackle. He was spotted a few months back by the FBI and the CIA hosting an al-Amin operative who was snapped up but hasn't been talking. What we do know is that Puchain set sail his freighter, the *Napoleon*, loaded, we believe with contraband."

When Bolan heard the *Napoleon* was due to dock the following night in the Port of Miami, he had a strong suspicion where he was headed next.

Price confirmed it. "We need you and Able to start squeezing Teddy the Titan."

"I'm sure he'll be happy to see Carl and the boys again," Bolan said.

"How you do it is up to you," Katz said. "Steamroller the guy, we don't care. We have a thumbs-up from the Man, given what happened in Croatia. Whatever it takes, if you have to impale Teddy's head on a stake, it's your call."

"Croatia. Where Kanbar and a Serb criminal were somehow swallowed up by the earth," Bolan said. "Another riddle."

"One we're working on, and I hate to admit it, but we're winging it right now," Price stated. "More questions than answers, but something's brewing in the jihad world, that much we strongly suspect. Puchain's ship is going to be delivered to Islip, according to an informant and the ship's manifest. Only you and Able will be attached to a joint strike force. FBI, Justice and a team of what is known in the Treasury Department as Jump Teams, or cash commandos.''

"I assume this has some connection to what turned up in Croatia?" Bolan said.

"Not sure. The black ops team in Croatia," Kurtzman said, "found something like thirty million dollars in various foreign currencies, including U.S. dollars."

"Counterfeit bills," Price added.

"That would put a definite new spin on hawala," Bolan said.

"Carmen and I are working on that now," Tokaido told him, "but what we don't know is why or where the counterfeit bills are being manufactured."

"We're thinking," Wethers said, "al-Amin is looking to flood various countries with funny money, hoping to destabilize economies perhaps."

"Or," Delahunt said, "they're low on legitimate cash, considering all the accounts of terrorists that have been frozen for the past while."

"Meaning they're out shopping for the Suitcase from Allah, or chem or bio weapons," Katz said. "Dump off bad bills, grab the goodies and scoot before the seller gets wise to the scam."

"The bottom line is," Price said, "nobody knows what contraband is stowed on that freighter. An informant in the Puchain organization claimed a special cargo is onboard, but before he could learn more—''

"He turned up shot, one to the head, in a Marseilles alley," Kurtzman said.

"You'll be attached to this strike force," Price said, "as co-leader, your usual cover is Special Agent Mike Belasko."

The Executioner sipped his coffee, then said, "When do I leave for sunny South Florida?"

"HOW COME I feel like we're pariahs at the Farm?"

"Gee, I don't know, Carl, let's see," Schwarz said. "Maybe it had something to do with us getting tossed into the can, with more charges hung over our heads than Jihad Johnny Walker, General Manuel Noriega, Mr. and Mrs. Clinton and Slobodan Milosevic all together now. Maybe it had something to do—"

Lyons winced from the bomb going off in his skull as someone leaned on a horn, then scowled over his shoulder at Schwarz. "I got the picture, and I'm not in the mood for anybody cracking wise. Both of you. Damn," he said, wincing again, the harsh sunlight seeming to lance straight through his shades, as it glittered off the towering glass monoliths of downtown Miami.

Able Team was shuffling and weaving its way through the surging sidewalk lunch mass, brushing here and there, past suits and skirts, many of whom saw them coming and made quick beelines around the trio. They were disheveled, sporting bristles, tussled hair and haggard, surly expressions. In general, Lyons knew, they looked like stepped-on crap, or three knuckleheads just coming out of the hole after an anxious stint where every minute behind bars could feel like an hour and a guy couldn't sleep no matter what, since a million-watt overhead light was forever burning down into the eyes.

Lyons tucked in his shirt, frowning around at the midday mobs, hating all sound and light, checking his six, brushing the flakes of peeling skin off his jacket. It didn't help his mood any being jammed up in an eight-by-five cell for well over thirty-six hours, waiting on Brognola to get it together, taking his sweet time. Then having to take attitude from the magistrate on the way out the door, the guy reminding them and repeating over and over how unusual a situation it all was. The guy giving them the evil eye as he returned their weapons, sans clips.

Not only that, but ten or twenty minutes out the door, he was certain they were being followed as he spotted the same black sedan, tinted glass all around hiding the occupants, down the block. It eased along, seemed to tail them, Lyons sure he could feel eyeballs following their every step. Or was he just being paranoid?

"Where the hell are we, anyway?" Schwarz growled.

"Downtown Miami, that's where. There, that's the Metromover," Lyons growled, pointing at the upraised silver streak in the distance.

"Will it take us to the new digs Hal got us up Biscayne Boulevard?"

"How should I know?"

"Well, you seem to know your way around all the nudie bars," Schwarz pointed out.

Lyons groaned, rubbing his face. "So, we grab a bite, get a cab. What are we supposed to do, anyway?"

"Call Striker, get an ETA and rendezvous site," Blancanales said.

"And what was the mission?"

"Striker has all the details," Schwarz said.

Lyons stopped, feeling mean and on the verge of exploding. "Look at this," he snarled, turning, nodding at the black sedan. "They've been dogging us since we caught our first breath of free air."

The sedan crept closer, rolling up to the curb, and parked.

"Carl, let's not push our luck," Schwarz said. "If we have to go back and face that magistrate again…"

"Don't remind me. Damn guy tossed Gigi's number, I'm sure of it."

"Could be something, could be nothing," Blancanales said, checking out the sedan.

"Yeah, well, I'm going to find out which it is. Fan out, both of you take the shotgun side."

Lyons was moving, stepping into the street, mind made up to go for the throat when the driver's door opened. It was hard to see at first who it was, since burning light was bouncing off the black windshield and the dark shades of a big guy looming up over the door. It took another step and two more seconds before Lyons recognized the face behind the cocked grin.

"If you ladies are done playing around," Mack Bolan said, "we have work to do."

RAHIM ABDUL BARUK, a.k.a. Theodore "Teddy the Titan" Islip, had been "asleep" for more than two decades. The long, secret struggle had its genesis in a *madrassa* in Cairo. At the tender age of ten he had been indoctrinated into what the West called fundamentalist or radical Islam. His father, a poor street vendor who had fought and lost a leg against the Israelis during the Six-Day War, had been responsible for his initiation at the feet of the cleric who had been known to him only as the Great One.

As he sat in his study, shutting down the laptop, the message sent to his cutout, he now recalled the final words of the Great One before he was shipped out to America, armed only with a student visa, some money and a contact in Miami where he would be taken in by a respected Egyptian physician and his family: "You will appear to become American in the coming years. You will immerse, even appear to embrace the sinful culture of the infidels. You will become educated, and when the time is right you will have help in becoming a successful and wealthy businessman. You will never go to a mosque, you will never pray, except in your mind. You will obey their laws to a fault, you will appear to us to have turned your back on the holy teachings of the Koran, never letting the enemy think you are anything other than one of them. You will wear the clothing of a sheep for the infidels, be polite and civil at all times, while grooming friends in their country. Cutouts and contacts will be provided over the years, but you will remain cautious and wary at all times, waiting for the day when you are called upon to initiate jihad in their country. Beneath the humble guise you are a hungry wolf. And when called upon to act you must show the courage of a lion. A word of warning, my young brother. Should your resolve weaken, should you decide you would rather cling to the comfort and the wealth and the pleasure of the infidel ways, we will send someone. He will come, an avenging angel of death, in the middle of the night, and he will show no mercy.''

Well, the time had come, Baruk-Islip knew, and he was wide awake, the torch to light the fire of jihad in hand. The Great One had long since passed on to Paradise, but others had stepped up to continue paving the righteous path, holy warriors who had more money, more operatives and more connections around the globe than even his teacher and mentor could have ever hoped and prayed for.

The jihad, yes, had indeed grown into a giant avenging angel of death, prepared to swoop and wipe out millions of infidels in one cleansing breath. A war, he knew, unlike anything the Americans had ever seen, was ready to be unleashed on their soil. He knew what was sailing into Miami on the *Napoleon,* and it gave him pause to consider the contents of the contraband. The encrypted E-mail had already been sent to the cutout in New Orleans, who would relay the message to Houston. They could expect delivery in forty-eight hours. It wasn't the counterfeit pesos, to be dumped off on unwitting contacts in Mexico, that troubled him. No, it was the winged—

He shuddered. If what he had heard was true about the Angels of Islam, so dubbed by the holy leader who was in hiding somewhere in the world, then life as he knew it would soon end. Indeed, he could well imagine that once the horror was turned loose on American cities, the mother of all infidel nightmares would become the ultimate dream come true for his brothers-in-jihad.

And if life for the hated Americans was soon to end, then life for him as well…

A part of him had serious reservations about what he was summoned to do, then he caught himself. It wasn't lack of courage, that heart of a lion mentioned by the Great One. Rather, it was regret and part anger that all he had worked for, all he had gained, could be gone tomorrow, his wealth, the pleasures he had secretly come to crave little more than a leaf burned up in an incinerator. Yes, he admitted to himself, he loved his life in Miami, but all of that was over. The money, the women, even the occasional dabbling in cocaine, throwing wild orgies at his Coral Cables estate. He owned policemen, judges, he had major dealings with Colombians, dispersing their cocaine, which, in turn, helped keep the dream of jihad alive and running. There were powerful men overseas, namely the Frenchman, who had been essential in seeing the worldwide Bank of Jihad, as he thought of his money-laundering operation, swell into a billion-dollar behemoth, while his bankers and lawyers kept cleverly outwitting the electronic long arm of the infidel law. He had, he knew, become something like his enemies, wallowing in money and sins of the flesh, but the charade had proved his greatest asset. If not for the Great One, he knew, he might still be floundering about in Cairo, railing at the West like many of his brothers, but unable through circumstance, such as lack of money, connections or true grit, to do anything other than rant and rave during some flag-and-effigy burning demonstration against the American imperialists.

And there were undetermined problems, namely the situation last night at his club, that made him wonder if the American authorities knew. Strange, he pondered, rubbing his goatee, how three men claiming to be agents of the Justice Department had been released from jail. No bond, all charges dismissed. How could that be possible? Paranoia had pushed him beyond heightened alert over this dark puzzle of the three so-called Justice Department agents. His man inside Miami PD didn't know what to make of it, since cops—undercover Vice he had unwittingly and stupidly employed—had been assaulted by the trio of mystery men, the next to worst felony other than shooting a police officer in the eyes of the law, but it was as if someone of high authority had gotten even those charges to vanish. In a way, that was the good news, the brawl rooting out lawmen who had slipped into his employ, trying, most likely, to smoke out his operation. The problem was, for those three to just walk out and breathe free air, all was forgiven, didn't make sense.

Or, perhaps it did.

If suspicions about the *Napoleon* had reached the secret corridors of some covert agency in Washington, then it stood to reason black ops, heavy hitters sanctioned to wax him and crush the operation, were closing in.

Which was why he had summoned forth a small army of sleepers, all Arabs, and why he was personally going to be on hand when the *Napoleon* docked.

He was standing, checking his Rolex watch, time winding down to go to meet the freighter, when he heard scuffling and muttered questions—were those voices raised in panic?—coming down the hall from the security room.

He swept out into the hall, found his head of security, an Uzi subgun in hand, running his way.

"What?"

"An intruder—or someone—was just at the gate," Ihrjaj told him.

"Show me."

He followed Ihrjaj into the security room where another armed guard was winding back the tape. Islip scanned the bank of monitors that covered all points around the estate, but didn't see any intruder until—

"There he is."

He was a big man, had to be, to reach up and spike whatever was in his hand on top of the spear-shaped tip to the front gate. There was a massive assault rifle in his hand, what looked like a grenade launcher fixed to the weapon.

That was no policeman's weapon, Islip knew, and something about the stranger, the way he moved, swift then disappearing into the night, flared up instinct that the man wasn't there to serve a warrant. The playback showed the guard rushing up to the gate. He made an awkward climb a foot or so up the gate, then grabbed whatever had been left behind.

Harried movement behind, as Islip felt his blood race, scouring the monitors, and he turned. The guard had what appeared a sheaf of papers in his hand.

"I don't know what to make of this," the guard said. "We are searching now."

Angry, Islip snatched the papers. One look at the familiar faces on the computer printouts, and his blood ran cold. Ragged holes were edged around the faces where the armed stranger had impaled them, but Islip recognized them all. Dead or alive at the bottom below their names, with alive crossed out, Xs had been slashed over the faces of Mullah Haroon Kanbar and Nawir Wahjihab.

"What do we do?" Irhjaj asked. "This could be a raid by the FBI."

"Find him," Islip snarled. "Take him alive, if possible, but it is your judgment call whether to kill him."

"But what if he is FBI and with—"

"Find him!"

Islip flung the wanted posters away, then saw the first of three monitors go dark. The mystery intruder was shooting out the cameras mounted on the south wall, then a dark face with eyes like fire was framed on another screen before the invader held some kind of box up and all the screens went blank.

Life, Islip thought, as he knew it, had just ended. The enemy knew, or thought they knew, and someone had come to declare war on him.

It was time, he decided, to take this to the limit. If he failed, if he was caught on the eve of jihad by American authorities, a military tribunal would be the least of his worries.

"On second thought," Islip told Ihrjaj, halting him in midstride at the door, "shoot to kill."

CHAPTER FOUR

"Dismissed, gentlemen. Make a final gear and weapons check, then saddle up. You three stay put."

Rosario Blancanales was halfway up from his seat next to Hermann Schwarz as Special Agent Alvin Ricker—second in command and supposedly sharing the show with a currently missing Mack Bolan—wrapped up the briefing. The forty-four man strike force, a combination of Justice-FBI-DEA special agents, rose from their metal chairs and began to file out of the large com center. Blancanales sat and glanced at Schwarz, who muttered, "Here we go. Thanks, Carl, for calling more unnecessary attention to us."

"I know," Blancanales whispered out of the corner of his mouth. "Why can't we all just get along?"

"I say something to piss you off, Agent Lemon? My brief bore you? Something wrong with the attack plan?"

The op center was located in what Blancanales assumed was a converted warehouse, used by the United States Coast Guard and the DEA at the Port of Miami. The com center was lit up with banks of glowing monitors, as the AWACS radar transmitted the position of the *Napoleon* to base. All systems were go, or so Blancanales—Special Agent Blankenship—hoped. The dark look on Ricker's face, as he scowled Lyons down, didn't inspire confidence that it was all for one and one for all here.

Blancanales turned, wondering how Lyons would respond to the lean, blond agent's questions. Lyons was peeking through the venetian blind, checking his watch, and Blancanales was fairly certain he wasn't gazing at massive cruise ships berthed against the sprawling concrete dock. Rather, as the clock wound down and they were minutes away from boarding one of five Black Hawks now grounded on a secured dock used exclusively by the Coast Guard, he figured Lyons was awaiting the return of Bolan.

The Executioner, Blancanales recalled, had laid out the two-pronged assault strategy when they made their new hotel suite in north Miami earlier in the day. Approved by Brognola, with the Farm laying out the groundwork to land Phoenix Force into combat on the next horizon, Bolan had gone to the Coral Gables estate of the owner of the Kitty Kat, a bad guy who had been brought to light just in time. Funny, Blancanales thought, how things, even the mess they had created for Brognola, had worked out to their advantage. Bolan was going solo, hoping to grab up Teddy the Titan, squeeze him for every ounce of information he could before returning to lead the strike force against the *Napoleon* and crew. Or so went part one of the plan.

Usually Able Team worked as a single unit, or with the other warriors of Stony Man, but sometimes they joined forces with other law-enforcement agencies when the need arose, something, Blancanales recalled from past experience, Lyons sometimes had a problem with, since he wasn't keen on authority other than his own. Reading the tight expression on Ironman's face, having wondered himself why the leader of Able Team had left his seat and gone to the window before the SAC finished his brief, Blancanales was hoping the big guy didn't find a dozen of more holes and flaws in the proposed strike, kicking up a storm of feces that would have every agent on the strike force squawking in Brognola's ear for days to come. Lyons, he suspected, was still in a foul mood about their stint behind bars, which could prove fatal to any bad guys aboard the *Napoleon,* but that was the good news. Where Lyons was concerned, Blancanales had come to expect the unexpected, braced for any sudden storm, verbal or otherwise.

Dressed in combat blacksuit like Blancanales and Schwarz, in full harness with webbing and pouches fitted with grenades and spare clips for the MP-5 subguns they would take into battle, Lyons walked up to the monitors, then looked over the wall map of the area in question out to sea. "No, no and no, Agent Ricker. Fact is, I think we can work something out."

"I'm hearing a change in strategy?"

Lyons stabbed the wall map. "Okay, you've got three first-class speedboats, armed with mounted M-60s, capable of sixty knots. Speed and power, so far, so good. The speeders and Coast Guard Cutter *Swordfish* intercepting and surrounding the freighter, eight miles offshore, right here as you indicated. My problem is this. You've got, according to your intelligence, close to forty crew members, all with small arms, and you believe there's a machine-gun nest in the rear that can be electronically raised from belowdecks. It's planted right over the cargo hold.''

''Your point?''

''They're not going to go quietly. The commander of the *Swordfish* isn't going to be able to just announce us and tell these pirates 'prepare for boarding.' No warning shots across the bow, either. You want to fly a holding pattern, but I say you go in prepared to shoot first, because that's sure as hell what I'm thinking they're going to do.''

''And you come by this enlightenment how?''

''Intelligence again, simple background checks on this Captain Bouchet and his scurvy bunch,'' Lyons said. ''Most of this crew have long and extensive criminal records, and they work exclusively for this Godfather of Marseilles. We don't even know what's belowdecks. We're thinking everything from drugs to a small tactical nuclear device. You've got the Treasury Department getting into the act, and I'm hearing counterfeit bills are likewise squirreled away belowdecks, but that's for the cash commandos to dicker over. We want the contraband, whatever it is, and my people are hearing 'special cargo,' which means likely it's more than a usual milk run for dope. These cutthroats will go down with the ship if whatever they've stashed is that valuable. I say swarm the vessel with the Black Hawks, drop the three of us off on the deck near the stern. We take out the machine gunner—"

"We're not looking for some long-running sea battle, Agent Lemon. And I'm not looking to fill up the water with a bunch of bodies for shark chum."

"As long as the right bodies splash down as fish food, you'll get no argument here. My hunch, you'll get a shooting war, whether you want it or not."

"How come I look at you and I get the impression you want one?"

"How come I'm trying to cover our asses by covering all bases? Okay, you're taking the vessel down well out to sea, the Coast Guard has diverted all ships well away from the AIQ."

"Those were my orders."

Recalling Bolan's standing order which came from Brognola, Lyons said, "That's because we don't want half of Miami Beach or some luxury liner heading out for Jamaica to witness the fireworks. We want Puchain and his thugs back home to think their contraband reached shore, in the hands of this Islip, who all but ruined my night and a sure thing, by the way, and is on the way to whatever its destination."

"In my mind, it's a stretch trying to keep a major operation like this, arrests of the crew, seizure of the vessel, from Puchain."

"Let us worry about that," Lyons said. "We only need a day or so to try and keep word from getting back to Marseilles."

Blancanales watched as Ricker weighed Lyons's words. "We're with him."

"So I would have figured. Okay, hotshots, but hear this. We leave in thirty minutes, with or without your man, Belasko, onboard. If this thing goes to hell because you want to play Captain Kidd…"

"I'll take full responsibility," Lyons stated.

"Damn straight you will."

"And I was always kind of partial to Blackbeard."

When Ricker grunted, pivoted and marched off, Blancanales said, "Sometimes I like it, Carl, when you get your way."

"Best the three of us go in solo," Lyons said. "I've got too many chiefs in the way as it stands. At least I know the three of us can, uh, how did you put it, Pol? Get along?"

"I believe I posed that as a question."

THE DIRECT HANDS-ON approach was the best and only way in Bolan's unwritten playbook when engaging the enemy. The wanted posters got the ball rolling, as he hoped it would, the soldier braced now for an avalanche of gunmen to come hunting. Islip was dirty, and the opening act, implementing psywar, would crank up the paranoia and fear if the Arab had something to hide, which, everyone on the home team strongly suspected, he did. The trick, Bolan knew, would come later, weeding out secrets, perhaps reversing the ghoul's act perpetrated on those CIA ops on Islip, though torture really didn't sit well with the soldier. Naturally, it would be the task of the Justice

Department and FBI to comb the estate in search of clues, hard drives, E-mail and so on that would keep the Stony Man war machine rolling. Clean-up chores were someone else's headache.

The psywar didn't stop at the front gate. After melting into the tropical vegetation near the south wall, Bolan had shot out three floodlights and a couple of cameras mounted on the wall. Before scaling the wall, he had used the Zapper, the mini-high-tech gizmo borrowed from Gadgets Schwarz. All Bolan had needed to do was aim the box at any camera, thumb the button and the microwave radioactive transmission superheated the works, generating a meltdown of fiber optics, cables and whatever else that had high-tech eyes watching, a blistering invisible inferno scorching its way throughout the entire monitoring system in the control room. When their screens winked out, he figured the enemy inside the huge coral-and-glass mansion would scurry out of their rats' nest, come running and looking to wax the invader.

They did.

Miami PD, he knew, could prove a problem, especially in light of Able Team's antics, but the FBI was in the vicinity, with orders from Brognola to hold back the men in blue. Two blacksuit pilots, on loan from the Farm's security force, were flying a holding pattern in a Black Hawk over Biscayne Bay, waiting for the call to swoop and scoop after they had dropped off the soldier in a jungle thicket east of the estate.

The Executioner was loaded down to take full-scale

war to the savages here, and beyond, when he finally hit the *Napoleon*. Wearing a combat blacksuit, harness and webbing, he was weighted with a variety of grenades, spare clips for the shoulder-holstered Beretta 93-R, with the big.44 Magnum Desert Eagle on his hip. An M-16 filled his hands, a buckshot round down the gullet of the fixed M-203 launcher.

It stood to reason Islip and shooters would begin a fighting march for the motor pool, six luxury vehicles lined up out front in the driveway, once the battle started and they realized this was a hell of a lot more than a standard raid on the premises. Phone taps and electronic intercepts from Islip to the captain of the *Napoleon* alerted the strike force that the Arab planned to meet the ship personally to receive the special cargo. If the soldier cornered Islip, the man boxed in and seeing whatever his dreams about to crumble, the warrior figured the hardforce would be ordered to go all the way in blood and thunder.

Bolan saw he figured right.

Three hardmen came running across the manicured lawn from the walled-in pool outback. Bolan was angling for the motor pool, homed in on the angry chatter out front, when the trio cut loose with subguns. That was as far as the soldier let them get, wild rounds flaying apart leaves from the palm trees he darted behind. They were exposed, packed together at less than arm's length, when Bolan hit the trigger, sweeping his assault rifle left to right, a lightning burst that appeared to kick them off their feet.

Another cluster of palm trees flanked the motor

pool, the engine of a Mercedes limo already gunning to life as armed figures scurried about, heads craned in the direction of the soldier's first three kills.

The front of the coral digs had no raised entrance, no pillars. For Bolan's money that nearly made for a perfect world for this killing ground. Four hardmen had nowhere to hide, except if they made the vehicles, so Bolan zeroed in on them as they charged for the limo. He bolted into the ring of palm trees, hitting the M-203's trigger, watching as the man-eating charge detonated on the limo's portside. Countless razor-sharp pieces of shrapnel scythed through. Two went down for the count, shredded to human hamburger, while a duo of mangled bodies cried out and thrashed through leaking gore.

Three more hardmen, standing outside massive gold-gilded double doors, argued with one another, clearly uncertain whether to run for cover or attempt a fighting dash for the motor pool.

Bolan had a 40 mm charge down the chute, triggered the weapon and sent the grenade flying. The limo vanished in a fireball, the trio getting it together, as sheared wreckage winged their way and banged off the facade. Before they could run for deep cover, regroup and try again, the Executioner dumped another hellbomb into the pack, blowing them back and out of sight.

Bolan rolled out of cover to nail it down, up-close and personal. Ratchet up the killing heat, and Teddy the Titan's kingdom, he thought, was about to tumble down.

TWO SECONDS or two more feet closer to the door, and Islip knew he would have been on his way to God, not enough pieces left to spoon inside a sandwich bag. As it was, the world blew apart, nearly in his face, the shock wave hammering him down the foyer. Laid out on his back, his bell rung, his guts churned with nausea as he breathed in the smoke and blood, trembling hands checking himself right away to make sure all the critical parts were still attached to his body. It was more fear than being punched out by the blast bringing on the sickness, he believed, then he saw what the explosion had done to three of his men. The sight of limbs, bloodied and torn, an arm on a corpse hanging by mere sinewy threads, the screams of at least two more of his vaunted operatives lancing his senses from the motor pool, nearly opened the floodgates of vomit.

A mental image of the dark man, out there, blowing up the night, wasting his people, shredding apart not only a midrange six figures worth of luxury vehicles and their way out...

No, he told himself, it couldn't be possible. But he heard his surviving force, shaved to less than half in a heartbeat.

One man? Was that what he heard them squawking near the boiling smoke at the front doors? Did this attack have anything to do with the drubbing his American security detail had taken last night at the club? Following the attacks on the WTC and the infidel incursion into Afghanistan, Islip knew the Americans had changed the rules. Their operatives had carte blanche these days to take an eye for an eye where and whenever they saw fit to shoot first and fling the questions out the window. They no longer needed judges to sign warrants for phone taps or raids. They—

This was no time to ponder the incredible or the outrageous, he decided, getting shakily to his feet. They needed to reach whatever vehicles were still intact, bail the premises, only that inflamed his imagination with yet more dire scenarios.

If they were being hit like the wrath of God at his own home, then it was possible they knew about the *Napoleon;* perhaps an army of American law-enforcement agents were prepared to seize the vessel. If that cargo was discovered, well, Islip had no intention of spending the rest of his life behind American bars. He would rather die first than face around-the-clock grilling by the FBI that might expose the entire operation.

He made a decision, reaching out and grabbing an Ingram subgun from the hand of the corpse at his feet. They were paralyzed at the door, he saw, searching the night, listening to those pitiful wails of pure agony. Then a brief stutter of weapons' fire rang out, and an eerie silence seemed to swell the smoke cloud with a portent of more doom and horror to come.

Just to make sure he wasn't having the mother of all nightmares, unwilling to digest the impossible, Islip shuffled up to his shooters and barked, "How many are out there?"

"One man. That's all we saw."

"Where?"

No one looked certain, or willing to peek outside or respond, but Ihrjaj crept up to the edge of the doorway. He pointed to his left, said, "South wall."

"We make a run for it," Islip told them, pinning them each with a burning eye, and God pity the man who didn't want to go. "Shoot and keep shooting."

Ihrjaj looked set to remind him the damn guy had a rocket launcher, but Islip lifted his subgun, put some challenge into his voice and said, "A running wall. On the count of three. One..."

THE SOLDIER HUGGED the south wall, a fresh clip fed to the M-16, another 40 mm charge ready to fly from the M-203. He heard the voices of fear and panic debating their next move. When they made a break for it, the soldier would drop the steel and hellbomb net, seal it with a one-two punch. The Ford Bronco was closest to their intended run, and he would blast the vehicle off the driveway when the shooting charge broke. Of course, he intended to reel in the big catch, and if Islip played true to form like so many other bad guys he'd hunted in the past and who didn't want to give up the ghost, he would let the others take the lead. While they died, Teddy the Titan would try to flee behind their flailing bodies and flying blood.

The war cry got it jump-started again, two then three subgunners lurching into view, another trio behind them and blazing away with autofire, the gang going for broke. Stretched out on his belly, bullets gouging out stone above his head, the Executioner sent the 40 mm missile winging away, aimed for the Bronco's grille. The bulk of the running stampede was close enough to take the brunt of the thundering firestorm, a head-to-toe mutilation that left no doubt who was winning the night. Lead hardmen, perhaps five in all, were pounded back into the others by storming wreckage and roaring flames. A tangle of limbs brought down three more gunmen, streams of wild autofire chattering for the sky as a domino effect toppled them down the line. One look at the downed pack, and Bolan glimpsed the face he had committed to memory. Shock and terror carved Islip's features, but as Bolan figured, he had lagged behind. Sacrificing his men had saved his skin from getting flayed to ribbons by the blast, but the warrior determined Teddy the Titan's woes had only just begun.

The Executioner rose, marched out and began slicing them up with long raking bursts of autofire. He ran the fusillade up the backs of grounded hardmen, dicing them to bloody rags, sparing not even the wounded or the one gunman who thrust his hands up and begged for mercy. Firing on, he drilled two more off their feet, spinning stick figures raining gore as they flew over Islip.

Bolan tuned combat senses into his surroundings, on even higher alert for any stragglers, but if earlier Justice Department intel was right, he was looking at a clean sweep.

Islip looked up at Bolan, rolled onto his side and started to reach for a discarded subgun.

"That would be your last mistake," the Executioner said, drawing a bead with the smoking M-16 on Islip's face.

"Who the hell are you?"

"Let's just say I'm not with the Red Cross."

"Do you know who I am? I'm a legitimate and respected businessman in this town—"

"You're garbage."

Kicking the subgun away, the soldier flipped the man on his stomach. One eye on the doorway, he fastened the Egyptian's hands behind his back with plastic cuffs, then took his tac radio to call in the pickup.

THE COAST GUARD assault chopper, what looked like a Marine Sea Knight CH-46 to Lyons as he stood in the hatchway of their Black Hawk, came under fire as soon as the commander of the USCGC *Swordfish* let the captain and crew of the freighter know they were about to be boarded and searched. Well, Lyons had warned the co-leader of the strike force they could expect a fight.

The good guys were taking serious small-arms fire ahead and below. The speeders, Lyons saw, had fanned out, two to port and one to starboard near the stern of the dark hulk of the *Napoleon*. The machine gunners in those speeders were hosing the railing with sweeping M-60 firestorms, Lyons glimpsing two shadows tumbling out of sight, weapons falling for the ocean. The cutter had a 78 mm cannon, but so far the big gun was silent. The Black Hawks and Coast Guard gunship began strafing runs over the deck, and

Lyons hoped they cleared the way some of armed cutthroats.

But he needed to get this under control in a hurry, he knew. Scratch plan one and go to option two on the spot, if Able Team was going to board and fight its way belowdecks, wade in without getting diced by their own people pouring on the fire from above.

He found Ricker squawking into his radio, the sounds of machine-gun fire rattling through the fuselage over the airwaves. MP-5 subgun in hand, Lyons rolled over to the SAC. "Ricker, this is what I want you to do. Have those speeders and the cutter fall back, then veer to the vessel's port. Same thing with all choppers except ours."

Ricker looked at him as if he were crazy. "I've got these bastards trying to shoot our people out of the water—"

"Do it! Pass on that order now."

Lyons returned to watch the sea battle. It took a good minute before the order was passed on down the chain of command, but the gunships, speeders and cutter vectored for the freighter's portside, firing as they sliced through the night. As hoped for, the enemy surged in that direction, triggering weapons over the railing. It was dicey, what he was going to do next, but there was no other way he could see to board that vessel.

"Ricker, have your flyboy go in low, I mean skim the goddamn water up the starboard side, hugging that hull on the way in. When he's near the stern, rise up and the three of us bail right over the railing. If we draw some fire, the cavalry can swarm that boat, stem to stern and it's your show.''

Ricker went to the cockpit and barked the order. The dark swell of the Atlantic rose up as the Black Hawk lowered and began its run up the starboard side.

Lyons's com link crackled as Bolan patched through. ''Yeah?''

''I'm en route, Able One, ETA is ten minutes.''

''We couldn't wait, Striker, the show's started without you.''

''I just caught the score from the commander of the *Swordfish*.''

''Then you might know we're hitting the vessel aft, near the machine-gun emplacement, just to let you know where the action will be on our end.''

''I'll be there.''

''How did you make out on your end, Striker?''

''Let's just say I bagged the catch of the day.''

''Good news for a change.''

''We'll see how it shakes out.''

''We'll look for you.''

''Keep the faith.''

BARBARA PRICE TOOK Bolan's sitrep over the sat com in the Computer Room with a mix of hope and trepidation. The warriors were in the mix, bulling on for the crew of the *Napoleon,* and Islip was Bolan's prisoner. That was the good news.

A stone-cold professional, the former NSA mission controller had been around long enough in the covert business to separate personal feelings from the facts of life where it concerned combat and the kind of bad folks the Stony Man warriors went up against. She cared deeply about each and every man and woman involved with the Farm's operations, but she was only human, after all. She would never show it to the others, of course, but Mack Bolan had a special place in her heart. She couldn't imagine a world without the Executioner, couldn't stand the thought either they might never share those rare intimate moments again, but what the cyberteam had just learned, during an electronic intercept from the CIA in Marseilles, put her on edge. This, she feared, could be it, the big fatal blow, a planned suicide stand that might take out Bolan and Able Team for good.

She listened to Bolan's report, feeling Katz and Kurtzman silently urging her to say it.

"If the joint strike force came under fire like that," she told Bolan, "it means they're onto something I don't even want to consider."

"Right, the short list is obvious," Bolan said. "Everything from suitcase nukes to containers of bio or chem weapons. Whatever's down there, we're in the process of getting it. I'm three minutes and closing. Able's already boarded and taking fire."

"Listen, Striker. We just learned something and you need to know."

"Sounds serious."

"It is. I'll spell it out quickly. Something like three hundred pounds of C-4, laced with uranium, is believed to have been smuggled onboard. Electronic intercepts by the CIA has determined that in the event that ship is boarded, the captain is under orders to blow that vessel.''

A pause, then Bolan simply said, ''I'll keep that in mind. I'll be in touch.''

Price offered a silent prayer of good luck and godspeed to the four warriors and the brave men of the joint strike force. She found Katz staring at her and hoped her expression didn't betray her concern.

''We wait?'' Katz asked.

''Call David,'' she said, referring to the big Briton who was the leader of Phoenix Force. ''Phoenix is on standby as of now. For the moment, we ride out the wait, and keep our fingers crossed they make it in time and out of there in one piece.''

CHAPTER FIVE

Even before his ship set sail from Marseilles, the pressure to succeed and safely deliver the special cargo was enormous, and frightening. The death threats—in person, by E-mail, fax, phone, and just now via the radio on the bridge—were subtle, carefully worded reminders the captain had to blow the vessel and go down with the ship in the event the *Napoleon* was to be boarded and seized by the United States Coast Guard. When his crew had been armed to the teeth in Marseilles—briefed and even trained for counterattack against a raid at sea in a vast training complex—he had nearly told his paymaster he could find himself another captain for this particular voyage. Between the death threats, the haunting ghosts of the sins of his past, and, of course, the money, meant for his retirement after this sojourn…

It was far too late for regret now, even though he longed in this moment of impending doom for the simple days of a dead and buried yesteryear.

Captain Renauld Bouchet had been a seaman most of his adult life, following a brief stint with the Foreign Legion in Algeria. That was a lifetime ago, fifty years to be exact, trudging through the sand in blistering heat, a foot soldier trading weapons' fire with Arabs who would have just as soon seen his head on a stake as look at him. After seeing men slaughter one another over what he considered nothing at all, he had come to yearn for a freedom he could call his own, or at the least where insanity on the mass scale of bloodletting wasn't the order of the day.

He was essentially a loner who longed to be his own man. He had never denied what really beat in his own heart, which was to be free to call his own destiny, charting courses for destinations yet unseen, hard men with more problems than they could count and were running from, under his command. The open sea, then, sailing into the wind, crossing vast expanses of ocean that had no end in sight, had once been all the dreams of romantic stuff come true he might have had as a boy.

The trouble was, he thought, the boy became a man, with a man's problems, the man unwittingly stumbling into needs and wants casting a devil's brew into dreams that once looked pure and simple of heart. Marseilles was infamous for bringing out the worst in even the best of men, and he had fallen prey to the vultures who sought to devour the weak and the fallen so they could keep on feeding whatever their dark insatiable hunger. Born and raised in the port city, the only son of a widow, he had stumbled into a life of piracy, due to one moment of madness for which he had spent decades thrashing through nightmares in torment and regret. And, eventually, the love and thirst for adventure on the high seas was cast aside by the most basic fundamental failing in men.

Greed.

Years ago, he had been bought and sold by the Devil of Marseilles himself. Having sliced the throat of a prostitute in a drunken rage when she demanded more money than services rendered, it turned out the whore was in the employ of René Puchain. Even worse—and what could be worse than murder?—it turned out Puchain was willing to forgive and forget. What was one more dead whore anyway? Or so the Devil's reasoning went. It was later discovered by Bouchet during a drunken night in a waterfront bar that the woman had left behind three orphans. In later years, he learned that night, the son committed suicide, and both girls, following in the footsteps of their mother's profession, had fallen victim to murder themselves.

Well, his crime had disappeared with the body, no grudge, no revenge factor on the Devil's part, but only if he was willing to invest his own freighter, give up and hand over his one dream that had come true only because he had scrimped and saved to get a loan for the *Napoleon*, which, as it turned out, was dumped in his lap through a banker under Puchain's pitchfork. His own export-import business, wine, olive oil and other goods, had been floundering up to that point, due to reckless spending, carousing, all those sins he had opted to forget over the years, and he needed fast cash. Chalk up his failings to keeping bad company, or the lonely heart simply in search of a human touch, but he knew better. He was weak when he wanted to be strong. He did that which he did not want to do, crying out to God, who he didn't think cared or was listening, wondering why he couldn't stop himself from charging down the road to hell. Well, Puchain had offered a way out, and Bouchet knew it wasn't God who had answered his prayers. The *Napoleon* wouldn't only become the crime lord's boat, but Bouchet would be the captain, hauling every manner of contraband the seven seas over.

Sins of the past.

And now, as the final battle raged on around the freighter, he knew the end had come, the gates of hell yawning wide and ready to take his wretched soul home for an eternity of accounting.

The relentless drumming of autofire rolled down the passageway, jolting him back to the present, jarring him with the sickening knowledge of what he had been ordered to do. If he went through with it, he knew there would be so much innocent blood on his hands, good men leaving behind widows and orphans—forget his crew, since they were handpicked by the Devil, the worst of inhumanity imaginable—that no amount of mercy from God would save him from eternal damnation. He felt like a man wading in slow motion through a bad dream as he made his way aft, looking for the ladder that would take him below-decks. His handheld radio crackled with the voice of his crew leader, Dupré, wanting to know if they should go ahead and do it. What insanity drove evil men? he wondered. At a moment like this, when suicide and mass murder was their only option, he couldn't help but wonder if God even existed, or if God was just some spectator who left men to their whims and wants, watching the whole sorry tragicomedy, betting on who would win and who would lose.

This, he thought, was a defining moment, and if he was going to die he was hoping to find an answer, the smallest of clues that God did, in fact, care before he was gone from this world of sorrow and pain. He had seen over the years the worst of cutthroats, killers, rapists and thieves running from the law, signing on for a voyage they thought would take them far away from the law, allow them to start a new life in a strange land, free of worry, but free to carry on their evil, since they were unwilling to change what was in their hearts. This time he had sailed on a ship of doom that had reached its final destination before it plunged into the abyss. To a man aboard, they deserved to die. No one, he knew, ever escaped sins unrepented. He believed in a cosmic justice, a benevolent all-powerful being, watching, willing to understand, but also ready to call in markers if a man believed he could escape the sins of his past.

The tab had come due.

The voice shot out over the handheld radio in rapid-fire French. "I will take your silence, Captain, as a yes!"

The radio was reaching his lips, the threat that if they mined the cargo hold he would personally shoot them all was on his lips, when it sounded like the wrath of God came thundering down on his head. The shock wave knocked him on his face, as smoke and fire shot down the passageway. Wreckage screaming and banging behind him, the massive invisible blow was bringing on the roiling sickness in his guts, darkness threatening to envelope him, take him away. His once-beloved ship, but a dream that had long since died, he knew, would be sunk, one way or another, as the moment of truth of what had happened slapped home. Someone, or something, had just blown the bridge off the ship.

LYONS HIT THE DECK, shooting from the hip, waxing two swarthy cutthroats with a sustained burst of sub-gun fire, pinning them to a steel container before they slid in a boneless heap. The Black Hawk was up and away, slamming rotor wash over Able Team, but hosing down the deck with a storm of 12.7 mm machine-gun fire. The gunship cleared the way some more as three pirates were riddled with heavy man-eating steel-jacketed slugs, bodies flailing and dancing back, eviscerated before they toppled beyond the crane, sliding away in a slick wash of crimson muck. The Able Team leader beelined for the steel container as he saw his hopes of a quick and easy boarding shot to hell in a ball of fire that left him wondering how long the freighter would stay afloat when the bridge was blown off the deck in a thousand and one raining steel chunks.

It was one of those ''what the hell'' moments, and he cursed the SOB who gave the order to blow the bridge. There was no other possibility, he figured, than the commander of the *Swordfish* had taken it upon himself to unleash the seventy-eight, which left the three of them one hundred percent on their own and wondering if they'd go down with the ship. To compound their dire straits, Lyons, Schwarz and Blancanales weren't only taking fire from a scurrying pack of five pirates charging them from amidships, but the machine gunner in the steel-enclosed revetment was doing his damnedest to turn the tide, sweeping his heavy man-eater around, cranking out the lead, the hurricane of bullets chasing the Stony Man warriors to cover behind the steel container. Sparks shot above Lyons's face as a storm of lead tore off the container.

Lyons returned fire at the running hyena pack, kicking one, then another cutthroat off his feet, the long fusillade stitching number two pirate back and forth across the chest before he twirled and pitched overboard.

As Schwarz and Blancanales took up firepoints at the other end of the container, Lyons told them, "I want that gunner out of the picture, and like five seconds ago!"

"Striker to Able One, come in, it's urgent!"

Lyons keyed his com link. "Bad timing, Striker!"

"I'm about a mile out! Don't go below until I hit the deck! Word is the opposition may try to sink the ship with a big dirty bang."

"A radiation bomb?" Lyons shouted over the thundering of the heavy machine gun.

"That's the story."

"See you in a few, and if you get a chance, plant a verbal foot up that commander's ass if he gave the order to start blowing up the deck with that cannon!"

"Roger."

Lyons crept closer to the edge of the steel container, saw three pirates vectoring for cover behind a line of crates. He hit the subgun's trigger, scored a lucky tag as a dark spray erupted from a hardman's leg, sent him thrashing and howling out of sight. That heavy machine gun, he knew, had to go, or they were out of the fight. And now, aware the crew was below, racing about and perhaps mining the cargo hold...

Silently Lyons urged the cavalry in the form of the big guy to arrive. Whatever was left of the bridge still raining fiery sheets to the deck, Lyons looked to his side, and he saw the Black Hawk streaking in. The two 12.7 mm machine guns began blazing, and Lyons hoped his prayers were about to be answered.

A standoff, while doomsday ticked down in his face, was unacceptable.

UNDER THE CIRCUMSTANCES it was the best plan. The blacksuit pilots had already been in touch with Ricker, who gave them the sitrep on Able Team's problems. The way Bolan heard it, Lyons had ordered all friendly craft to one side, the enemy moving in that direction while the three Stony Man warriors boarded on their blind side. The bigger picture nearly shot that plan to hell, since all hands on the *Napoleon* were bent on not only fighting to the death but taking the ship down with a dirty bomb. It told Bolan the enemy had something nasty to hide.

The Black Hawk cut back on speed, Bolan in the hatchway, M16/M-203 combo loaded. He was taking in the problem spots—aft—and raising the *Swordfish,* keying the frequency on his com link that tied him into the Coast Guard. "Belasko to Admiral Locke, come in!"

"Locke here!"

"I've got my own people onboard, Admiral, or had you forgotten? I want that seventy-eight to stay quiet from here on, you copy?"

A pause, as Bolan saw the flaming speedboat on the far side of the massive cargo ship, the Coast Guard cutter pulling alongside the wreckage. The rest of the gunship armada was scissoring the length of the vessel, unleashing machine-gun fire on targets the soldier couldn't make out. The Executioner had already given the word to his blacksuit pilots where and who to hit, as they lowered and began opening up with their own 12.7 mm barrage.

"I just lost three good men, Agent Belasko."

"I understand that, but since I'm in charge, I'm ordering you to not fire that seventy-eight again. Something else, and if you don't want lose any more men, you'll follow orders. There's a bomb below, a big ugly one, so get the HAZMAT team suited up. Me and my men are going down. Hold back the troops from going below until it's clear. Have them board, but wrap it up on the deck." Another pause, then Bolan growled, "Admiral?"

"Aye-aye."

Bolan glanced at his prisoner. Before vacating Islip's estate, the soldier had called in two of Brognola's agents to sit on the Egyptian. "I don't suppose you want to tell me about this special cargo?"

Islip shrugged. "Luxury automobiles, rich men's toys."

"We'll talk later. For your sake you'd better have a little more to offer than the obvious."

As the Black Hawk sprayed the machine-gun nest, Bolan picked out the foursome behind the crates, pinning down Able Team in an exchange of weapons' fire.

The Executioner drew a bead on the four pirates, slipped his finger around the M-203's trigger and let the missile fly.

THE OPENING HE WAS looking for to take out the machine gunner came in a flash of fire and a thunderclap from beyond his point of concealment. Schwarz was pulling back for deeper cover behind the container as the machine gunner locked in and kept pounding out the big slugs. He heard the rotor wash, glimpsed the Black Hawk lowering and pouring out twin streams of machine-gun fire, dousing the steel revetment. It was another glimpse, the big guy jumping from the gunship, but it was the window of opportunity he needed.

Striker had cleaned out some of the cutthroat garbage.

Thrusting his subgun around the edge, the bearded

pirate lurched up, manning the heavy machine gun when Schwarz hit him in the face with a burst of subgun fire. The obliterated face and skull vanished from sight beneath a dark halo.

"Scratch the big gun, Carl!" Schwarz shouted.

"About time! Move out!" Lyons ordered.

Withering autofire sounded in the distance, Schwarz figuring the remnants of the crew were dropping, one by one, as the Black Hawks kept up the slice and dice from above, searchlights holding the halo over the vessel. He looked up at the jagged smoking teeth where the bridge had stood. So far no fire breaking out, threatening to consume the ship and see them all diving overboard, but that was about the only good news, in light of what Lyons had just informed them.

Schwarz ran for the revetment, scaled the short ladder, then cautiously looked in and down. His kill confirmed, he found Bolan, Lyons and Blancanales splitting up on the deck, toeing bodies.

"Gadgets, you want to get with the program?" Lyons barked over his com link.

Schwarz quickly swung himself over the rail and settled in behind the big machine gun. He keyed his com link. "Guys, I have a suggestion."

THE EXECUTIONER knew their personal Armageddon clock was ticking as he made the hatch nearly amidships and armed a frag grenade. Lyons and Blancanales on his heels, Bolan heard voices shouting in French and peeked inside at the galley. So far, there was no interfering linkup with the rest of the joint strike force, but he made out the weapons' fire rattling on, sternward. Bolan needed to get belowdecks in a hurry, or all was lost.

Bolan pitched the steel egg into the galley, rode out the explosion, then charged in, low and peeling off to his left while Lyons and Blancanales surged right. Bolan counted three pirates standing, subguns raising in shaking hands, two mangled bodies stretched out over steel bolted-down tables, bleeding out. The Stony Man warriors opened up as one converging leadstorm, chopping up the pirates, then surged on as spinning bodies slammed off the bulkhead.

The Executioner hit the hatch of a passageway thick with churning smoke where the seventy-eight had blown a hole in the roof above. It was clear of armed combatants, and the Executioner heard the groan, spotted the figure clawing his way up the wall.

"Freeze!"

Bolan recognized Captain Bouchet from the intel pac. The French skipper threw his arms up.

"I surrender!"

"You cooperate, Captain, and you might make it out of here alive," Bolan stated.

"That sounds like a noble plan, however..."

"We know. Your crew is ready to blow us clear to Miami in a dirty cloud of radioactive waste," Lyons growled as Blancanales snapped plastic cuffs on Bouchet.

Bolan told Lyons to touch base with Schwarz.

"You want to tell us what you're hiding and where it is, Captain?"

Bouchet nodded.

"Striker, Gadgets is down there laying waste to whatever's still standing, but he says he could use a little help from his buddies."

Bolan shoved the prisoner ahead. "Lead the way, Captain."

ON THE RIDE DOWN, Schwarz had fed another belt link to the big machine gun, figuring about three hundred rounds of 20 mm flesh shredders were at his disposal. Before the revetment jounced to a halt in the cargo hold, Schwarz let it rip. He didn't bother counting up enemy numbers, but figured close to twenty shooters were still on the loose. It was the pirates fixing big slabs of explosives up and down both walls and rolling out the det cord that received the first wave of attention.

Schwarz hammered out the first of several long salvos. He hosed down the pirates along the starboard wall, bodies erupting in scarlet clouds, it looked, from head to toe. It might have been a little overkill, but the Stony Man commando wasn't taking any chances a badly wounded cutthroat could set off the suicide blast as he swept a line of big slugs back over the fallen pirates.

As Schwarz swung the big gun to port and began pounding the next batch of wannabe martyrs to grant them their death wish before they could do the dirty deed, the enemy began scurrying for cover down the parade of roped luxury vehicles and sports cars. Autofire swelled the cargo hold with a thunderous echo, swarms of rounds hissing past Schwarz or drumming the steel nest. He held on, recoil jarring him to the bone, as he raked the lines of autos, taking whatever he could get. A typhoon of glass began bowling through the surviving rank and file, two pirates screaming, clutching their eyes as they jigged out into the open before Schwarz gutted them and sent them flying.

Schwarz poured it on, shearing off fenders, cleaving engine hoods, hurling hurricanes of lethal glass shrapnel around the hold. Still, armed figures kept darting between the vehicles, firing on the run, closing the distance.

He fired on, turning men to bloody sieves and luxury cars to battered scrap.

BOLAN SLUNG Bouchet to the deck. One look at the man, as he heard the weapons' fire swelling the massive cargo hold with a sense-splitting din, and he knew the captain would stay put. Whether he would fully cooperate when the smoke cleared...

First things first.

Another look at the revetment, as bullets sparked off steel with mounting intensity, and the soldier knew the pirates were closing fast and hard on Schwarz. Armed shadows darkened to near invisibility, Bolan noted, the farther they moved from the wire-encased lights hung on the bulkheads, the brigands looking to outflank the Able Team warrior.

Bolan gave the order to split up, while he'd take the middle line of vehicles. It was hard to tell how many shooters were left standing, but at least Gadgets had taken the demo team out of play, as he glimpsed the bodies piled up on the floor beneath the packs of uranium-laced C-4, blood still pooling in the light.

They might have made it in time to stave off the Apocalypse at sea, but Bolan determined to keep one eye peeled for any hardman who might attempt a return to mining duties.

Lyons and Blancanales split off from Bolan's flanks, their subguns chattering as heads popped up over fenders. Two came running the Executioner's way, assault rifles blazing down the center line of autos, when Bolan nailed them on the fly, his M-16 chewing dark silhouettes to bloody shreds before they bounced off a Mercedes limo so riddled with 20 mm rounds it was destined for the junkyard.

"Guys!" Bolan heard Schwarz shouting over the com link. "We've got three on the run, sternward, and that looks to be about it."

Bolan, hunched low, weapon searching for live ones in the spaces between vehicles, was filling the M-203 with an HE round when someone beat him to the kill.

The explosion ripped apart two BMWs, enemy bodies sailing away. Through the ringing in his ears, Bolan strained to make out any sound of wounded hardmen, or any shooter scuffling and still in the mix, as he closed on the smoke cloud.

Lyons lurched up from between two vehicles close

to the rear, kicked the fresh corpses. He turned and told Bolan, ''I didn't think you'd want us to malinger with this bunch, Striker, since Admiral Locke's proved he has an itchy trigger finger.''

''Let's walk through it,'' Bolan told Lyons and Blancanales. ''Then we'll go have a chat with the good captain.''

CHAPTER SIX

After the cargo hold was cleared of armed opposition, Bolan gave the order for the joint strike force and HAZMAT teams to move belowdecks to find and secure whatever the contraband. DEA, FBI, Treasury and Justice agents were now wrenching panels off the vehicles, blowtorching metal and carving up seats with commando daggers where Bouchet indicated nonlethal contraband was hidden. The search teams moved with a sense of urgency, perhaps even a good degree of anger, Bolan noted, since the strike force had taken three KIAs, two more agents badly wounded and barely hanging on. Minesweepers, metal detectors, Geiger counters, thermal imaging, and bomb-sniffing dogs were being used to comb the hold, bulkheads, steel containers for contraband and boobytraps.

Following the takedown of the *Napoleon*, it took ninety-plus minutes, while the soldier grilled Bouchet, but Able Team searched the vessel stem to stern, including all quarters, with Gadgets using a thermal imaging, heat-seeking monitor to point to any crew stashed away in compartments or behind bulkheads.

A rough head count of enemy dead, including pirates bobbing on the ocean surface, and Bouchet insisted it was a clean sweep, all cutthroats dead and accounted for. Other than the captain, no survivors meant no prisoners for further interrogation, and Bouchet wasn't exactly proving a gold mine of intelligence, though he knew where the contraband was stowed.

"I tell you, *monsieur,* I was not informed of the contents of the special cargo."

M-16 slung across a shoulder, Bolan looked at Bouchet. "I suppose the ship's manifest isn't rife with particulars."

The captain hadn't squawked for any sweetheart deal or special consideration in return for his cooperation. If Bolan didn't know better, the Frenchman looked defeated, but relieved it was over, as if a ghost that had been haunting him over the years had been put to rest. There was a sorrow and remorse in Bouchet's eyes that picked at Bolan's instincts this was a man who wanted to help point the way to the bad guys, if only to clean his own slate. Good enough for the time being, Bolan determined, but the captain had a lot to prove, and the soldier knew they all had a long way to go. This campaign had only just begun, with more unanswered questions and bad guys piling up with each shot fired in anger.

"The way Islip and Puchain alluded to its importance, I came to believe it is very nasty stuff." Bouchet shook his head, his face pinched with some grief only he seemed capable of understanding. "I assume it is some weapon of mass destruction. I know for a fact Puchain has had dealings with certain Arabs lately, two of whom I believe I have seen on your CNN as wanted terrorists. Before we sailed, they were on hand to personally supervise the loading.''

''We'll get to that in short order.''

''Believe me when I tell you, I am sorry. I...I had no choice.''

''There's always a choice,'' Bolan said.

''In my case, I am not so sure. I was delivering this cargo under threat of death.''

''Family they could get to?''

''It is just me in the world. And suicide was never an option. It goes against my religion.''

Bouchet had already indicated where the nasty stuff was hidden behind the bulkhead in the hold where the majority of the dirty C-4 had been planted. Right then, HAZMAT team was using laser torches at the base to cut through the steel. Others were sweeping the walls, vehicles and the boxed-up contents in steel containers with radiation detectors while Schwarz and Blancanales, likewise toting mini-Geiger counters, made a walk-through. So far nothing shot the needles up on monitors other than the C-4 blocks. When the dirty plastique was removed, stowed in lead containers, it was carefully lugged up top to be secured by the Coast Guard and flown to their base in the Port of Miami.

''What do we do about him?'' Lyons asked Bolan.

''He comes with us. Islip, too.''

''You know, whatever we find here, Striker...''

Lyons let it trail off, the Able Team leader looking

as grim and mean as Bolan had ever seen him as the steel wall was removed and what looked like the first of six small lead containers was hauled out by their thick metal strap handles.

"I hear you, Carl. This is one war that's only just heating up. It's a safe bet it'll get worse before it gets better."

"Yeah, the usual. Thing is, as messy as this was, with this bunch willing to blow themselves and us to kingdom come in a radioactive waste cloud..."

Bolan allowed a wry grin. "You're not wishing you had one more day of R and R, are you? Or were maybe still in the slammer?"

"I hope to hell I never have to count on Hal like that again. And if this is my sentence for the error of my ways, I'll take it."

"Over here," Blancanales called to Bolan and Lyons.

Marching down the middle line of vehicles, the soldier saw the Treasury agents slicing open plastic-wrapped bundles of paper notes. Several notes were slid under a microscope that jutted from a laptop with a digital monitor.

"Pesos?" Blancanales queried.

"Counterfeit," the Treasury agent said, then held up a thick packet of brand-new U.S. hundred-dollar bills, then took a sniff. "Ink's barely dry on these."

"I thought the new bills," Schwarz posed, "were counterfeit proof?"

"Not a very good job," the T-man said, as several agents began hauling away the sacks of bills. "But at a glance they'd pass. Several things I can see wrong with them already. The magnetic strip, for one thing, is off-line, just enough, a hair say. The transparency implant of old Ben's face is a little too dark, to put it in terms you might understand.''

"Thanks for the consideration on our ignorance," Lyons gruffed.

The T-man shrugged. "You know what they say about where there's a will. All you really need is the requisite paper cloth, plates, ink and a press, and of course the technical expertise. A little more to it than that, but if someone's pumping out this much funny money, it tells me it's a sophisticated operation.''

Bolan read the flurry of questions the Able Team warriors wanted to throw out, but they knew better than to stand around and try to solve this riddle before developing any leads, either on their own, or through the Farm. As usual, Bolan knew any clues to this puzzle would come by grinding up the enemy.

"Agent Belasko!''

Ricker, obviously having just gotten the clear from the HAZMAT team that the contraband wasn't radioactive or booby-trapped, was waving for Bolan and Able Team to share the revelation.

"What in the hell is it?" Lyons asked, as the Stony Man warriors stood and looked down at the shiny steel cylinders in the lead containers.

Ricker shook his head, reached beneath the steel straps that held the cylinder in place and pulled out two fan-shaped objects that Bolan thought looked like insect wings. "My guess...drones. Could be unmanned, flown by remote or satellite guided,'' he said. ''Meant to fly and disperse whatever the contents. We won't know until they're taken apart.''

Bolan felt his guts clench with anger and foreboding over what they were seeing.

''Six altogether,'' Ricker told Bolan. ''I think we need to question the captain and Islip a little harder, and I'm talking taking off the gloves.''

''We'll take care of that,'' Bolan said. The soldier was moving away with Able Team falling in, his sat phone in hand, and told Ricker, ''Get them up top and ready to be moved. I'll tell you where they're going.''

''Striker?''

Bolan turned, read the stone-cold anxiety on Schwarz's face.

''Are you thinking what I'm thinking those things are and what their purpose was?''

The Executioner nodded. ''I've got a few ideas, Gadgets. None of them pleasant.''

WHY WAS IT, Hal Brognola wondered, whenever he choppered to the Farm the idyllic setting that housed the world's most powerful covert agency never looked as tranquil or inviting as it should have? Even though he knew why, Brognola, for once, would like to try to deny the reason.

It was a short flight, eighty miles, give or take, from Washington to the Shenandoah Valley where Stony Man Farm was nestled in a ring of wooded hills of the Blue Ridge Mountains. Just once, for God's sake, he would liked to have landed, breathed tension-free air, taken in the sights, a nature buff, in his dreams, carefree and traipsing through the tulips, even though he knew this Chinese box of tranquility of a simple farm with apple orchards, a poplar pulp plantation and a wood chip mill was all a whopping smoke screen meant to keep the locals from wondering what really went on in a place so secure and heavily guarded trespassing wasn't taken lightly. Everything here was beefed up and fortified for maximum security, even counterattack in the event the Farm came under siege, as it had in the past. Sensors and cameras and every conceivable watching and warning device laced the Farm, perimeter and clear up into the foothills. Bulletproof, steel-grated windows all around, with anti-aircraft batteries that could be raised from beneath the retractable roof of the mill. Farmhands who were really blacksuits, armed with HK subguns, were gleaned from various special forces branches and sworn to a secrecy that would have been the envy of Area 51. Never, he recalled, had he come here in recent memory without the threat of a major, national security crisis hanging like a sledgehammer over his head.

This day, Brognola feared he was on the verge of a truth so horrifying, so mind-boggling it gave him doomsday visions of what could possibly signal the end of the United States of America as he knew it.

Unless, of course, swift and decisive action was immediately launched.

The big Fed was trying to grab one last moment of

silence while attempting to quell the bubbling caldron in his gut by chomping down half a pack of antacid tablets when the Bell JetRanger touched down on the helipad. Within minutes, he hoped to know what, exactly, they were dealing with and how to proceed.

Briefcase in hand, weighted down with the latest batch of intel his people in the field and behind the lines would need to get it cranked up into high gear, he stood, moved for the doorway and opened the fuselage hatch. He knew, given the ominous ramifications of what had been discovered on the *Napoleon*, he would be spending restless, sleepless, nervous days, perhaps weeks to come at the Farm, until this suspected nightmare was rooted out and crushed by the Stony Man warriors.

The steel cylinders had been whisked back to Washington on a classified military flight as soon as Bolan had given him the update on the strange contraband. An agonizing limbo of roughly ten hours had ground by while the six suspected drones—or whatever the things really were, he thought—were analyzed by the best weapons experts Uncle Sam could find. After hashing over the situation with the President, then getting full sanction to do whatever it took to track down and eliminate a football-field-long list of enemies believed behind this catastrophic scheme and growing by the hour, the Man had ordered the cylinders divvied up for dismantling and analysis by weapons and other high-tech experts at various agencies. Two went to Brognola's special science and analytical team at the Justice Department. Two for the

CIA, and one each for the NSA and a nuke-chem-bio crew at Fort Detrick, Maryland.

He stepped out into the rotor wash and saw Barbara Price headed his way from the farmhouse. Normally a team of blacksuits would be on hand to greet any arrivals, but the mission controller had already informed him she would meet him personally, skipping the SOP of confirming his identity. That alone, he knew, didn't sound like she was coming to laud the moment with good news. In fact, judging the tight set to her mouth, Brognola braced for the worst. Truth was, he almost thought she looked afraid.

Brognola walked up to Price, who froze in mid-stride, giving the big Fed a dark stare that sent a chill down his spine. "One look at you, and something tells me we have major problems."

Price simply nodded. "The A-team of microbiologists from the CDC was flown to Fort Detrick to analyze the contents of the cylinder. I didn't tell you earlier, since I was holding out some hope."

"The Centers for Disease Control?" Brognola said, and was almost afraid to push any further for an explanation.

"Come on," Price said, turning and leading him toward the farmhouse. "I just received a full report from sources of mine at the CDC and Detrick." She stopped suddenly, stared Brognola dead in the eye. "Hal, this is something beyond a worst-case scenario. In fact, I wish what they had found on the *Napoleon* was as simple as suitcase nukes."

Brognola felt his stomach churn over, drop straight down to his bowels. "Let's get to it," he said, marching past her.

THE SIMPLE SOLUTION was always on the table, but Bolan had gone ahead and tried to give Islip the option to play ball without soiling his Italian silk slacks. A no-go silent middle-finger salute shot back at him over and over, and Bolan had finally decided to shake some answers out of the man the old-fashioned way. The threat of death, or torture, sometimes worked better than acting out the lethal drama. Not only that, dead men didn't sing. Most people didn't want to die, and fewer still, the soldier knew, enjoyed pain. Despite the fact the Executioner didn't believe in torture, he was at least willing to dole out a minimum of pain for the sake of realism, and, of course, to make Islip a believer. They had to do something, he knew, to pry some answers loose from the enemy about their operations, since the Egyptian was proving himself the penultimate stonewaller who acted like he really believed his own lies.

The Stony Man warriors had been sitting on Bouchet and Islip at the Coast Guard command center while the strange steel cylinders were being disseminated and analyzed. It was a waiting game at present, while Brognola and the Farm determined what the contraband was, where the field ops went from there. Bolan and Able Team had spent the time wisely, piecing together an attack plan, sifting through intelligence seized at Islip's estate by Justice agents, the Farm decoding encrypted faxes, computer hard drives transcribed to the cyberteam, among other paperwork found in a wall safe at the Egyptian's estate. They had some ideas on how and where to launch the next phase, but until they heard back from the Farm for a brainstorming session they were on hold. During the interim, Schwarz, who had earned his nickname for his electronic wizardry and love of high-tech super-toys, had pulled off what Bolan hoped was the mother of all state-of-the-art gizmo magic acts. It involved voice-synthesizing and alteration using his computers and the wiretaps on Islip. Some phone calls would be made, in the hope the bad guys were going to be duped and stalled until their walls came crashing down in a blitzkrieg moment determined by the Executioner. And Bolan wasn't counting on the Egyptian to bluster through a forced charade to inform Puchain and whoever his cutouts that the shipment of funny money and strange cylinders were safe and en route. With all the faith in the world in Schwarz's ability to make him sound like Islip, the con game, Bolan knew, would stand up.

It had to.

They were more than two thousand feet in the air, the Black Hawk sailing out over the Atlantic Ocean. It was a technique the Executioner knew some CIA operatives and Special Forces had used on Vietcong prisoners, but it was still murder in Bolan's eyes. Lyons, playing the bad cop, stood in the hatchway, returned Bolan's nod with a thumbs-up and a wicked smile. All set to start twisting the thumb-screws.

"Bye-bye, Teddy," Lyons said, chuckling. "See

you at the big Kitty Kat Klub in the sky, but you first. I've still got a hot date with one of your dancers, which, by the way, asshole, you might have ruined for me. Maybe Allah will grant you some wings on the way down.''

"You through?" Bolan said.

"Launch his ass into space, boss!"

"Wait! Wait!"

A running step, and Bolan slung Islip down, a human missile flying fast and hard across the floorboards. He was sliding for the open hatchway, the Egyptian nearly on his way out the door, skimming on his belly for the swan dive and crying out, when the Able Team leader snatched him up and away from the edge. They weren't going to take it all the way, but Bolan found Islip's eyes going wide as he stared down at what he feared would be the last bit of sunshine he saw on Earth, dancing off the ocean like an endless field of diamonds that would mark his watery grave. Perhaps they had just found a chink in the man's armor, Bolan hoped.

"This is where we are, Teddy," Lyons began. "No more Mr. Nice Guy. Take a look down there." Lyons slapped him on the back of the head. "Take a look! From this height, you'll splat like the bug you really are. Whatever's left, well, let's just say you won't be around while the sharks make Teddy the Titan their lunch special."

"I told you, I am a businessman...a mere club owner. You can't do this...."

"That right?" Lyons kicked the man in the back

of the knee, the cuffed Egyptian buckling with the blow, then thrust him down in the prayer position. "Toss him, boss?"

"Not yet. Here's the story, Ted. My friend there, he's had a few real bad days, and I can only hold him back from tossing you so long. Minor point here, but he thinks, for one thing, you purposely ruined his vacation the other night, got him tossed in the can, and he hasn't had a vacation in ten years."

"Fifteen! And that's what you call a minor point?"

"I stand corrected. Fifteen," Bolan said, forced to nearly shout above the rotor wash pounding into the doorway. "I don't want to have to dump you off as shark chum, but unless you start talking…"

"I am a club owner, a legitimate American citizen! I have rights!"

"What the hell is this on your ear?" Lyons snarled. "What the hell you supposed to be anyway? Some kind of closet Liberace fan?"

Then Lyons ripped off the diamond earring, held it out for Islip to behold.

The Egyptian howled and tried to squirm back on his knees, cursing next, but Lyons wrenched up a hand full of ponytail. He flung the diamond out to sea, the gem winking sunlight as it arced away.

"I can help you, Ted," Bolan said, continuing in his good cop role, "but you have to give me something in return. We know you're involved with a terrorist organization called al-Amin. We've already decoded all the information you kept on your hard drive. We know where your cutouts are, and we have some idea on where the shipment of this special cargo was going next. It all points back to you, Ted, the big sleeper al-Amin has roused from slumber. But what I'd like to know, and here's where you can at least show some good faith, is what those cylinders are we found, and what's inside them. We'll go from there. Or we'll stop here. Full stop. Dead end. A shark lunch special du jour.''

Islip stared down at the glittering ocean, appeared to be on the verge of hyperventilating. Bolan thought he was breaking through, the man about to give it up, then decided to bring Blancanales into the act as scripted.

Bolan stood, nodding at Pol who was nicknamed the Politician. Blancanales, a psy-ops master, had a knack for reaching into the hearts and minds of the enemy when the rough stuff failed. Sometimes, a kinder gentler touch worked.

"I suppose I am on deck, as you Americans might say?"

Bolan looked at Bouchet sitting on the bench and told him, "You're along for more than just this joy-ride, Captain. Standby. I might need you to try and talk some sense into the guy yet.

"How are we coming along, Gadgets?"

Schwarz was tinkering with his computer, reading the squiggly lines on the monitor, adjusting knobs. "Final touches, Striker. A few more minutes, you're center stage, and you'll sound just like Teddy, that's a solemn promise. If not, you can toss me out the door next."

"That could end up being my pleasure, the mood I'm in," Lyons growled back. "My vacation might not be a total wash after all."

Bolan watched and listened as Blancanales dropped to a knee beside Islip.

"Listen, my friend. You can save yourself, you might even be able to keep some of the life you've come to know here in America, with restrictions. I can tell you don't want to die. I saw you at the club the other night. You might not think it, but you're more American than you know. And what's so wrong with that? I'm sure it's something you've asked yourself over the years. Educated in America, a taste of the good life, glad to be here, be what you want, free to find your own way, and it's not so bad. We all make mistakes, and you won't burn in hell for being human, despite the diatribes and the anti-West rhetoric some of the people you work for spew about the evils of Western freedom. We look like devils to you? We're human, too. We'd just like to hold on to what we have, same as you, pretty much, only we don't want to see our families and friends and the families of friends slaughtered by whoever is scheming whatever against us, and if you know the whoever and whatever about what we found on that ship, now's the time to come clean." Blancanales held Islip's stare as the Egyptian appeared to consider his words.

"We have freedom here, yes, something I believe you have come to cherish, but we also have laws, and speaking for myself and my friends here, with freedom comes responsibility, and freedom doesn't include undermining our way of life or allowing others to slip into this country and murder innocent women and children. Take your time, think about it. We've shown you we can be merciless if we have to be, if we're forced to, but we can also show mercy where it's warranted. You can have a new life. Not the one you knew, but it beats the alternative.''

Islip twisted his head, stared at Blancanales. "As what? An informer?''

"You can call it that, but I call it atonement.''

The Egyptian snorted. "You put me in the Witness Protection Program? They would send someone. They would find me and kill me.''

"There's always that possibility, but you've left yourself no choice. Right now, it's life or death. Play ball, and we can make some moves, see you don't spend the rest of your life in an American prison. Informers—as you call them—have been known to get the chance for a fresh start, and sometimes, at least the smart and the grateful ones, are damn glad someone bailed them out of the fire. You'll never run another strip joint or sell rich men's cars. The old ways are gone forever. But you also won't spend the rest of your life eating bologna-and-cheese sandwiches every day and wondering when you'll get passed around the cell block as a sex toy.''

Islip made an angry face. "I have heard them called Angels of Islam. They are unmanned drones, similar to those CIA Predators you used in Afghanistan.''

"What's inside them?'' Bolan asked.

"I wasn't filled in on many details, but I know they contain nerve and biological agents. Something far more deadly than anything ever created, if I am to believe what little I heard."

When Islip paused, Lyons shook him by the ponytail. "Keep talking and don't force us to ask the obvious questions, Teddy! I don't give a damn what my pals said. I'll still fling you out this door!"

"Okay, okay." He looked at Blancanales, his new friend, and said, "Do we have some sort of deal, this Witness Protection Program?"

Blancanales nodded. "We can work it out."

"I have your word...."

"What did he just say, Teddy?" Lyons bellowed in Islip's ear.

When the Egyptian began spilling his guts some more about the Angels of Islam and the horror they were meant to unleash, Bolan felt his blood turn to ice. No matter what was promised, the man was as guilty as whoever had created and shipped these high-tech weapons of mass destruction to be used on unsuspecting American citizens. The soldier wouldn't do it, but he had a damn good mind to still toss the man out the door.

One less terrorist today, the Executioner thought, was one less murderer to deal with tomorrow. It was all Bolan could do to keep himself from becoming a butcher of the helpless like Islip and his operatives were intending.

THE WAR ROOM BRISTLED with raw anger and nerves, but Hal Brognola could appreciate the emotion that threatened to burst around the table, if what he suspected was true. The facts weren't all in yet, but judging the faces around him, Brognola dreaded the worst.

The revelation of the horror they faced began as Kurtzman snapped on the wall monitor. A series of photographs showed both the assembled and disassembled steel cylinders. The HAZMAT suits hovering over the pieces in some of the pictures didn't escape Brognola's eye as he stuck a cigar into his mouth.

"In one piece," Brognola said, "they look like big metal insects."

"Drones," the computer expert began. "Approximately six feet long, four feet around at their belly. Stainless steel in parts, titanium in others. Weight is eighty-two pounds, fully loaded."

"Loaded with what?"

Kurtzman forged on as if he hadn't heard the question. "Rocket fuel gets them off the ground."

"Rocket fuel?"

"Horizontal takeoff, then the wings and two gas-powered propellers take over just like a plane. Then there's a guidance system in the head of what you referred to as an insect we're still trying to figure out, but we think somehow keeps them airborne. It comes complete with GPS, all the trimmings of a state-of-the-art computer system and database that hook into a satellite. Striker just interrogated Islip and called right before you stepped in, Hal. The Egyptian confirmed some of what we already know, and a few things we didn't.''

''I can always count on Striker's powers of persuasion,'' Brognola said. ''Continue, Bear, and feel free to answer my original question anytime.''

Kurtzman's expression seemed to darken. ''With the initial but still sketchy reports we've gathered or intercepted from the CIA, NSA, Fort Detrick and your own science detail, we were able to work up the specs in the Computer Room. The parts are similar to an unmanned Predator drone, right down to battery pack, and that database that allows them to be laser guided.''

Brognola found himself growing impatient for the bottom line, as Kurtzman clicked through a run of computer graphics. Just like that, some of the awful truth began to sink in. The big Fed groaned. ''Oh, God, these things not only fly, but you're telling me they can be steered from outer space by some rogue nation's satellite?''

Price and Katz were also present in the War Room, but Brognola noted they were too quiet and grim up to that point for his liking.

''I'm thinking they sail best with a good wind on their aft.''

''Wait a second,'' Brognola said. ''You're saying…some terrorists stake out a city rooftop…Barbara? What was found in the containers of these things?''

Price paused, then answered, ''Three had nerve agents, a hybrid variant of VX and sarin. Four to five times more potent than anything UNSCOM discovered in Iraq.''

When Price fell silent, Brognola gruffed, ''I'm waiting for the other shoe to drop.''

Price cleared her throat. ''The other three were determined by the CDC to have contained a bioengineered mutation of Ebola Zaire, designed to be dispersed as an aerosol.''

CHAPTER SEVEN

René Puchain found the overseas call somewhat strange. The voice of the end user in Miami sounded sincere enough in his praise and gratitude for the services of his ship, and the line itself was scrambled to avoid eavesdropping by Interpol or the American FBI. So, why then, was he troubled by the call? The captain of the *Napoleon* could just as easily radioed in to the warehouse office down at the port and confirmed delivery on the man's behalf, standard procedure that had always been observed in the past. Why would the Arab see fit, he wondered, to make such quick personal contact when surely the vessel had only just docked? And who could be assured anyone on either side of the Atlantic was out of the law enforcement danger zone yet? He had never done this before, calling right after delivery, no less, but Puchain knew the cargo was the most important and dangerous shipment of both their careers, and lives. Perhaps it was nothing more than the man in Miami giddy with triumph, having pulled it off, letting his French connection know all was well, fear not. Still...

He settled the phone back on its cradle, steepled

his fingers, eased back in his chair. Looking around his office suite, distracted, he considered various possibilities for the flare-up of a sudden bad gut feeling, sifting through a mental list of enemies, known, suspected or imagined. He lived in a world, after all, where paranoia and keeping his friends close but his enemies closer was the mother of all necessity when it came to survival. He hadn't made his climb to the top by being careless, or by allowing his enemies or the competition to remain on the loose for long, searching for the window of opportunity where they could stick a knife between his shoulder blades.

Thief. Pimp. Drug dealer. Pornographer. Extortionist. Loan shark. He had been called all of those odious tags by various elements of the public and legal community over the years, even though he had his humble origins as a teenaged assassin and leg breaker working for a smuggler who also happened to be his uncle, the only family he had ever known, the only man he had ever feared. Assassin had never been bandied about by the French media, but there were days when he craved to announce to the world he had once been a front-line street soldier. Not, in "their" eyes, or so they wrote and reported in the tabloids, some aging self-indulgent mobster swilling Napoleon brandy around the clock, consuming Viagra like candy before sweating up the sheets with high-priced call girls, calling the shots from his Jacuzzi whirlpool, a corrupt slug who had never gotten his hands dirty in the mean streets of Marseilles.

Puchain had to chuckle, aware that what they saw

wasn't what they got. If "they," all the little people who lived in his world, he thought, only knew what he was capable of when the heat was on, his back slammed to the wall. Yes, there were those who still called him a gangster, even after he had clearly gone respectable with the expansion of several businesses growing and spreading from Nice to Barcelona and all the way to Paris, restaurants and night clubs mostly, with a smattering of shops that sold everything from computers to pornography. Then there was his export of luxury automobiles, which carried the bulk of his contraband to and from far and near Asia, to and from North and South America.

And the black market had always proved more lucrative, in terms of fast, easy, monster cash on the hoof and off the books than any dabbling in legitimate endeavors meant to throw the authorities off the scent. Anyone who knew him could smell the smoke that shrouded the giant money machine behind the facades, and that included the local, national and international authorities. To some greater degree, he still took pride in the fact that he was something of an outlaw in the eyes of many of his countrymen, forever skating the icy edges of the law, an entire country bribed and bought so he could maintain a worldwide criminal empire and keep on indulging every whim. To hear Interpol tell it, though, he was a renegade throwback to the days, he mused, when he might have rivaled the titans of American gangster lore the likes of Al Capone. Well, his enemies, both civilian or backed by the law, were always smoked out of the shadows. They came, they went, and usually to a watery grave. Some, namely reporters, those hack journalists looking to make a name for themselves and advance floundering careers, had written whole series of articles on him, snooping around Marseilles, trying to discover how his empire really worked, as if, he thought, flush with pride, they were on the verge of finding the Holy Grail or something equally mystical or supernatural.

Eventually a fellow newspaperman always ended up writing the reporter's obituary. Nothing ever so bold or obvious as a car bomb, or a bullet to the head while they sipped espresso at the local café to raise the red flag at Interpol. The subtle touch, Puchain knew, worked better, his ghosts in the night seeing the loose of tongue slipped in the bathtub, or had some unfortunate drowning accident while vacationing on a Mediterranean beach, or bad brakes saw him or her flying off a cliff along the rugged coastline. Fortune was fine, but fame, he had come to accept, was simply the cost of doing business.

No, it wasn't the curious, the starstruck or those looking to make a public name in legitimate circles by bringing him down he had to fear.

It was the men he had lately taken it upon himself to aid and assist for riches not even he had ever dreamed possible. They needed close watching.

He picked up his cigar, puffed, pondered.

Why fear? He was the most powerful man in all of France. The little people were right about one very important matter, he thought. He owned politicians, judges, policemen and Interpol agents. He was, he thought, the Pablo Escobar of Europe, his empire, beyond narcotics, could rival the glory days of the Medellín cartel. So why was one simple phone call of confirmation and thanks disturbing him? Why did he feel as if he were on the eve of personal destruction from faceless enemies? Could it be the fact that the special cargo, now in the hands of what he knew were terrorists, would come back to haunt him somehow? That his own desire for more wealth would prove his own Achilles' heel?

He punched the intercom to the bar downstairs in his club. His evening dinner jacket on, he normally made his way downstairs for a specially prepared meal from Jacques, dining with cronies, high-ranking businessmen and distributors who helped keep the Puchain empire running behind the scenes. But this evening he was more thirsty for alcohol than hungry, wishing more to be alone than among the familiar faces of hyenas looking only to suck up to him or scheme his demise, as some undefined and ominous scenario wanted to prick his thoughts. "Send up Answain immediately," he told the bartender. "Tell him he does not need to knock."

While he waited, Puchain went to the bar and built a whiskey. He was halfway through his drink, twirling the ice in the glass, then pouring another when Antoine Answain entered. Puchain looked at what he considered a younger, leaner, more handsome version of the man he used to be. Where he was balding, Answain had a full head of wavy dark hair...

He caught himself, aware his own vanity was making him long for a past that would never return. Puchain grunted at the bottle. "Join me, Antoine. Please." While his top lieutenant helped himself, Puchain said, "I just received a curious call from Miami. The end user wanted me to know the shipment arrived without problems, he was all gratitude, something he has never done, or at least not this soon. He inquired, rather abruptly, how soon could he expect more merchandise to be delivered. I want your opinion on a few matters, one of which regards this Miami situation."

"You already know how I feel about our dealings with the Middle Easterners."

"Yes, yes. How it is too dangerous. How they are terrorists, a rapidly spreading scourge, one that has even found a breeding ground in our own country. I believe you even referred to them as a nest of festering maggots."

"They will bring unwanted attention us."

"Perhaps. I simply asked, hoping your opinion has changed. As long as their money is good, Antoine, not the counterfeit garbage we ship to America and Mexico for them, we will accommodate them."

"I see there is no point in my attempting to change your mind."

"None, not until I am proved wrong, which I doubt I shall be. Antoine, hear me. I look at you, and I see myself many years ago, when I first began my rise to the position I am now in. Tough, strong, loyal, the heart of a lion. I have no children, though I am told by several whores they have born me sons and daughters from here to Tunisia. Who knows? I pay them to keep quiet. I could go through with the DNA ritual, but what man wants the offspring of a whore?'' He paused, stared at his drink, then continued. ''We have discussed before how when I leave this world, you will step up and inherit the kingdom.''

Answain nodded, sipped on his drink. ''I am honored you would choose me. I have no words to express my gratitude, my respect, even…my love for you as the father I never knew.''

''It is all I could have asked for from you in return. Loyalty and respect. Without those a man is nothing. I tell you all of this again, because if there is trouble, whether from the Arabs, Interpol or the American authorities, I will go out the way by which I came into all that I have worked so hard for. With blood on my hands.''

''If you are asking if I will stand by you in the event of a war…''

Puchain smiled, waved him off. ''Yes, yes, I do not question you would sacrifice your own life to save mine. The thing is, no war was ever won because soldiers marched blindly to their deaths. There are those who seek to do us harm.''

''You are referring to Rousiloux?''

''Well, he is our main rival, a greedy little man who is never content, an odious monster if ever there was. He is like some hideous evil caricature out of a Dickens novel. Ahhh…perhaps it is time I excise this boil. However, for now, I am thinking our informants on the street need to monitor him closely. And we likewise need to maintain a close relationship with the Arabs in Marseilles.''

Answain shook his head. "Forgive me for being so blunt...."

"Please, feel free to speak your mind."

"What we shipped for them still has our organization's name attached to it, even though the manifests and other paperwork regarding the cargo and its origins have been 'rearranged.' What just landed in America—and there is no 'if' they will use it—when it is used will, I fear, trace back to us. War will be declared on our organization."

Puchain shrugged. "We deny everything in the event of seizure. We claim Captain Bouchet, a man with a sordid past and many money woes, was acting on his own. The Arabs are not so different than some of the others we have done business with in the past, Antoine. Colombians, Iraqis, Sudanese, the Russian and Mexican and New York crime syndicates, even North Korean intelligence operatives..."

"All dangerous people, granted. And we are still standing, thriving, yes. But for how long? I agree, the Arabs have put outrageous sums of money into our operations, and we have moved their counterfeit currency, their small and large arms safely for a long time, among other high-tech surveillance and countersurveillance and communications equipment, but now this—what I understand is a horror that... that..."

"That what?"

"Ask yourself what would happen if that shipment is seized by the American authorities. We have pledged ourselves to deliver still more of these things to America, to Mexico even where their organization has many cells. There would be a vast ripple effect, since we know the Arabs of this al-Amin have ongoing dealings with the Russian Mafia and North Korean operatives. They think they are clever where they are really devious. They work several groups at once, a juggling act where they get what they want on several fronts, not caring who they leave behind to twist in the noose. Where do we fit in if it all goes bad? I know, we deny responsibility and point the blame toward Bouchet, but my problem is this, and I tell you with all due respect, there is one glaring difference between the Muslim extremists and the other groups you mentioned. They hate the Americans, but they also hate anyone who is not Muslim and is of the West."

"I have no great love or need of America anymore. The truth is, I am in the process of severing ties with New York as we speak."

Answain balked at that but forged on. "My point is, what would happen if they smuggled one of those things into France to be used on us? So there is a large Muslim community in our country. So their operatives would die in the process of unleashing that weapon, but these people, they do not care if they die, as long as they take as many infidels—and, I believe, that includes us—with them."

Puchain nodded. "You have just brought to mind

a disturbing point. Say the shipment is seized and we decline to continue to do business with their people here in the city, citing too much risk. Unfortunately they have handed over a hefty seven-figure advance for future services. I do not think they would take kindly if I suddenly decided the risk outweighed the reward.''

He watched the younger man as Answain paused in the act of drinking, his stare hooded, head bobbing. ''Ah, yes. They would blame us for the seizure, for one, since we guaranteed unmolested delivery. Secondly, they would not forgive us if we reneged on our obligation, whatever the circumstances, perhaps seeing us as timid children, or back stabbers. They would become our enemies.''

Puchain smiled. ''Now you understand. Our enemies are most likely everywhere, in everyone we see, and deal with. The world has changed, Antoine, and many days I think it has gone completely mad. Suicide bombers, weapons that could exterminate entire cities in a matter of minutes or hours. It is a different game out there, where our business dealings have become entwined with the sale and shipment of merchandise I would have never considered moving when I was younger. The same has been true of our Russian and Central and South American counterparts for years. We had to advance our operations, or fall behind to the competition, which inevitably would have signaled our own extinction. Yes, the times ahead may be full of peril, but we can profit greatly in our dealings with the Arabs, but only if we stay the present course. What do we care what they do in America, or to Americans anyway? We are thousands of miles away. And in response to your scenario of some doomsday in our country, I do not believe that will happen. They probably have more to lose by not dealing with us than the other way around.

"Here," he said, filling both glasses. "Drink up and be of good cheer and strong heart. The future is ours, and if it is all to end tomorrow, then we have had a good run. If we go down, then I pity the poor bastards we will take with us on the way out of this world. To us, Antoine, my heir, to the future, and the defeat of anyone foolish enough to try and take away our world."

They clinked glasses. Puchain watched Answain drink up, liking what he observed. The man who would claim the crown of his empire someday looked buoyed by new confidence, a light of inspiration shining in his eyes that told Puchain he would defend the kingdom at any cost.

René Puchain decided he had made a wise choice for a successor.

EBOLA.

The name alone of what was the most dreaded hemorraghic contagion probably ever known to man, incurable, almost always one hundred percent fatal and could spread faster than the bubonic plague, which had wiped out one-third of Europe's population centuries earlier, froze Brognola with fear. Price, he considered, was correct, even in her momentary lapse of dire pessimistic analysis. Being vaporized in a nuclear fire cloud was one thing, painless, he had to imagine, over in less than an eye blink, unless, of course, victims on the outermost ring of ground zero were stricken by radiation sickness, a slow dying that could linger for months. As terrifying as the thought of nuclear annihilation was, it was at least quasi-acceptable in some form of abstract horror, since humankind had been living with the fear and the images of incinerating mushroom clouds for more than fifty years. A virus, invisible to the naked eye, was indefensible. One thing to die instant and painless, here one nanosecond, gone the next, but...

Ebola.

Against his will Brognola's fear of the future for America conjured up horrific images of the world's most powerful nation dying a hellish agonizing death.

Ebola.

An unstoppable, unquenchable fever would literally liquefy a human being's insides, until blood ran freely from every orifice and the afflicted howled for the mercy of a quick death. He saw the streets of major American cities thrashing with falling, screaming, bleeding hordes, lobbies of skyscrapers and hotels, restaurants and theaters and office buildings choked with the dead and the dying like stacked cordwood. He saw the steel shadows of these Angels of Islam rolling over New York, Washington, Chicago and Los Angeles, skirting clouds of doomsday, spraying down a rain of tasteless, odorless poison. He imagined water supplies, major rivers, the Great Lakes contaminated by the raging virus. He saw anarchy sweeping across America from sea to sea in a madness so uncontained it would defy the most heinous visions by Nostradamus or John the Divine about the end of humankind. There would be looting, riots, armed citizens taking to the streets, crazed with terror or fear of their families and neighbors who were infected, gunning them down, burning the bodies just to buy themselves a few more days. He saw tanks and armed HAZMAT teams, some with weapons, others with flame-throwers torching the living dead before they could contaminate—

"Hal?"

Brognola looked up, grunted, as Kurtzman's voice snapped him out of his reverie.

"Seventy-two pounds."

"What?"

"To answer your original question," Kurtzman said, and repeated himself.

"Ten pounds of chemical and biological death inside each of these things, and I bet," he said to Price, "you're going to tell me a single pinhead of the virus can probably kill hundreds of thousands in about the time it would take CNN to make the scene."

"Genetic analysis isn't yet complete," Price replied. "But from what we know already, it is far more deadly and contagious than Ebola Zaire, by as much as three to five times."

Brognola scowled, squeezed the bridge of his nose. "Mother of God," he muttered.

Price went on. "I was informed this particular engineered strain needs no incubation period, and like any virus it simply requires a living host to keep replicating.

"Airborne contagion?"

"Highly likely," Price said. "No exchange of bodily fluids required. A simple intake of air breathed out by an infected individual could spread the virus. Released in aerosol form there would be no stopping an initial outbreak."

"Kill the slide show, Bear," Brognola growled, chomping on his unlit stogie. "I've heard and seen enough. Okay." The big Fed rubbed his face, heaved a sigh. "Who created these drones? Where are they being produced? And how the hell did our vast intelligence network miss this horror show up to now? Well, they did it, they somehow got their hands on what I can only call high-tech crop dusters. And I mean to tell you, people, we are staring down the gun barrel of Armageddon here."

No one had an answer, but Katz said, "As we speak, there are satellites parked over the big seven of state-sponsored terrorism—Sudan, Somalia, Iran, Iraq, Yemen, Syria and North Korea. We're tapped in and watching whatever they watch."

"The problem is," Price said, "we could tack on another seven to ten countries that are possible suspects."

"Meaning we're nowhere," Brognola said.

"Not exactly," Katz corrected him. "We have two definite starting points overseas."

"So, I'm assuming Phoenix," Brognola growled, "is off their own R and R stint in Italy?"

"Phoenix is already in place and ready to move on two fronts," Katz answered.

Brognola lifted an eyebrow.

"I wasn't bucking your authority, Hal," Katz said, "but I went ahead with a judgment call once I heard about these drones."

"I'll take the heat, since I gave Katz the green light," Price said. "Also, DNA tests of the bodies found in Croatia didn't turn up Kanbar or Zharjic among the dead. Blame me for getting the ball rolling for Phoenix, but we need to find the mullah and the Serb butcher, since the group consensus was they may be the key to tracking down Wahjihab and the source of these drones."

Considering the crisis, Brognola let it go that the Farm's tactical adviser and mission controller had jumped the gun. "You two made the right call, but now I'm hearing two top snakes are still slithering around in the Balkans?"

"We don't know. What we do know is that they haven't been spotted, either on the ground, from the air or outer space," Kurtzman said.

"If they play true to specter form, hell, they could sashay out of Croatia disguised as women."

"A distinct possibility," Price admitted. "Katz and I decided to split up Phoenix for now because we've got the short list narrowed down to a hand full of targets we can maybe get our hands on. Word from the CIA and the NSA says that Croatia is still hot with al-Amin operatives or Muslim sympathizers in-country, with some Serb war criminals looking to maybe latch on to Zharjic's taxi ride out."

"That's assuming he and the mullah haven't boogied already," Brognola pointed out.

"Bottom line, we need a quick track on the where-abouts of Wahjihab," Price said. "He's the money behind this operation, and where the money is, I'm betting the drone store—lab—is close to wherever he hangs his keffiyeh. With luck, we hope to take a key operative of al-Amin there or bag one from René Puchain's organization alive."

"Good luck," Brognola said. "We know the mar-tyr's play that went down on the *Napoleon* and in Croatia, and from what I've heard most of them on that ship weren't even Arabs. Which means the stand-ing orders, Arab, French or whoever, are kill or be killed or don't come home." He raised a hand before anyone could speak. "Here's the deal, folks. We are at war with these animals. It's nothing new for us, only this time out there are no rules, even if that means blasting and blowing up these bastards on American soil in full public view. Even if that means violating some lawyer or accountant or banker's civil rights who may well be aiding and abetting the en-emy. That comes straight from the Oval Office. Pa-tience, like tracking and freezing their assets, profiling and rounding up Arabs for endless Q and A sessions, forget about it. This is hardball time like we've never done before."

"Then you know Striker and Able have put together a hit list that reaches all the way to Texas, where they believe al-Amin cells are monitoring our border with Mexico,'' Price said.

"Right, I briefly discussed it with Striker earlier. Gloves off, both barrels blazing, even if that means we take this thing south of the border. Whatever messes they make, I have teams of special agents from my Terror Task Force ready to move in behind them and clean up and seize whatever intel is on-site. So, what's the story on Phoenix?''

"Gary and T.J.,'' Katz said, referring to Gary Manning and T.J. Hawkins, "have already landed in Marseilles. They will meet, be briefed and armed by a CIA operative. They are looking for a way either to infiltrate the Puchain organization as potential sellers of weapons-grade uranium and plutonium they purchased on the black market from the Russian Mafia, or make some noise as the new bad guys on the block, flush out whatever al-Amin operatives are in the neighborhood. We've created a solid background to send them to Puchain's doorstep with all the right credentials as over-the-edge mercenaries with a track record that shows they don't give a damn what they sell to whom as long as the price is right, and that they can deliver as advertised. Dishonorable discharge from the Army Rangers for T.J. for assaulting an officer. Manning canned from the Canadian army, suspected of having 'the wrong sort of acquaintances,' such as drug dealers and suspected terrorists. Mercenaries with forays into Angola, Sudan, Indonesia, having peddled everything from diamonds to

U-235. The package comes complete with placing them on the FBI and Interpol's most wanted list as arms dealers."

"Thin, and slim chance Puchain will bite. It sounds to me like a colossal waste of effort, especially if Puchain is already dealing with al-Amin thugs. We might have bought some time, or so we hope, that he doesn't discover his Miami connection is severed and the drone cargo is in the hands of the Coast Guard, but I'd prefer a straight-on blitz at the French connection, Katz."

If Katz was offended, he didn't show it. "We're hoping, Hal, Puchain will send them packing."

"So, you're painting a bull's-eye on their backs?"

Katz nodded. "If they strike out with Puchain, which we're counting on, they'll take their sales pitch to the man's competition, Vincent Rousiloux. If word gets around Marseilles there's new and bigger and better kids in town, al-Amin operatives might crawl out of the sewer and have a few words with Gary and T.J."

"Okay, I see where you're headed, Katz. Bait all the players, maybe start a war between Puchain, the extremists and this Rousiloux character. Maybe someone gets a bad case of the nerves when the bullets start flying and wants to bail, with Manning and Hawkins offering a way out."

"Or so goes the strategy. Now David, Calvin and Rafe," Katz said, mentioning the other three commandos of Phoenix Force, "have a CIA paramilitary contact on the ground in Croatia to point the way to any more suspected armed nests. Word from our intelligence sources is that the counterfeiting lab could be right inside Croatia.''

Brognola looked each of them in the eye. They all knew the score, and their silence told the big Fed there was nothing more to report for the moment. Suspicions that more of these Angels of Islam might be out there on American soil didn't need their collective voice for them to know it was a real and horrifying possibility. In the hours to come, he knew a lot was going to change. But how? And how bad would it get? In the final analysis, he knew that all the intelligence gathering and battle-mapping and strategizing would open enemy doors, but it was the Stony Man warrior who would have to go through the gates of hell into combat.

And God help them all, he thought. God help America if they didn't pull off the seemingly impossible before the doomsday clock struck twelve.

''Okay, get back to work. Keep me posted.''

They filed out, and right then Brognola almost wished, watching them go, that he wasn't alone. He tried to keep the word out of his mind, fought back the visions creeping into his solitude.

Ebola.

God help us all, he thought.

CHAPTER EIGHT

The Tamiami Trail, or U.S. Highway 41, slashed an arrow straight course from Miami, through the Everglades and Miccosukee Indian country to Fort Myers on the Gulf Coast. From there Islip's road warriors ran their haul north by 18-wheeler, finally catching Interstate 10, heading west for New Orleans, where confirmation of the cargo was made by a cutout, before rolling all the way to Houston where the end receivers waited on delivery. Based on the word of Islip, and Bolan had little reason to doubt the Egyptian after his harrowing chopper jaunt over the Atlantic, three previous journeys had been made to Houston, after the terror financier either faxed the particulars to several cutouts or rang them up by sat phone. According to Islip, no Angels of Islam had made prior trips west, only counterfeit money, high-tech surveillance and countersurveillance equipment, and small-arms caches, complete with C-4, det cords, timers. Sleeper operatives—armed Arabs—were used for these runs, once the 18-wheeler left Hobart Trucking in Glades country. Some hacking into and decoding by the Farm of Islip's encrypted files had unearthed a treasure trove of intelligence gems—phone and fax numbers, addresses—to get Bolan and Able Team blitzing on. The running scheme was to lay out the ruse in turn for the next cutout up the line, on the way west, with the soldier placing the phone calls as Islip. A playback of his earlier conversation with the cutout on this first stop, and Bolan was amazed at how much he sounded like the man. The Farm, meanwhile, following a money trail, discovered electronic transfers in the neighborhood of five million dollars had worked their way in cyberspace from Miami to Houston to a bank in Mexico City where it disappeared into a shell company in the Caribbean. Bolan didn't want to look any further than this next stop, but the stink of corruption sure seemed to be drifting his way from Mexico the harder the Farm looked at each batch of seized laptops, computer drives, address books.

However it began again and where it went from there, it was a perfect fit for Bolan's game plan to start the next leg of the campaign by following the flow of the enemy's prior sojourns. Each stop, and the Executioner intended to lop off one head of the terror hydra, all the way through Houston, then south of the border.

First they would wipe Hobart Trucking off the Everglades map.

Using the GPS monitor fixed to dashboard, Bolan saw they were closing to within a mile of the compound. Blancanales had the wheel of their rolling com center, delivered to them by Brognola's Justice agents right before they set out from Miami. Lyons was hunched up at a console in the back, perusing the sat and aerial images of the trucking complex both the Farm and the Justice Department had provided. From his shotgun seat, Bolan took in the oversized black van on their rear as Pol navigated the lead vehicle down a narrow dirt strip that paralleled the paved road to the front gate of Hobart Trucking. The attack strategy was basic, standard keep-it-simple but with one exception. Rock and roll, blast and burn.

Schwarz, sitting on seventy pounds of C-4, all of it wired in to one radio frequency, would be the point man into Hobart. It was a bulldog play, what the warriors had on the table, but the Executioner and his teammates had agreed to brazen it through, search and destroy. And Schwarz had volunteered his special delivery services while his three comrades in combat split up the sniping detail for Blancanales, while Bolan and Lyons marched in from a predetermined entry point to the east.

They were minutes away from giving the terrorists an incinerating bang of their own poison.

"Amazing and sickening," Lyons growled.

"What's that?" Bolan asked.

"This Dennis Hobart. Convicted of possession with intent, sale weight, according to the package on this scumbag, that should have landed him in the same cell as Manuel Noriega, only he somehow gets a free pass."

"Courtesy of Islip's connections in the wonderful world of judges and juries for sale," Blancanales said.

"Makes me wonder how many more native-born Americans are running around, sucking up to Islip and ready to sell their souls to the jihad for a few bucks."

"All we need to know is that Hobart's dirty," Bolan told them, his M-16/M-203 combo canted against his seat in the space between himself and Blancanales. "What we know is that the regular work force has been sent home for the day, and we're expected."

"Right, those homegrown American workers on Islip's payroll, replaced by armed extremist imports," Lyons said. "Only we don't have an accurate head count of shooters on-site. And the way this whole complex is laid out, we might have to spend half the night digging them out of all these office complexes when this thing blows up and sends the rats scurrying inside."

"If you want easy, Carl," Blancanales said, grinning into the rearview, "I can always take you back to the Kitty Kat."

Lyons scowled, but for once didn't have a snarling comeback.

The four of them were loaded down in full combat blacksuit, com links now fixed in place as Bolan signaled for Blancanales to pull over and park in a ring of cypress trees dripping Spanish moss. In the dying light, and with the wall of prehistoric vegetation that ran a good hundred yards down the south face of the chain-link fence, Bolan had chosen this spot as the best way in for a nearly invisible encroachment.

The Executioner, the big assault rifle combo in

hand, was out the door, Lyons and Blancanales falling in, weapons ready, van locked down. Bolan moved off to have one last word with Schwarz, then it was time to deliver the goods.

THE PANIC SWIRLING around Dennis Hobart was so strong, so alive it felt as if it might knock him out of his chair. Whatever was happening, and he had to assume the worst, the Arabs were coming unglued, human cyclones raging all over the offices and their maze of cubicles, torching hard drives, filling his nose with the biting stench of melting rubber, shredding documents, speaking to one another in the machine-gun staccato of their native tongue.

"Would you like to do something besides sit there and smoke cigarettes and look stupid?"

Hobart, lounging back in the rolling chair, feet propped up on his desk, just another day at the office, held his hands out and put on his best innocent act. "Like what?"

The Arab he knew as Salimin swept over the desk, drilled a boot heel into his legs. This looked serious, Hobart decided, legs flying, spun halfway around in his chair, cigarette snapped in two in his fingers.

"Go monitor the cameras. We're going to be hit!"

Oh, man, this wasn't good, he thought, wishing to God he could break out the stash of Jack Daniel's and that ounce of blow in the bottom drawer of the file cabinet to which only he had the key, float and fly away instead of dealing with this unholy reality. "Hit?" he sputtered.

The subgun came up, Hobart staring down the barrel, as Salimin repeated his order, all visions of freebasing the night away while they played their macho games snatched from his thoughts. Hobart knew he was one wrong word away from being shot to hell and dumped in the swamp for gator food.

Life presented a series of flashbacks all of a sudden for Dennis Hobart. Life, he thought, hadn't been very good to him, as he considered all the failures, foul-ups and fruitless endeavors to find his own stroll and subsequent niche on Easy Street. He saw that DEA raid in his mind, subgun-toting storm troopers crashing every door simultaneously at his Coconut Grove digs, one of many nightmares from the past, but that was the big bad roaring gator that had led to his present dire straits. Three keys of blow at his disposal and he had found himself slammed up against the system, staring down twenty to life, unless he started singing about who was higher up the food chain. He saw himself washing out of the U of Miami for possession a few years before the bust, wondering where it all went from there when the old man knocked him on his ass and out of the will of a real-estate fortune that would have seen him own half of Miami, a shoo-in as a pharmaceutical superstar among the rich and famous of South Beach.

Life sucked, always had for the most part or so it seemed, and he wondered if he was simply destined to keep on playing a losing hand. He wanted to see more of the distant past and sort it out, wondering why life had taken the Godzilla of all dumps on his head, then stared at the subgun next, Salimin nearly foaming at the mouth and cursing him in Arabic. Was the crazy Arab's finger tightening around the trigger? He figured he'd better go with the program, or else. There might be a way out for him yet, if he survived the next few minutes. Trouble was on the way, and if it was DEA, FBI or the United States Marines, he believed as long as he was unarmed and under maximum stress by way of death threats, he could concoct a plausible story of deniability. He was an unwitting dupe. He was a pawn in some sordid game of smuggling. He was a hostage of international terrorists, for God's sake.

Of course, he knew some of the facts, like their midnight runs hauled illicit contraband for Teddy Islip, stuff, he believed, that was meant to make the World Trade Center a footnote in American tragedy. He knew what they were up to, and who these Arabs bowed to the east in Miami.

And his own unholy alliance with Islip? Well, that was another sad story all by its lonesome.

A few years back, he briefly recalled, the judge had mysteriously thrown out the drug charges, citing any number of violations of his civil rights, illegal phone taps, bad warrants and police brutality that had him sashaying out the court, and right into the waiting arms of Islip. Having used his ill-gotten gains during the glory days of distributing a controlled substance, he had ventured out into the legitimate world, starting a small trucking business. A front, naturally, so he could expand his pharmaceutical dreams of a vast empire westward. Only Islip had other ideas for his trucking pot of gold, and since Teddy the Titan had yanked him out of the frying pan he owed the man. And Islip was fond of reminding him about that.

Hobart held his hands up. "Okay, okay, chill."

The tac radio was held out, the Arab barking at him to watch the front gate and surrounding environs, alert him to any approach or suspicious activity. Standing and grabbing the tac radio, Hobart was glad to be free of their menacing presence, glancing once at the file cabinet to heaven, then continuing his hurried stroll to the watch room down the hall.

Work now, smoke later, he figured. Time now to conjure up a good story to sell to whoever was coming to crash the gate.

He had to admit something was seriously out of whack. Salimin had been on the phone, faxing New Orleans and Houston for the past hour. In between these frenzied duties, he rounded up the fourteen Arabs brought in on the heels of the departing work force. Some sort of military-style briefing, the assault rifles and subguns broken out of the crates in the main warehouse. Hobart knew they were set to receive some special shipment from Miami that night, and supposedly it was en route already where it would be transferred and stowed in an 18-wheeler. He'd seen this gig before, a small convoy of armed Arabs heading out, staggered around the rig in a phalanx of SUVs and luxury boats on wheels, as they departed the premises. Only once had Islip been on hand to supervise, then place the necessary calls and faxes to the end users. If this shipment was so important, mass hysteria bursting all over the place now, why wasn't Teddy there to calm the troops?

He was firing up another cigarette, moving up to the bank of cameras, visions of coke smoke filling his thoughts again when—

Two cameras framed the disturbance, and he found himself torn between the monitors. The smoke slipped from his fingers, his stomach fell straight into his bowels as a sickening reality hammered home, and a voice from the past told him he was body-slammed into another losing night.

The oversized van had blasted through the gates, that much was clear, sections of chain link all gnarled and flapping in the rampaging wheelman's wake. Two of the Arabs were spraying the runaway vehicle from behind, on their feet for all of a microsecond, before a dark spray burst from their skulls and they hit the ground so hard it looked to Hobart like a sledgehammer had felled them. Beyond the doorway he heard the shrill cries of panic as the stampede of Arabs, he saw on the warehouse monitor, surged en masse for the open maw of the receiving bay. Another camera showed the van rampaging on, a beeline for the armed contingent that was now cutting loose with weapons' fire. A dark figure then tumbled out the door of the runaway van, rolling up and taking sanctuary somewhere in the motor pool.

This was more than he wanted to stick around and ride out. Hobart was stumbling back on trembling legs, the tac radio tossed to the floor, when something happened that told him whoever was invading the premises wasn't there to serve arrest warrants.

The unmanned and impromptu bulldozer was obliterated in a fireball that ripped the guts out of the Arabs on the bay. The flash was so intense on the monitor, Hobart cried out, fearing he was temporarily blind, but even more afraid to stick around and discover the truth behind the coming scourge. Whoever was hellbent on blowing up the store wouldn't be in the mood to buy any plausible deniability snow job.

TWO DARK FIGURES came running for the gate when Schwarz eased off the gas, forty yards out and easing closer. They were swarthy types, lean and mean, angry faces framed in his headlights. And they were also armed with Ingram subguns, looking antsy to open up without warning. No facial hair, no keffiyehs, of course, nothing to betray the origins of nationality. They could have been Italian or out in the Miami sun too long, as Schwarz put them to profile. But he knew, as did the other Stony Man warriors, that blending in as just another good American citizen was part of the terrorist war manual.

Seeing was believing right then, so Schwarz mashed pedal to the metal.

The van rocketed forward, engine thundering, tire rubber squealing in his ears. He blasted through the gate on a screech of metal, the hardmen throwing themselves to the side, screaming something in his slipstream. Then the back windows erupted in a momentary hail of flying glass. A check behind, and

Schwarz glimpsed the special delivery, hidden under a tarp, unscathed and ready to be billed as advertised. It was his show to start, but his comrades in combat got deadly serious right away, making sure he succeeded in dropping the hammer on their doorstep.

One last glance into his sideview mirror, and he saw both subgunners laid out by Pol's HK-33 sniping chore.

Focusing on the task ahead, Schwarz saw the bay and immediate complex beyond laid out just like the photos depicted, only the entire place looked bigger and more intimidating in terms of size in reality. A motor pool of maybe ten vehicles, SUVs and rich man's rides, staggered to his nine o'clock. That would be his bailing point. From the wide-open mouth of the receiving bay he counted eight or nine shooters piling into view, pouring on the autofire. One last eyeful of the 18-wheelers and those massive double-decker open steel behemoths for transporting autos, and Schwarz took up the radio remote. Taking his foot off the gas, he slowed enough to let him tumble to the asphalt without needing a few nights in the ICU. The van rolled on, bullets tattooing the windshield, spiderwebs obscuring his view of the hardforce, but he knew he was on-line for the big bang.

Schwarz threw open the door as slugs drummed his shield. MP-5 subgun grabbed at the last instant, the Stony Man Commando launched himself airborne.

THE ROCK AND ROLL started with a bang that would have been the envy of all heavy metal bands taking center stage for the opening number. Lyons was surging through the section of fence cut away by Bolan, both warriors racing across a stretch of no-man's-land when the van blew its payload, and right in the faces of the terror horde. Even Lyons was amazed at how tremendous the blast was, an instant swollen dirigible of screaming fire that appeared to knock out nearly the entire wall of the two-story warehouse. A large force of shooters had come running onto the receiving bay to greet Schwarz with weapons' fire, and Lyons would be stunned if anything was still moving after the shock waves finished pounding through the interior.

But, of course, even the most precise plan, even the biggest bomb sometimes, he knew, left a few cockroaches skittering about, crawling out of the cracks.

They were scraping themselves up along the concrete docking, two figures, at least, Lyons saw, staggering through the smoke cloud and vanishing inside the warehouse for a sanctuary they would never find in this world.

Lyons and Bolan veered away from each other, the Executioner signaling for Ironman to take care of the walking wounded on the dock. The massive SPAS-12 autoshotgun leading his charge, Lyons locked on the reeling soldiers of terror, who were choking and trying to lift subguns his way.

Two quick blasts of 12-gauge meat grinders, and Lyons blew them apart where they staggered and wondered, most likely, what wrath of God had just sent the sky crashing on their heads.

As Bolan waded in to aid and assist Schwarz, who was taking enemy fire near the motor pool, Lyons keyed his com link and told Blancanales he could come on down and join the party anytime he saw fit.

ABDUL SALIMIN KNEW it was over, at least for him. The truth was, he had feared the worst since his man who had gone to the Port of Miami to make sure the shipment arrived safely reported back about the armada of helicopter gunships that began landing hours after the *Napoleon* should have docked. That call included the worst of all worlds. Islip and the vessel's captain had been spotted cuffed and taken into the Coast Guard command center.

It was incredible to the point of outrage, he thought. He had come so far, endured so much, a stunning victory of Koranic proportions merely days away but now snatched from his grasp, the cruelest of fates.

Salimin knew others would carry on the jihad, even after his martyrdom. In the al-Amin chain of command he was the number three operative on American soil. As a cutout, he was deemed expendable, and he was aware other sleepers would rush to fill his slot and bring to fruition the greatest, most ambitious war plan against the infidels yet. Arrest, according to al-Amin's manual, was unacceptable. Should the authorities attempt to drop a legal net over his head, he was ordered to stand his ground and fight to the death. He, for one, wouldn't end up in their Camp X-Ray, waiting for the humiliation of the American military tribunal to begin, paraded about as some savage to be hanged, a degrading spectacle, in his mind, that perhaps wouldn't even land him in Paradise. No, he would die here, on his feet, taking as many of the enemy with him as he could.

Well, he decided, that was pretty hard to do at the moment, a great warrior charging into the guns of the infidels, since he was crawling on his belly, senses ripped apart by a blast so strong it had flung him clear back across the warehouse, left him now wondering if he even had the strength to stand and attempt a martyr's play. The devious enemy, he thought, choking down a bitter laugh, had torn a page from al-Amin's manual.

A car bomb.

He looked back across the warehouse, rising somehow, blood in his mouth. At least seven, maybe more of his fighters, had rushed to their deaths, he saw, bodies heaped in the opening, several corpses minus arms and legs, the blood still pumping out in spreading pools. Still, he heard shooting from some point beyond the pall of smoke, figures hazy, dashing around, but he was hopeful. They were still in the fight, at least a few survivors outside, willing to hold their ground and—

He saw two shapes materialize, rushing from the smoke, backs turned to the threat beyond. He recognized his men, wondering why they were running when they should be shooting, then the cloud was punched open by a stream of bullets.

They slammed to the floor, weapons flying, and the shooting abruptly stopped.

So close, he thought, now the end was staring him down. It didn't seem right.

He was looking around at the floor, when, miracle of miracles, he saw and scooped up his Ingram MAC-10. The chiming bell in his skull lessened enough so that he made out the groaning from wreckage splintered to matchsticks behind him. Like some slug, Salimin found Hobart crawling out of the debris, knees and elbows crunching glass, the man crying out for help. It crossed his mind to simply shoot the American, then he spotted a tall dark shadow boiling out of the smoke. One look at those eyes, as the big man with the massive assault rifle combo strode deeper into the warehouse, and Salimin knew he wouldn't live much more than another minute, two tops.

If he was going to die...

It was worth the gamble. Salimin hauled Hobart to his feet, locked an arm around his neck. "Shut up!" he hissed into the American's ear, as he marched him closer to the dark man.

A few more steps, attempting to bluster a standoff, steal a few seconds and cut the distance, and Salimin figured he could at least kill the dark man who had stolen his dream.

THE EXECUTIONER saw and sensed what was coming next, trained the muzzle of his M-16 on the face of hate. They were the same set of eyes he'd seen for years in the killing fields, and more recently plastered on wanted posters or shown during CNN roundtable sessions about the new war, which was old news for the Executioner. Cold, dead eyes, no soul, only the fire of the fanatic revealing the slightest flicker of any life staring him back. A quick glance around the warehouse, and the soldier didn't spot any armed stragglers around the crates, tool benches, forklifts and catwalks as he stepped toward the new situation. The extremist had to have thought Bolan cared whether a traitor like Denny Hobart lived or died, since the Arab kept barking how he'd kill the American if the soldier didn't drop his weapon. Behind, Bolan heard the Stony Man warriors moving inside, his com link crackling with Lyons's voice as Ironman told him they'd check the store for hostiles.

"I'll handle this," Bolan called out to Able Team.

"The weapons, all of you, lose them, or I kill him now!"

"Hey, pal, do what he asks, huh! For the love of—"

"Shut up!"

"Go ahead," Bolan told the fanatic. "Shoot him."

Eyes bugged out, Denny Hobart was shrieking how that wasn't going to make his day, and the change Bolan anticipated fell over the terrorist's face. It was a ploy, the soldier knew all along, the enemy hoping to stall him long enough, hoping to pluck some compassionate string, before shooting anyone within sight in a martyr's homerun swing. As far as Bolan was concerned, anyone who slept with the enemy could face the same swift justice.

The Ingram was sweeping around, Hobart wailing when Bolan held back on the trigger of the M-16. It was a short burst of autofire, but the 5.56 mm rounds obliterated the terrorist's face left a mess no plastic surgeon or mortician would ever scrape together.

Hobart toppled to the floor, shimmying as he rose to his knees. When he found the corpse behind him, he sobbed, then looked up at his savior. "Oh, God, thank you, buddy. You don't know what I've been through, you don't—"

"I know enough."

"Yeah? Hey, I can explain—"

"No need."

The Executioner felt a cold anger well up from his gut, the sight of a cheap hustler who had sold his soul to enemies of America enough to make him to want to puke.

Hobart grinned, bobbing his head. "So, you understand?"

"I do."

Bolan slashed the butt of his assault rifle across Hobart's jaw and put out his lights.

BROGNOLA JAMMED a fresh unlit cigar between his teeth as he took the sitrep from Bolan in the Computer Room.

"Okay, that's another clean sweep, Striker, but the problem the way we see it is that now they'll be waiting for you up the line. Locked and loaded, once they realize Miami is out of play."

"I was sort of counting on that."

Brognola grinned around his stogie. He had known Bolan long enough to understand the thinking. "Is this Hobart giving you anything you can use?"

"Other than a song and dance, zero. Claims he was forced to tap-dance to Islip's tune if he didn't want to end up gator bait."

"Hand him over to my people."

"Already taken care of."

Price walked up to the sat com, a sheaf of papers in hand. "Striker, the next cell is in New Orleans, and what Hal is saying is that they might have already been warned."

"And fled."

"Right."

"I have the address in the Big Easy. It's worth checking. We know Islip moves Puchain's vehicles through New Orleans to Houston. From Texas, there's a distribution point that fans out to New York, Chicago and Los Angeles."

"All of which are being watched by my people," Brognola said.

"We're on the clock, Hal. There's no time for any Big Brother surveillance. The facts are in."

"We understand that, Striker, but Puchain, we just learned," Price said, "dumped his car dealerships six months ago to a group of Saudis through some sort of tax shelter and shell company. It's shaping up to be an all-Muslim extremist operation once you hit New Orleans, but they have some financial backing, legit on the surface, here in America."

"So I gathered from the intel package. These dealerships also funnel cash through this United Front in Houston, a charity organization that primarily handles relief aid for Mexico and Central and South America. A bunch of Johnny Jihads have been bought and sold in our own backyard to keep this going. The United Front is where a lot of the money's dumped off to finance whatever their final war plan. I don't think food and medicine for the needy is part of some benevolent undertaking. We'll see how it shakes out, but down the line we're going after any front men, bankers, lawyers, any wolf in sheep's clothing that's part of the laundering operation. The bulk of the cash is going south, whether it's counterfeit or real, we know that. My guess is someone in a suit and tie for this United Front has answers about any Mexican connection."

Brognola knew Bolan was asking for him to make the final call. "All right, it's your play, Striker."

"I'll be in touch."

Brognola listened to the silence when Bolan signed off. He gnawed on his cigar, felt some relief they were getting results. One or two battles, though, didn't win a war.

"Hal?"

Brognola turned toward Kurtzman, thought he spotted some hope in the man's expression that they maybe caught a wave.

"We've got something. You might call it breaking news."

"Please, tell me it's good news."

"I don't know how good it is," Kurtzman said.

"We've been monitoring the Moscow CIA station chief's reports to Langley. Akira and I tapped into their sat transmission—"

"Skip all that. What do you have?"

"Well, we all know how many out of work, disgruntled, starving Russian nuclear physicists and microbiologists were left wandering about and wondering…"

Brognola was as edged out as he could ever recall, but managed to keep the anger out of his voice when he said, "I'm hearing more problems, Bear, so out with it."

Kurtzman paused, grim, as he ripped a printout from his computer. "We might have just found a big piece to the Angels of Islam puzzle."

Brognola stifled the groan. Now, he knew, they had the Russians to deal with.

CHAPTER NINE

The visions of glorious victory over the infidels stopped blessing his sleep three nights earlier. It was troublesome, to say the least, why God no longer spoke to him. He had to wonder why.

Alone in the tight confines of the communications office of the counterfeiting factory, he should have been hammering out the details, alerting his contact they needed to secure the alternate route out of Croatia, since the Serb war criminal was on the verge of forcing his hand. Zharjic, this Butcher of Slavic Muslims, had been issuing implied threats, flailing about since their narrow escape in the mountains in near hysteria unbecoming of a man, fuming for hours on end now over the unforeseen delay. It was disgraceful, he reflected, forced, even if it was the order of the Successor, to carry out the wishes of the very same godless barbarians who had so brutalized his nation for ten years.

Haroon Kanbar was distracted, yes, he admitted to himself, troubled and angered by some feeling of abandonment and impending doom he couldn't define, but which he wanted to attach some dire omen to, in light of the previous night's vision.

Kanbar wasn't sure what to make of the sudden end to what he had thought of up to then as the divine calling. In the caves of eastern Afghanistan, the visions had been discussed, he recalled, several of the meetings even filmed by video camera, to be delivered to al-Jazeera by a series of courier cutouts. This was done, he knew, to rally the Muslim world at large, encourage the faint of heart or warn those who believed the infidel crusaders had embarked on a just cause by ridding his country of the Taliban. After his meetings with the sheikh, he had come to attach divine significance to the dreams, all of them believing God was speaking to them in their sleep, the prophet himself invading their subconscious, inspiring them in his supernatural visitation, filling them with courage and wisdom on how to proceed with the jihad.

Where the sheikh discussed soccer games and pilots, Kanbar had other visions that he'd openly tossed into the discussion. His own philosophical insights had fueled the mirth as they sipped tea in the bunker of Zawar Kili, all of them proud, feeling blessed by God over recent triumphs but looking to the future, planning bigger, more grand and holier operations to come. And when he learned the truth about the strange winged drones his visions became like living entities in his sleep. They were so alive, it had seemed, it was as if he were watching a movie playing out while he slept the sleep of the righteous.

In those visions he had seen the beauty of the Angels of Islam as they took to the skies, launched from rooftops in Manhattan or Chicago or Los Angeles or Houston, or lifting off from empty soccer fields on tongues of fire. Where the shadow of death washed over the infidel hordes on their city streets, a radiant light broke across the sky, a band of gold so bright the enemy fell to their knees, blinded, crying out for mercy, a voice like thunder pealing from heaven, so loud it drowned their screams. Then the rain of hell showered down on them, and blood began to flow from their mouths and ears and eyes, their brains eaten up by fire raging from within, God looking down, deaf to their wailing for deliverance from the plague and their horror and their agony.

The sheikh, he recalled, told him this was surely a sign from God that they would prevail. There would be a fierce struggle ahead of them, perils unforeseen to come, but they were all told to be patient, pray and keep their faith in God and the jihad, no matter what hurdles loomed in the near future.

The problem, he remembered, as the bombs rained down and he fled through the vast underground network of caves and tunnels that took him to the Pakistani border, would be finding safe haven in a country far removed from both Afghanistan and his often shaky alliances to the south. The task would be to live long enough, while being hunted by the crusaders, to see his dream come true. Prearranged escape corridors had been established by a then little known but rising organization that would pick up the sword where al-Qaeda and his own doomed Taliban appeared destined to fail. From Karachi to Cairo by freighter, malingering in the desert wastes of North Africa, back and forth from Morocco to Tunisia as operatives filtered the intelligence to him by sat phones or cutouts, it had been an agonizing wait for the calling.

There were many details about the Angels of Islam operation he wasn't privy to, such as where the high-tech drones were created, or who were the architects behind this marvel of engineering. Not that he needed to care especially, as long the operation succeeded. Blessed with new life after his harrowing close encounter in Afghanistan, scuttling through the refugee camps while Pathan tribal warriors and ISI contacts opened the magic doors out of Pakistan, he was to receive and follow the orders of the sheikh's Successor, without question, without fail.

So what, then, was bringing on the fear now? Why had the divine calling turned into a vision that he even now dreaded to ponder while awake? Kanbar knew he needed to focus on the crisis before him, but the vision—the nightmare—swelled his mind's eye, turning him to ice. Where there had been the winged angels he saw the black dragon, swooping from a flickering dark sky, slashed by blinding bolts of lightning that seemed to hold the behemoth aloft. Where he had seen the infidels falling in the streets and screaming in terror and sweet excruciating agony, he saw himself and his followers, some living, but most having been killed in Afghanistan, crying out in fear as the dragon unleashed a funnel of fire. He saw the living flames sweep in a massive wave for him as he tried to run, but found he was paralyzed. Then the fire…

Perhaps, he reconsidered, he had been placing too much importance on mere dreams. After all, they were only dreams, they were only…

Kanbar became aware of another presence in the room. Turning from the laptop and banks of surveillance monitors, he found Nuri in the doorway. The large nylon satchel, he saw, was open, revealing the blocks of plastic explosive, det cords.

"It is done?"

"Yes," Nuri answered.

Kanbar thought he saw fear in the Taliban fighter's eyes, then dismissed it as simple haste to perform his duty, leave this godforsaken country of mixed religions, seething hatred and return someplace where they were accepted, understood by their own. "Hurry then and finish."

Kanbar stood, as Nuri began planting small globs of C-4 around the room. "The Serbs, Nuri, where are they?"

"I do not understand their language, but I could feel my ears burning with my name."

Kanbar wheeled, glared at the Serb colonel and his guards as they filed into the com room. Their weapons were out, pointing down, but Kanbar read their cold expressions, knew all of them were thrust to some threshold of mindless fear and rage where it could erupt into violence at any second.

"This is not, I believe, what we agreed on, Mullah Kanbar. Another delay, while you count your funny money, while you mine this factory to blow clear into Bosnia. I am tired, I am angry and I demand we leave this instant.''

''You demand?'' Kanbar said, ripping off the fax printout and slapping it against Zharjic's chest. ''Here, read that. That is from your Russian comrades. They have turned around. They will not be landing. Yes, the mission has been aborted because the Russians became nervous about the airspace monitored by the Americans. It is understandable, I suppose, since there are thousands of American soldiers and UN peacekeepers and CIA operatives scattered all over the Balkans with their AWACS and their continual electronic and radio intercepts alerting them to our every step.''

Zharjic read the fax, cursed, wadded it up and flung it across the room. ''And this was something you people did not factor in?''

''Understand something, Colonel, so we are clear between us. I did not want this mission to come here and help a murderer of Muslims flee to the safety and bosom of your Russian gangster friends in Moscow. The operation here can be connected to one of our cells in a Russian breakaway republic, a little piece of Islamic soil I do not think you would ever care to see, nor they you.''

''Chechnya?''

''Chechnya.''

''And?''

''I had my orders, however, a mutual pact between my organization and the devils in Moscow who are interested in continuing to do business with us. But they wanted our help in coming here to see you remain free in their country, a gesture, I understand, of good faith on the part of our organization. My coming to this country of heathens had more to do with destroying the operation here than making sure you did not end up in the custody of the Americans. Where you would either share a cell the rest of your life with your former president or be hanged for the entire world to see.''

Zharjic began trembling with rage. ''Are you telling me we are stuck? What's more, that we are trapped, hunted and soon to be cornered as the Americans come—''

''To kill or capture us, yes. I would not do that, Colonel,'' Kanbar warned, as the pistol began to rise a few inches. ''There are nothing but Muslims beyond that door, many of whom are my men, Taliban and al-Qaeda fighters who will fight to the death. Then there are Slavic Muslims, men, I am sure, who would gladly skin you alive as your reputation has preceded you here. If you want to live, and perhaps leave this country, you will think before you react. There is still hope we can make it out of Croatia.''

''How?'' he asked, nervous eyes darting at Nuri as he fixed blocks of explosive to the walls.

''By rail. If we can make it out of these mountains I have a contact in Zagreb. We take the train through Slovenia to the Austrian border. There was a backup plan from the beginning. It involves a private airfield my organization has access to.''

"So we go now!"

"Not yet. We must make sure the infidel dogs do not continue to bark and foam on our heels."

"We do not stand a chance against them, not when they have Apache gunships."

"The factory is mined, Colonel. When they come, and I am informed they are already on the way, we simply draw them inside the factory."

Zharjic shook his head, his jaw hanging. "If you're thinking about blowing this place up with us in it, I am not about to commit suicide!"

"That is where we differ, Colonel. Should I die here, I will go to Paradise, but I do not intend to die this night."

"I assume there is a way out of here?"

"Right out, as you might say, the back door. A short run across open ground, but there is another cave complex on the other side."

Zharjic clearly didn't like it, bobbing his head. "Okay, we do it your way. For now."

Kanbar watched as they whipped themselves out the door. He had drawn the line in the sand. If the Serbs so much as squawked once more in protest...

He decided he'd better arm himself soon, and with more than just righteous wrath and the will of God pumping in his veins.

DAVID MCCARTER WAS on the verge of erupting into a tirade fit to shame the worst megalomaniacal despot. All the intelligence brainstorming, high-tech chicanery, fine-tuned battle-mapping wouldn't save all the

CIA's men or perhaps even their own hides that night. Not when, the Briton thought, some glory hound had already shot out of the gate for a solo race to the finish line.

McCarter, Rafael Encizo and Calvin James were standing over the bolted-down metal table in the belly of the Black Hawk. It would be an uncommon, unseemly display of temper, but the leader of Phoenix Force had a good mind to sweep the table clear of sat, aerial pics, photos of bad guys, the guesstimated blueprint of the counterfeiting factory in question and bombard the CIA paramilitary operative with a tongue-lashing they might have heard all the way back to Stony Man Farm.

McCarter shook his head, glanced at Encizo and James. Beneath the soft glow of the white overhead light, both the Cuban and the black ex-SEAL looked angry enough to chew uranium-depleted bullets and spit them down this Colonel Joe's gullet.

The Briton scowled at the CIA man. "Your good Colonel Joe, mate, could just queer this whole mission."

Dean Harker held out his arms. "I told him to wait, I swear I did, but once our AWACS boys discovered Zharjic and Kanbar were at this factory... What can I say? He doesn't answer to me or the Company."

"Then who?" James asked. "The Almighty? If he didn't want us on board, we could have pulled some strings and had his chain yanked and jacked him right off this mission so fast whatever medals he's won would have rattled the teeth out of his mouth."

"All I know is that I have my orders. I don't know who you work for, don't even want to know, but I was told to give you one hundred percent cooperation."

Encizo tossed in his opinion. "Thanks for the big consideration, but at least we know who we can't count on."

"All right, we deal with it," McCarter gruffed, checking his chronometer. "We're pretty much on our own, nothing new. Tiger Force 12 is in the neighborhood and moving in, but I want you, Harker, to raise the colonel before we bail, find out the score and let him know we're coming to kick butt whether he likes it or not. And, my good CIA mate, if we take friendly fire I will do more than read him the riot act on collateral damage. Our own ETA is roughly ten minutes. Now," he said, stabbing a finger on a sat pic, "this stretch of the Dinaric Alps is, according to you, laced with tunnels and caves. This factory is nearly butted up against the foothills. Since no one has seen the inside of this factory, I see one huge fiasco in the making. This Kanbar has a history of blowing things up behind him while he runs."

"Understood."

"Then understand this. If Colonel Joe and his Tiger commandos try a full frontal assault, I'm thinking they'll be walking straight into the same setup that saw American Marines get killed in Afghanistan."

"Unfortunately," Harker said, "we're not equipped to deal with a chem or bio scenario."

"Which is why," Encizo said, and glanced at the

Briton, "I get the impression you want us to flush them out of the factory and into our open arms."

"Precisely," McCarter said. "We're here to attempt to take either Zharjic, the Marine-murdering mullah or one of their extremist flunkies in one piece for interrogation. This Wahjihab, is who we're after, but we need someone singing more than just the blues and not bleeding out."

"What I don't understand," James said, "is how this 'clothes-making' factory went undetected for so long when the CIA has been over here digging around and watching Muslim fanatics and Serb war criminals for years. You're telling us there may be as many as forty to sixty armed fanatics, many of whom are these al-Amin operatives who slipped like eels through the CIA surveillance net, and waiting for us infidels at this factory. We're looking at the University of Terror here and right under the CIA's watchful eyes."

Harker shrugged. "It happens."

"So does a tsunami," Encizo muttered, shaking his head.

"Hey, we only now just learned that they acquired the plates, ink, cloth and presses to pump out funny money from an Indonesian freighter that's made three runs to the port of Split in the past year. We only just learned there was a camp in the jungles of Indonesia that trained some of their people in how to counterfeit paper notes. A very sophisticated, high-tech operation, it came complete with Euro-trash criminals who had taken long vacations in prison for counterfeiting. They were recruited to pass on their knowledge. This al-Amin is a lot bigger and more connected than even the CIA originally thought. They might be the rabble and the leftovers of the Taliban and al-Qaeda, but they are a viable and powerful force to be reckoned with.''

McCarter perused the layout around the factory, gorges, ridgelines for a decent LZ, piecing together an attack strategy. It would prove seat of the pants, thanks to Colonel Joe, but the ex-SAS commando knew sometimes winging it was the only option. The three Stony Man warriors were togged in blacksuits, weighted down with an array of grenades, clips for their MP-5 subguns and hip-holstered Beretta 92-Fs. The multiround projectile launcher, dubbed Little Bulldozer by the creator of the weapon, John ''Cowboy'' Kissinger, Stony Man's number one armorer, was Encizo's 40 mm pit bull to unchain when the need arose. No matter what the odds, McCarter knew they were ready to fight. The Black Hawk was no Apache army slayer, he knew, but he trusted Jack Grimaldi in a pinch to mop up any ground troops with the 12.7 mm machine guns.

''And while we're circling the fort, Harker?'' McCarter asked.

Harker cocked his head at the M-60 inside the closed hatch.

McCarter didn't like it, a sarcastic remark leaping to mind, but Harker said, ''Hey, I look at you guys, and despite my orders, I'd rather ride with you than Colonel Joe. I'm not going to stand here and sound like some used-car salesman, 'trust me,' but beyond this factory I've got some critical intel I'm more than willing to hand over to the three of you.''

"We'll see," McCarter said, then told Harker he could call on Colonel Joe whenever the mood struck him.

THE ATTACK on the factory began just as Kanbar hoped. Beyond the forty-foot-plus open steel doors, rolled back in folding sections to now create a massive black maw, Kanbar heard the shouting of his men, weapons' fire directed at the sky before the bulk of them retreated into the first maze of the factory. The attackers might attempt to seal off the building's perimeter, a total siege by gunships and swarms of commandos, but it looked for the time being as if they would blaze their way in with a frontal assault. Kanbar would worry about gunships and commandos in the night when he ventured out the back, and even then he had a surprise waiting, in case all looked lost. He took his tac radio, aware the Serbs were on his back and watching, and ordered Yusef to fall back.

Phase One.

His fighters knew the plan. Put up ferocious resistance, make the enemy believe they had something so worth fighting and dying for. The attackers would invade straight through the front opening, chase them back, thinking they were on the run. The factory's working bowels had been sectioned off by steel walls, narrow passages crisscrossing the main works areas, plenty of hiding places and firepoints, Kanbar knew, to maintain the ruse. The first ring, he saw, watching as two of his fighters toppled under a hail of bullets, appeared like any other warehouse storage: crates and machinery, forklifts, catwalks. Rings two and three, however, once the attackers were drawn in, would prove their abattoir.

As Kanbar brushed past the Serbs, he marched through a narrow door that led to the first of the main labs, Zharjic barking at the back of his head about something how he didn't appreciate being ignored. It was a shame, he thought, glancing around, forced to lop off a chunk of an intricate network that had taken several years to develop and launch. Presses, ink vats, the laser printer that had cost the Successor a small fortune, the line of microwave dryers…

Then there were his own fighters, trained in the art of counterfeiting in a jungle camp in Indonesia, all that technical expertise they were about to take with them to Paradise. He knew they were more than willing to fight, even die in battle against the American crusaders, their righteous hatred of the infidels every bit as strong and unflappable as the fire that burned in his heart. They were much like, he briefly recalled, the young lions he had taught, whose character he had molded in his religious school in Kandahar, only these were seasoned warriors, not boys who needed their souls ignited by the holy fires of Islam. The Americans, he knew, would say the *madrassas* taught hatred of anything not of Islam, and to some extent that much was true, but for reasons far different, Kanbar thought, than anything they could possibly ever hope to understand. The enemy would also claim these young boys came from desperately poor families, no hope, no future, in search of anything and anyone who could give their empty squalid lives meaning. What in life, he thought, meant more than worship of God, utter and unquestioning obedience to the strict tenets of the Koran? What would the Americans have him do? Allow them to chase their own secret desires, the whims of ignorant youth chasing them into the arms of material wealth, yearning more for the flesh than the spirit? It was because of the potentially corrupt influence of the West that Kanbar and the other mullahs taught defiance of the crusaders. And if that meant honoring the will of God was to kill Americans, even in the ultimate sacrifice of martyrdom, then their place in Paradise was assured.

Kanbar had no doubt that even the Slavic Muslims, brutalized by what he knew they considered little more than carbon copies of Americans, would fight on to the last man.

Could they pull it off again? he wondered. Much like what had happened when he'd fled the caves in Afghanistan, he believed—or hoped—the Americans would replay the death march he had created for them. The only difference here was there were no mines stuffed with VX nerve gas, those plastic-coated bombs, undetectable by mine sweepers, which had spewed their poison and taken out a squad of crusaders, he later learned from an ISI contact.

"I need something more, Mullah, than a pistol!"

Kanbar was thinking along the same lines, but he was heading for the armory to take care of himself.

If this was the end for him, then the Serbs would also die here. The only difference was that Kanbar intended to soar to Paradise while seeing his enemies, anyone who wasn't Muslim, on their way to hell. He was a mullah, after all, a holy priest who had schooled the young to seize the future of Islam for the jihad. If he couldn't practice what he preached...

Kanbar moved through the doorway of the armory. He opened the steel door, took and handed Zharjic an AK-47, spare clips, then likewise armed himself. Delving into a drawer, he was shoving two Russian F-1 frag grenades into his coat pocket when he heard Zharjic growl, "I'll take a few those, if you don't mind, holy man."

Kanbar relented, gritting his teeth at the contempt he heard in Zharjic's voice. None of them, he believed, was destined to live out the next hour. What God gave, he thought, God could take away, if that was His will. With that thought in mind, he cracked a magazine into the AK-47, ready and willing to shed his own blood but only if he could take his enemies with him on the way out of the world.

THE SLEEPY LITTLE village on his map, Zibnek, McCarter saw, was stirring to life. Lights flared on in the distance, block-shaped structures with sloping red-tiled roofs, staggered in rows up the foothills of the Dinaric Alps were far enough from the dangers of the battle raging below to escape collateral damage, but close enough for its occupants to venture outside and fear the night.

The Briton had more to worry about than a few Croats sounding the alarm. Any commando operation, he knew, demanded precision teamwork, utmost faith and trust in the other to the point where the fighting unit was such a well-oiled machine. The mess they were now thrust into bucked the most basic of operational logic, but there was no way he would see himself or Encizo or James fall because they were "unwelcome and untrusted" expendables, he believed, in the colonel's eyes.

Glory hounds usually got the wrong guys killed.

He was squeezed into the hatch next to Harker and found that Tiger Force 12 was already rushing through the front opening of the factory. With the Apache having shot a Hellfire missile into the guts of the factory, smoke boiling over strewed corpses, McCarter wanted to believe the black ops stood a fighting chance. But some dark instinct gnawed away at his thoughts, making him more angry at the bullheaded play the longer he stood and watched and took rotor wash in his face.

James and Encizo were standing over the thermal imaging on the heat-seeking monitor. The black ex-SEAL, using McCarter's handle, called out, "Hostiles are forty-eight strong, Mr. D. Falling deeper back, to the north. About half are lagging behind, roughly fifty-yard line, the rest on the run."

McCarter was on the tac radio, as Grimaldi vectored on a west-by-north path to seal off any escape from the rear of the factory. "Phoenix One to Tiger Leader, come in!"

Harker had raised Colonel Joe just as the shooting started, but had been abruptly cut off. McCarter didn't care if the Colonel was under fierce fire or not. He had to try to alter the attack on the ground. It felt wrong, and every combat instinct kept screaming at him they were about to be spoon-fed a devastating wallop.

"You better have damn good reason if you're going start pissing and moaning in my ear, mister!"

"Fall back, Colonel."

"No chance of that! We've got these assholes running like the scared punks they really are! You people hit the back, you want to help my team flying that way now to seal off their exit—"

It was the last order Colonel Joe would ever give. McCarter was swallowing the outburst he wanted to vent, saw the black specters of the Apache and Tiger Force's Black Hawk sailing right over the roof of the enemy's lair, when what looked like the entire massive outline of the factory was obliterated in a series of thundering fireballs.

Grimaldi instantly hollered over McCarter's com link, "Fall to port, all of you!"

And McCarter knew the reason for that even before Grimaldi warned what he had to do next. A flying volcano of debris erupted for the Black Hawk, spewing its own form of molten shrapnel that could bring down the gunship as little more than a crushed steel coffin.

McCarter grabbed Harker and hurled him across the fuselage as Grimaldi banked away from the coming storm.

ZHARJIC DIDN'T KNOW when it would happen, but he was ready with his own scheme when the factory blew. It was high time, he had decided, on the way out of the factory, he took matters into his own killing hands. The mullah, point-blank, was so full of Islamic fundamentalist crap he should have read the writing on the walls days ago. This plan of escape from Croatia was as dead as the Muslims the mullah had left behind in the factory. Zharjic was no man's sacrificial lamb.

The AK-47 held out and ready to blast away, Zharjic followed the contingent of fanatics up the rocky incline. Try as he might, he couldn't see a cave up above, but the slopes were thick with black pines and beech, stubbled with sharp promontories, able to conceal any way into the mountainside. This was tough Alps country, he knew, cut by the Danube River, the way to Zagreb a grueling hike through steep gorges, dense forests, and if the Americans were still dogging them...

Zharjic's mind was set, his heart cold, a piece of stone in his chest. Up to then the great mullah, this hunted fugitive, made it all sound like a stroll through the woods, all that keep the faith nonsense, meant, he was sure, to fuel the con job. Like Croatia, Slovenia wasn't exactly in his tourist manual of places to see, since he'd likewise done some ethnic cleansing in that neck of the woods. In this part of the world, grudges and undying hunger for revenge could be passed on for generations, vengeance the only thing that kept a family going even when they were starving to death. Already, he'd seen the manner in which the Slavs had viewed him, glancing, turning away, but he believed he could read their thoughts. Well, the Slavs were in his coming plans, too.

Zharjic grunted at Burprija and Vojvod leading the trudge up the gully. Slowly, with each advancing yard, they fell farther behind. The Muslims were bunched up, assault rifles and a few RPGs in their hands, Kanbar taking point. Toss a couple grenades into the pack, while his men cranked out the autofire, and Zharjic would be free of this scum. He should have gone straight to the Russians on his own, instead of allowing himself to get talked into this nonsense by a mere underboss from Moscow. He had contacts and connections all over the Balkans, and with enough money thrown around, they would see—his own kind—that he landed in Moscow, a villa waiting with Ukrainian beauties and all the vodka he could drink. The Hague would just have to take out a little more anger and resentment on Slobodan in his absence.

He turned toward the factory, heard the fury of weapons' fire still pouring out the back door. When would the Americans come? he wondered, then heard the familiar and dreaded tune of rotor blades, saw the winged flying killers boiling out of the high darkness over the factory.

Zharjic was on the verge of ordering his men to do

it, when the night blew up. He thought he saw the Muslims dropping for cover—enraged for a heartbeat that Kanbar hadn't bothered to warn him—then a firestorm was rushing across the no-man's-land. Zharjic was bowling into his men, about to dive for cover behind a boulder, when something cracked off his skull and carried him into the dark.

WONDERING WHAT THE HELL, Harker whoofed like a kicked dog when he hit the floor. He felt the gunship dip and pitch to port as the flyboy he knew only as Mr. G. gave the aircraft all the yaw and pitch he could to avoid getting pummeled by the firestorm screaming to starboard. He was tangled up with Mr. D., Misters C.J. and R.E. tumbling off the wall, all of them holding on, hoping they cleared ground zero, counting on their guy to pull off the aerial acrobats. Whoever these commandos were, he briefly thought, they were the real thing, had come to the Balkans with backing from so high up the chain of command he didn't even want to consider the possibility his job might hinge on the whims of the Oval Office. Not only that, they clearly gave a damn, not just about the mission, but making sure the other guy on the home team walked away breathing. Whoever these stand-up, balls-to-the-wall ironmen were, Harker decided he was going the distance with them.

Mr. D. was rising, offered a hand. ''We're clear!''

Harker took the help to get up on his feet. ''Thanks.''

''Don't mention it.''

There was no time to contemplate the disaster, but Harker followed Mr. D. to the hatch and took in the holocaust. The blast had boiled up over the Apache and the Black Hawk, no hope, he could see, that Colonel Joe and his Tiger Force commandos would walk out of that smoking graveyard of wreckage. They were either blown to smithereens or buried and crushed under tons of brick, concrete and steel.

Not a snowball's chance under Satan's hooved feet.

He attempted contact, just the same, barking for Colonel Joe twice, then gave it up as radio silence told the whole truth. Feeling the angry heat radiating from Mr. D., they could only watch, as the gunships, swathed in flames, collided in a screech of rotors and rending metal. Two magnetized fireballs blossomed out as one inferno, then plunged for the foothills.

"Now we're definitely on our own," Encizo said.

"We always were," McCarter growled. "Get ready to bail, mates!"

IT NO LONGER mattered if he survived to keep the jihad dream alive. He was simply one link in the chain, and considering the fires of vengeance that had swept through the world of Muslim warriors since the infidel bombs began pounding Afghanistan, he knew there would be no stopping the Angels of Islam operation.

God's will.

What Kanbar wanted most now was the blood of his enemies on his hands, and that went double for the treacherous Serbs. If they had believed he hadn't read the murderous intent behind their eyes, they were fatally mistaken.

The mullah was on his feet, as the sky rained debris and fire, bringing the AK-47 to bear on the two big shadows down the gully. Serb autofire was eating up his fighters, shadows howling, falling. A large black shadow was sweeping behind them to the west and north, Kanbar aware next his message from God hadn't knocked all the gunships out of the fight.

So be it.

There were Serbs to slaughter, payback, as far as he was concerned, for past atrocities committed by them against his own, albeit loose and distantly connected, blood.

Kanbar held his ground, bellowing the familiar war cry he had taught the young. *"Allah akhbar!"*

He hosed them good and bloody, the two Serbs flying back under his lead hammer. Where was Zharjic?

It didn't matter. He would find the infidel, but first, he needed to address the not-so-small matter of the infidels above and coming to fight. One second he had the gunship in sight, high above, then it lowered on some rocky precipice walled by trees. How many more attackers could he take with him on his way to Paradise?

He would soon find out.

He rallied his surviving force, maybe a dozen fighters, and ordered them up the hillside.

Kanbar plucked a grenade from his pocket.

A MAN COULD RUN, even hide from justice, Rafael Encizo thought, but not this night.

This night belonged to a few good men who were willing to face down evil. So Encizo, taking his cue over the com link from McCarter, began slaying the jihad dragon.

A check of McCarter and James to his nine o'clock and he found they had chosen their firepoint behind a row of big stone teeth. Grimly aware one well-placed missile could bring down the Black Hawk, he wasn't anxious for any of them to face the same hard lesson those brave Americans had...

But Croatia wasn't Somalia.

Encizo chose his targets, groups of twos and threes, leapfrogging rocks and narrow gullys, and began to pump out 40 mm rockets from Little Bulldozer.

Pounded by subgun fire and fireballs scything through their ranks, the enemy tumbled down the hill, flying off in all directions. Still they came, their war cries flaying through the din. Grimaldi and Harker jumped into the act, the Black Hawk veering around in a hairpin turn, miniguns flaming, the CIA man dousing the armed shadows with long bursts from the M-60.

Three, then two, then one last extremist went down, smoke and dust, an eerie shroud backlit by the inferno that used to be the factory folding over the dead.

Just when he thought it was over, a dark figure bounded over a boulder, below McCarter and James. Encizo had all of a split second for his mind to register what was in the fanatic's hand, then swung Little

Bulldozer. The extremist was landing on his feet, about to charge the last twenty or so yards for their roost, when he was blown back by subgun fire and twin blasts. McCarter and James followed through with the subgun barrage, lifting the fanatic off his feet, but he was already gone and flying, a second explosion splitting the air after Encizo plowed a 40 mm missile into his chest. The little Cuban knew they could forget about identifying the remains, unless they wanted to comb the hills and scrape up body parts and spoonfuls of goo for DNA analysis.

McCarter patched through, Encizo shooting the Briton a thumbs-up.

THE WONDERS of intelligence gathering and the use of military satellites, he thought, wasn't the sole domain of the American imperialists. In the past few years, his country had launched its own satellite program, in secret, all of the electronic, radio intercepts and monitoring of their enemies from outer space now paying off.

He scanned the battle, winding down to death throes, switching from infrared to standard field glasses depending on how close or how far the three shadows strayed from the firestorm. When he had a clear fix on their faces, he took the camera, adjusting the high-powered lens for the three hundred meter distance. Snapping each face in turn, he then stowed the equipment in a small nylon pouch.

He stood, watched the gunship that had averted disaster maintain a holding pattern over the carnage while the three commandos walked a line down the hill to search for wounded.

Impressive, he thought. He would be dealing with pros, and if they had gathered more intelligence on the men he needed to find and kill, he would shadow them.

His fellow operatives had only days before discovered they had been cheated by the Arabs of al-Amin, and it was his duty to exact a blood debt, return to his nation the high-tech merchandise already in their filthy thieving hands. But they weren't alone, holding the bags of counterfeit money, seething how they had been outfoxed by minds more devious than their own.

Lieutenant Jong Din of the North Korean special forces melted into the night to return to his vehicle. It was time, he knew, to go and have a conversation with the Russians.

CHAPTER TEN

Former KGB Major Sergei Kilcotchkin, veteran of his country's ten-year Afghanistan debacle, knew it was a mistake from the very beginning. The truth, he thought, was as brutal in its naked reality as the million-plus land mines he had ordered planted from Kabul to the Uzbek border before the tanks rolled out with their legions of weary, beaten, shame-faced young Russian soldiers.

And he wasn't a man prone to repeat the mistakes of the past.

As he settled on the divan for the first of several morning vodkas, the mere sight of what he thought of as the "Bruce Lee triplets" was about to confirm one of many suspicions about the current operation. All he needed to do was to glance at the large nylon satchel, practically overflowing with the Euros, displayed on the coffee table for his viewing displeasure, as if he had something to do with the ream job the Bruce Lees had taken.

Oh, but he had tried to avert what he knew all along would be a series of explosive future disasters that could topple the entire Family. Time and again he had vehemently warned Petre Kykov about falling into bed with madmen who had nothing but suicide on the brain. And more times than he cared to count, with a belly full of vodka, he recalled urging, in near unseemly imploring of a man of his stature, then failing in his attempts to sway the boss from trading off common sense for the love of money. Kykov wouldn't hear of it, seeing only his bank accounts fatten, forging on to barter with duplicitous, inscrutable Asians.

When this unholy alliance was formed, he had found it baffling and unnerving to the point of outrage. Kykov, an aging former KGB man himself, insisted on holding hands with Mongol devils, sworn enemies, no less, as bad as the Chinese, but who bowed to a leader they actually believed came down from heaven on a UFO to save them from poverty, mass starvation and imagined oppression by American imperialists. Who could figure this insanity? These Bruce Lees were special forces operatives, thrown to lions by their pudgy drunken buffoon of a president who would lead them, or so they believed, while swilling brandy and watching *Star Trek* reruns, to become a nuclear megapower that would conquer the world.

Humankind was becoming, he concluded, not more complex, but more strange, insidious and desperate. From Beijing to Washington it was all just a devious quest, plowing on into the uncertain future, he thought, to gobble up more natural resources, stake out more fertile turf, grab up more power on a planet dwindling in everything by the day like some walking dead skeletal refugee while the world's population exploded with more mouths than ever that could possibly be fed. As far as he was concerned, the rich and the powerful could only keep the other world's misery contained by outright force or sheer apathy, just so it didn't spill over onto his doorstep.

Then there were those willing to die in the name of religion, an incendiary Factor X having glued itself to the seat of the pants of his own organization, these thieves and liars, sons of jackals who now had in their possession perhaps the most hideous of all weapons of mass destruction. All these problems and fears to ponder, or simply forget with another glass of vodka. It was beyond him, no doubt about it, a world gone mad, which was why he would just as soon sit on the sidelines and watch the rest of the planet consume itself, a great snake eating its own tail. As long as he could, of course, stay his own course, hold on to the good life he could remain indifferent. The trouble was, the past forty-eight hours had seen him lurch off his gilded throne of creature comforts and pleasure, plunging headlong into a boiling crisis.

No, he wasn't so certain anymore he could just spectate, since madmen were, in fact, circling the organization, these Arab and Asian hyenas skulking in to steal the choice meat where the lion had already made the kill.

As he smoothed his white silk robe, Yuri, Boris and Dmitri, his soldiers, took positions at the bar across the massive suite, focusing on the three Koreans in their identical cashmere coats, black slacks and buzz cuts. Kilcotchkin drank deep and slow. A little more vodka, and he might calm an anger that had churned his stomach since this most unorthodox and disturbing undertaking began. He listened for a moment, ignoring Bruce Lee One, who was boring ninja needle eyes into him from across the coffee table, to the bustle of street life stirring beyond the balcony.

He shut then opened his eyes, finding himself wishing it was just another day strolling the streets of Belgrade, window-shopping, hopping from café to café, or listening to American rock and roll as his Mercedes limo took him on a tour of the city where he was never alone with his vodka in the back seat. Whiling away the morning, yes, spending money on more clothes than he could possibly wear in a whole year, throwing more of it away on all the fine young tourist girls who flocked here to become, or so they believed, culturally enriched. Since his reputation preceded him from Moscow to Brighton Beach—and his track record of conquests over the fairer sex proved it—he was talked about in every important circle from his soldiers to the Kremlin to the CIA, and more for his prowess as a swordsman than former assassin with more blood on his hands than all the khans combined. He was considered, and proud of it, so he heard, as the gangster version of some American movie superstar or sports hero for his sexual appetites.

Ah, but he longed to be anywhere but where he was at the moment. Still, this was business, and Moscow had sent him here to do more than rack up another string of natural or unnatural sexual victories.

Since the end of the American bombing campaign, the Family had bought and fairly taken over the Hotel New Belgrade. In the cultural heart of the city he had a view of cathedrals, the Kalemegdan Fortress where the Sava and Danube rivers met. He had two Norwegian girls waiting for him in the bedroom for more cultural enrichment.

Bruce Lee One snapped his fingers. It was all Kilcotchkin could do to keep from erupting as the man glared at him. The Moscow underboss raised his glass for another. While Yuri brought the bottle and refilled him, Bruce Lee Two produced a small can of lighter fluid. Kilcotchkin felt the ripple of tension reach clear to the bar. He ignored the anxious questions from his men, sat calm and quiet as his nose was assaulted with the stink of lighter fumes. Two took a matchbook, lit one, torched the whole pack with the flame, then tossed it onto the banknotes. As the money burst into flames, Kilcotchkin stared and grinned at One while his soldiers flailed about, filling water pitchers at the bar, racing across the suite, trailing curses. With the side of his shoe, One pushed away the bonfire, sliding it down to the edge of the coffee table.

They were dumping water on the fire, swearing at the Koreans in Russian, when the underboss simply told them in their native tongue, "Take it into the bathtub."

The Bruce Lees blamed Moscow for getting duped by counterfeit currency.

"Yuri," Kilcotchkin said, as the smoking bag was hauled away, holding up his glass.

"Garbage," Bruce Lee One said.

Kilcotchkin smiled. "Your lips move, but I can't hear what you say."

"If that is some form of Russian humor, I do not find it amusing."

A fresh glass, Kilcotchkin sipped, smiled, nodded. "If you are finished with theatrics, I assume there is a reason you phoned to interrupt my morning."

"I took these last night. Three potential problems I foresee down the road."

Even before One flipped the grainy photos on the coffee table, Kilcotchkin was nodding, glancing at the blurry faces in the pictures. "I have my own intelligence sources inside Croatia. Every bit as good as yours. I know about the attack on the factory. I know it was where some of the counterfeit currency was produced. I know these three operatives, the only survivors, are Americans. I know they have taken prisoner a Serb colonel who, if broken under interrogation, could bring a lot of trouble to Moscow. That must be prevented at all costs. Unfortunately my woes have become entwined with your predicament." Bruce Lee One was about to squawk, but the underboss threw up a hand. "My organization was cheated likewise with Euros. Of cheap quality, it didn't take us long to discover what had happened, but it was too late. You are not alone, my Korean comrade, in your distress, or desire to correct this abominable situation."

"They came to our operatives, on bended knee, in Indonesia…"

"Did they? I understand it was your cutouts who sought them out. Unloading these drones for outrageous sums so your president can further his own ICBM dreams, do more than rattle his saber over brandy and Rambo movies."

"Whatever you choose to believe is your affair. Our problem is we accepted, a foolish mistake on our part, to give in to their claims their assets around the world were being frozen by the Americans."

Kilcotchkin sipped his drink. "You took cash instead of an electronic transfer of funds as we did."

"Our man in Singapore was arrested by the American FBI when he attempted to deposit their fake currency. By then, the Arabs had what they wanted, believing they could simply abscond with it to parts unknown. American operatives, the same ones who walked away from the battle last night, we believe are also hunting for the same treacherous snakes."

"If you know so much, you must know we went through considerable risk and expense to haul, by rail, all the way from a Siberian laboratory to Kazakhstan their matériel, along with delivering the human technical expertise to further their operation. What has been weaponized, I understand, is something so horrific…well, like you, I have my orders. So, what are you saying? Do you want our help in finding the Arabs responsible for stealing from you?"

"We already know where some of them are. And

there are reports even that the leader of this al-Amin is in this very country."

Kilcotchkin lifted an eyebrow. "Really? Would it be Chechnya?"

Surprise flickered through One's eyes. "Then you understand what must be done to rectify this matter."

"I do, and it will be done. As we speak, people in our organization are infiltrating what is perhaps the next most dangerous place on Earth outside Afghanistan. Naturally they are getting assistance from those we have inside our military and intelligence circles."

One leaned up, an edge to his voice. "Some of this technology we acquired from your organization..."

"It was against my better judgment, so I suggest you do not sit there and cast accusations, my Korean comrade. It has all become like some maelstrom swirling faster and faster, this doing business with people with their own insidious agendas."

"If you are referring to my nation, this is no time to kick around bitter differences between our countries."

"I agree. It would be wise to track down these terrorists at this juncture and take back the merchandise."

"While teaching them the hardest of lessons."

"What are you asking exactly?"

One sat back. "My orders are clear. I am not to return to my country until this situation is resolved. We need whatever your contacts and connections to help slip myself and a small commando team into Chechnya."

"A suicide mission, do you realize that?"

"I have no say in the matter. We have operatives in other countries where they are presently attempting to expand their jihad. The enemy, these Arab snakes, are, as you might say, on a suicide watch. Americans, French, I have no pity for those who get in our way."

Kilcotchkin killed his drink. "Very well. I anticipated your visit, but an operation by my organization has been set in motion to hunt down these Arabs. You want in, well, I have phone calls to make, so, if you will excuse yourselves. I will let you know something, one way or another."

They stood, One glowering. "Make it happen. In two hours I will contact you."

"Oh, I can make it happen, Comrade. If you want to commit suicide that badly, go ahead and pack your bags for Chechnya. Make sure you three have a change of shorts."

Bruce Lee One looked set to issue some threat, insulted, hesitating, glaring, then led his clones for the doors.

They were gone, finally, Kilcotchkin grateful to be alone with his own thoughts, one of which was the bedroom, where he could rid himself of pent-up alpha male aggression. A covert war against the Arabs in question was already arranged, and little did the Koreans know how ugly it would become. Only now his hand was forced, in the interests of maintaining the status quo with the Mongols, to land them in Chechnya. Not a problem. He would be more than happy to oblige their death wish.

Chechnya, he thought, envisioning the North Koreans getting themselves blown away and clear into Dagestan or Georgia in a land where not even Russian soldiers dared venture unless there were five divisions of tanks, thousands of soldiers and gunships with nerve gas. Oh, but he'd help Kim Jong Il's bootlickers commit suicide, if only to rid his future of one more pack of hyenas on the prowl.

Two hours, plenty of time, he decided, to set what they wanted in motion. First, another vodka, then a thirty-minute or so romp with his Norwegian beauties.

Business could wait. The world—Kykov included—could kindly kiss his ass.

Kilcotchkin lifted his glass, told Yuri to throw a certain tape into the CD, volume ten. He believed he could he see the future, a hell on Earth where there was no place to run, or hide, if the Arabs succeeded. He imagined tea leaves on the table where the ashes of treachery remained after the Korean melodrama, wondering if he hadn't just looked into the future.

Death for one, death for all, was essentially what the Korean had stated, going for broke, attempting to take back what they—both of their countries—had dumped off in the hands of fanatics.

The world, he knew, had just become nothing more than the Devil's lair.

Chechnya.

OF ALL the godforsaken hellholes on the planet, David McCarter couldn't imagine a worse place. What little he knew about the former Soviet breakaway republic was all bad. A ferocious independent state of Islamic guerrilla warriors, mountain-bred and hardened by years of kill or be killed with Russian soldiers, McCarter knew they were headed into country where not even the Kremlin wanted to march in the troops unless they had an overwhelming force. The Briton knew the brutalization of Chechens went back to World War II, where Stalin did his damnedest to exterminate what he called Nazi collaborators, and to this day Moscow, he imagined, probably wouldn't like anything more than to nuke it off the map if they could get away with it. Like the Afghan mujahadeen, the Chechens, as mean and vicious as a spitting adder, believed in nursing grudges, and living only for vengeance was a way of life. Hop a train to Moscow, and they could keep on ripping off big bloody chunks of Russians before slipping back into the armed womb of some of the most inhospitable terrain in the world. They were more than just a colossal pain in the rear and embarrassment for Moscow. They were armed fanatics, the ex-SAS commando thought, with the same jihad mentality as the worst of the worst to ever come out of the Taliban or al-Qaeda.

A fresh wave of terrorist attacks in Moscow, apartment buildings gutted by bombs, discos and night clubs shot up by machine-gun-toting lunatics, had prompted the Russians to stake out a base, Fort Pavel, in neighboring Georgia, Spetsnaz and FSK paramilitary ops prepared to go in and hunt down Chechens believed behind the rash of terror, and who were believed connected with al-Amin. McCarter shook his head, standing amidships in the C-130 that two hours earlier had lifted off from Camp Bulldog, wondering just how more fouled up this mission could get. The three Phoenix Force warriors had set up their sat links, Zharjic farther down the fuselage, getting grilled some more by Harker. Headphones on, McCarter, James and Encizo listened to Hal Brognola and Barbara Price give the brief as intel scrolled off the fax line.

He perused the sat pictures of the terror compound in question. Chechnya, he knew, was little more than the Devil's playground, near impossible to get to mountain villages where every male over the age of ten was armed with an AK, where drug lords from various clans fought for control over narcotics trafficking, where outsiders came under instant suspicion as black ops shipped out from Moscow and were often shot two steps inside the borders with Georgia or Dagestan. Not even traditional Muslims, called Nakh, they claimed their heritage as sons of Noah. Each clan was headed up by a spiritual mystic, Chechens embracing the Sufti brotherhood, a bizarre combination of mysticism and Islam. To say the country was an outlaw, anarchic mess was the understatement of the year.

"Please, tell me," McCarter said, "we won't be falling into another fat mess like we just put behind. Tell us we won't be dealing with some Russian version of Colonel Joe."

"No guarantees," Brognola said. "Forget Colonel Joe. We know he was a CIA paramilitary operative with a track record as a mercenary. I'm thinking he was in it for the bucks.''

''Wouldn't surprise us, since it sure looked like he just wanted to get his hands on some fast seven figure blood bounty,'' James said, ''the way he tried to cut us out of the game.''

''Unfortunately he took a bunch of good Special Forces warriors with him,'' Brognola said.

''Makes you wonder,'' James commented, ''who's running the show at Langley.''

''What happened is Langley's headache,'' Price told them.

Enough said, McCarter knew.

''The way we read it,'' Brognola said, ''the Russians are embarrassed they allowed the Kykov *mafiya* to get their hands on weaponized Ebola. Spell international cooperation on this, and the CIA has paramilitary operatives at Fort Pavel to, hopefully, assist the three of you when you hit this terror camp.''

''Fort *Gazavat?*'' Encizo posed.

''That's Nakh for holy war,'' Price said. ''The intelligence rumor mill is churning with reports that Wahjihab and several top lieutenants are in this village compound in southern Chechnya.''

''This great big armed minefield called Dhujar,'' Encizo said. ''We're looking at maybe a hundred to two hundred fanatics.''

''You won't be going in alone,'' Brognola said. ''Jack will have a crew ready to hammer down and soften the way in an AC-130 Spectre. Throw in some Russian Hinds, and I'd say the odds are better than fifty-fifty it could be a clean in-and-out sweep.''

"You hope. You didn't see the fiasco in Croatia," Encizo said.

"Report to General Mytkin and a CIA operative called Chino," Price told them. "They are getting last-minute intelligence, according to our sources and intercepts from the CIA station chief in Georgia, and they're ready to move. Now, we've cleared the way for you to bag Wahjihad and the other top henchmen whose mugs and background we faxed. The Man has been in contact with the Russian president, and it's been agreed they're yours."

"If that's dead or alive," Encizo said, "I wouldn't hold out hope we'll take them standing. The further this goes, the bigger the bang they have ready and waiting to take out anybody who crashes the front door."

"However it shakes out," Brognola said, "they're yours, and if there's guff about that, you can tell them to phone Moscow."

"And Gary and T.J.?" McCarter wanted to know.

"Feeling things out in Marseilles," Price said. "Take care of business first in Chechnya, then you're France bound. One more thing."

"How come I don't like the sound of that already?" McCarter said, watching as a black-and-white picture rolled out of the fax.

"His name is Jack Arnold," Brognola said.

McCarter saw a grizzled, bearded face framed in long black hair, a burly figure sporting a dark green fatigues.

"He's former CIA. Word is he scoffed up some

drug and gun money over there, used it to help arm and train Chechens.''

McCarter sounded a mean chuckle. ''I suppose you'll tell me he's converted to Islam?''

''Close enough, but I don't think he's in it for the ideology.''

James swore. He looked back at Harker, called out, ''Hey, you know about this clown, this Jihad Jack Arnold?''

''He's one reason I'm tagging along for the ride,'' Harker said.

''He's an embarrassment to the Company, that it?'' James said.

''He's a lot more than that, friend.''

''Have Harker fill you in some more about this traitor,'' Price stated, ''during the ride.''

''Count on it,'' McCarter said. ''This is getting better by the minute. Any more surprises?''

''Nothing more to report,'' Brognola said. ''In the interest of all this interagency cooperation, you'll hand Zharjic over to Chino's people when you land. The way it sounds, you've gotten about all you're going to get from him. We established his connection to the Kykov Family, and their affiliation with al-Amin. Good luck and watch your backs.''

When Brognola signed off, McCarter looked at the weapons bin. ''Let's break out the hardware, mates, and do a little brainstorming.

''Harker!'' he called out, holding up Jihad Jack's mug. ''You care to fill us in a little more about al-Amin Arnold?''

CHAPTER ELEVEN

The passport and visa stated he was Jacques Puersaux, in the U.S. on business in the food and beverage industry, with interests in establishing a chain of cajun restaurants in the French Quarter of New Orleans. He could speak perfect French or English, even knew a little Creole now after his few dealings with drug smugglers out in the bayou, whichever language depending on what group of infidels he needed to dupe to further the jihad. His real name was Rashim Akhman, and he was a Syrian national, formerly of al-Qaeda misfortune when he was chased out of Afghanistan by American bombs and commandos in search of the scalps of bin Laden and Mullah Omar. The fortunate part, though, he recalled, was fleeing the caves, the crushed ruins of the camps of eastern Afghanistan, barely clearing, by hours, the same gruesome fate of the fearsome air strikes that had decimated hundreds, perhaps thousands of al-Qaeda and Taliban warriors he had trained, eaten and rejoiced with over the great victories of 9/11.

It was a bad dream even still, those days when he was on the run, the window of escape closing rapidly behind him before he found comfort and aid through ISI commiserators, catching the long boat ride out of Karachi to Marseilles where a new organization, he discovered, had arisen out of the ashes of al-Qaeda and the Taliban. The magic al-Amin carpet ride, he thought, had flown him clear to New Orleans where a storage-office complex of Hobart Trucking Inc., connected with Islip Foreign Automobiles Inc., was ready and waiting in the Warehouse District on the muddy shores of the Mississippi River. Beyond the false front of crates and steel containers, tools and machinery out in the warehouse proper, the smattering of imported autos, the place was actually a bomb-making factory.

And the whole building, in light of very recent dire developments, was now primed with enough C-4 and wired-up four-second delay dynamite to clean out half a city block. It was strange, if he thought about it, the organization selecting southern Louisiana—with its mixed bag of various cultures, religions and pagan rituals passed off as festivals, and where he was sure he would be found out long before now as Arab by what he believed were called rednecks—as a main transshipment point for money, troops, matériel. Occasionally he had strolled Bourbon Street, found himself enjoying the sounds of what they called jazz, wondering in a sick sort of amazement over the open and shameless displays of American debauchery. He had been tempted, yes, to wander into any number of saloons or strip clubs, immerse himself in their subculture. If nothing else, he should to try to understand his enemies by reveling with them, these debased people he was going to kill someday soon, knowing if he was to succeed on the massive scales of jihad and justice for Islam required he would need to see them only as soulless animals. But he had been warned to keep primarily to himself, stay focused, not get swept away by the sins of a city that was essentially a bawdy free-for-all of excess in everything from food to sex. That would be no problem, he knew, since he found it easy enough to isolate himself from and despise a people who practiced some pagan religion they called voodoo, curses and such where pins could be stuck in dolls to torment a hated enemy.

Shameless heathens, he thought, pandering to superstition that fairly bordered on prayer to the Devil.

He had work to do, and they could play, unaware their next Mardi Gras could well be their last.

Rashim Akhman was a cutout, plain and simple, with orders that came by express mail from France through other middlemen higher up the pecking order, none of them knowing from where the dictates came down or who they directly reported to. In his office cubicle, sometimes the occasion called for a fax, E-mail, Internet or direct contact by sat phone. Every word was, naturally, coded to disguise its true meaning.

Right then, Akhman, setting back the phone, suspected something was wrong with the voice on the other end. Twice the man had called, once to let him know he was thirty minutes outside New Orleans, and just now to inform him he was coming down to the

French Quarter. The caller claimed to be Baruk, the Miami connection and his ticket to moving westward the Angels of Islam. Akhman suspected it was highly unlikely he had heard the real Baruk, since he knew for a fact the Egyptian had been arrested, the French freighter seized by the Coast Guard, its cargo, most likely, discovered.

Which meant that either Baruk was now under extreme duress and constant threats by their FBI to place the bogus call, assure him of its delivery, the jaws of disaster about to clamp...

Or what? The devils had ultrasophisticated high-tech equipment, which, he'd heard, could even alter a man's voice. The voice sounded enough like Baruk's, but there was something subtly tinny or slightly off-note he couldn't discern, enough to make him wonder about a lethal ruse that was set in motion. When the reports first reeled off his fax from Hobart Trucking about the seizure and arrests, Akhman had put in a most dangerous call to Marseilles to another cutout, hoping it wasn't monitored by the enemy, alerting them that he knew the worst, and was prepared to act in accordance on unwavering faith in the jihad.

It was made clear, in no uncertain terms, what he was expected to do. The jihad would go on, with or without him soaring along with others on the wings of victory.

Akhman took up the Ingram MAC-10 subgun, the pockets of his jacket filled with grenades. If the American law was coming, there would be no more arrests. They would find a surprise waiting for them when they broke through the doors.

Out in the warehouse, he found twelve of his most trusted operatives waiting, assault rifles and subguns in hand, the collective mood tense. He ordered Hamaj to kill all but the office and loading bay lights. Then, remote in hand, he walked out the back door, his soldiers trailing him, ready for war. It took a good minute to assemble in the loading bay, then Akhman took the remote, armed the explosives, wired to pressure plates in some spots, trip wires strung along the base of other doors. Should he make the final call himself, he could radio activate the works with one push of a button.

A check of the sprawling lot revealed they were alone as night dropped over New Orleans, and he set his sights on their secondary office-warehouse directly ahead.

There was nothing left to do, he thought, but wait, watch who showed up and turn the Big Easy into the Big Jihad Bang for the enemy.

NEARLY A FULL DAY was burned up getting to, then setting the stage for the New Orleans phase of the campaign. Between the long haul to the Big Easy, a recon of the target premises in the Lexus rental Bolan had picked up in the city, a debrief with Justice Department special agents surveying the terror shop on the Mississippi, callbacks to the Farm...

It was time again to ignite a firestorm on the enemy's doorstep.

The Executioner and Able Team had agreed to spend as little time, sweat, and hopefully expend only spilled enemy blood on what they considered a pit stop but a key link in the terror chain before rolling on for Houston. Quick and easy, though, was always a big question mark, rarely happened, and the soldier had been around long enough to anticipate the worst, expect the grim unexpected.

Like now.

According to the monitor on Bolan's handheld thermal-imaging unit, no heat from live ones was reflected back from inside the warehouse in question, the rooftop, or flanking alley corridors. Bolan stowed the IR box, decided a closer hard probe was in order. He grabbed the small portable explosives detector from the back seat. Tapping a button on his chronometer, he illuminated the dial, figured another two minutes tops for Schwarz, Blancanales and Lyons to get into position, then he'd call them over the com link. Brognola's agents had been sitting on the warehouse, keeping it under surveillance from a nearby office window during the day. Bolan had already pulled them off the watch detail, but not until he learned at least a dozen armed men were on-site. In thirty minutes, since the agents vacated, there was no way the targets could have bailed, and their fleet of luxury vehicles was still parked out front.

Which signaled ambush to the Executioner. By now surely word of disaster on two fronts had found its way here through cutouts on the loose. If Islip was still being truthful under duress, there were spies on the fringes watching to make sure all cutouts and operatives carried out their orders.

With Able Team covering him to the south and northeast, Schwarz having burglarized his way into an adjacent warehouse with his high-tech tools for a rooftop perch and sweep of the area with his own IR monitor, the Executioner would take the hunt forward from what he hoped was the enemy's blind side.

The soldier, togged in blacksuit, M-16/M-203 platoon killer in hand, was out of the rental car, having concealed it as best he could behind a Dumpster garbage bin in an alley. Familiar with New Orleans from past blitzes, the Warehouse District of the Central Business District appeared renovated somewhat by city planners and various institutions perhaps sick and tired of keeping abandoned the eyesore of an industrial garbage heap, or so Bolan judged the halfhearted refurbishments on the ride in. Tucked between the French Quarter to the northeast, the Superdome to the northwest and the grimy run-down immigrant nest of the Irish Channel, it was still a sprawling maze of imposing stone, steel or hollow behemoths of concrete and iron spread before him. With the Public Belt Railroad still chugging its mercantile course along the Mississippi, Bolan could see the more things changed—the addition of quiet residential neighborhoods and art galleries lacing the perimeter—the more they had stayed the same.

Dark, grim and run-down, with plenty of hiding places or pockets of resistance for shooters to hold out or lay in wait.

Combat radar screen alive and blipping, the soldier padded for the huge steel back door. The small wand of the detector out and scanning, the sensor could pick up even the most minuscule amount of nitroglycerine or any nitrobenzene concentrates. According to the needle on the monitor, the digital readout of 1 through 10 flickering all the way to maximum alert, the door was mined with enough explosives, the soldier knew, to launch him clear to Lake Pontchatrain. No need to pull out any sample module for analysis, even if he was so inclined to test the booby-trapped brew, Bolan knew enough.

The Executioner fell back, reaching up to key his com link.

THIRTEEN RED GHOSTS lit up the monitor on Schwarz's IR handheld unit. Packed in a staggered line behind a row of windows in what the Justice intel stated was a secondary Islip office at dead twelve o'clock from the main warehouse, Schwarz read the darker outlines of weapons, darting movement as the specters went from window to window. Panic or pre-combat nerves, they were feeling something raw and unnerving, he knew, as they hunkered down in the shadows, waiting.

Either way, it was about time to rock their world, a Mardi Gras riot of bombs and bullets in their face that might splatter them clear to bayou country.

The Zapper had done its magic, the alarm system to what was some sort of storehouse for Mardi Gras floats and costumes, melted down. Up the stairwell, then onto the roof. A check of his watch told Schwarz he was on time for the party. And ready to let it rip with his M-16/M-203 combo. The problem was Warehouse Main was clean of enemy traffic, letting him know the targets were expecting a whopping armed encounter of the worst kind. Given their track record, he had to believe Main was rigged to blast into the face of anyone first through a door.

"Gadgets."

He keyed his com link. "Striker, it's an ambush," he told Bolan, and laid out the score.

"I'm driving around the front. The warehouse is mined. Carl, fall back and cover the rear of that building and take out any rabbits we might chase your way. Pol, get a clean line of fire on those front windows. Mark it now, thirty seconds and counting, then hit them with everything you have, even if I'm a few seconds behind."

They copied, then Schwarz found a disturbing development on his IR screen. Lyons, he saw, rearing up over the lip of the rooftop, was shadowing down an alley, crouched and hugging the southern face of the office complex. Two specters were up and heading in that direction, one, then two more peeling off from the mob. Schwarz had no idea how they knew, figuring hidden minicams had Ironman lodged in their gunsights.

He pressed his com link, checking the digital readout that gauged their flight to Lyons down to the foot. "Carl, look alive. Two bogeys coming your way, to your eleven o'clock. Twenty-two yards and closing in hard. They're all yours.''

A glimpse, and Schwarz saw Bolan cruising out of the alley, the Executioner's idea to take cover behind the motor pool, pour it on from there. His chronometer already set, he heard the beep to cut loose in tandem with Lyons and Blancanales. Lyons was copying the warning, Blancanales unloading Little Bulldozer on the windows, explosions marching through the enemy ranks, then Warehouse Main went up in a blast that momentarily blinded Schwarz with piercing needles of light and shock waves that punched the air out of his lungs.

Worse, he saw, horrified, the Lexus was pounded by the gushing firewall, lifted off its wheels, flipping over, and hurtled through the air.

WHEN AKHMAN SAW the tall heavily armed dark figure on his monitor, using some sort of small bomb detector and discovering the truth, he determined to change his original plan to blow the warehouse only in the event of a raid by an army of American lawmen. Part of his reasoning to level the building involved more than just crushing any attackers who would storm the place. Invaluable intelligence on computer hard drives, reams of paper too many to shred in a few hours that detailed bank accounts, phone and fax numbers of other cutouts and operatives in Texas and Mexico had to be destroyed. What the monstrous blast would not wipe out, fifty-five-gallon drums of gasoline and diesel fuel, left open on the way out and placed strategically around the warehouse, would consume as a firestorm ignited. He had to assume the attackers had managed to intercept the Angels of Islam shipment because information about the freighter and the entire Hobart-Islip connection to New Orleans had fallen into their hands. No more. The operation had to be protected from there on, at all costs.

"One more, coming up the alley!"

"Go, go! Take him out!" Akhman raged, wondering how many were coming, and if he should stand his ground and fight. He had seen the attached rocket launcher in the hands of the dark invader, knew they didn't stand a chance if one or several attackers began lobbing in grenades, blasting them out of the office, rats in a barrel.

The cameras were well-hidden, near invisible pinheads, mounted high up the walls of the main warehouse and office complex. Foresight was about to pay off, using the Islip office as backup to launch an ambush, but he was hardly grateful for looking into the future several months back.

Akhman had visions of bombs raining from heaven to churn up the earth around him in waves of hellfire, those fuel-air explosives that could vaporize legions of jihad fighters for thousands of yards, suck the oxygen out of their caves, sear the eyeballs out of their skulls. He had no desire to get ground up now, suddenly thinking there might be a way out for him. Let his troops do the fighting, escape for him had been

God's will before, hadn't it? Why should he die now, after having survived so much?

He palmed the remote, saw the Lexus vector for the motor pool through the crack in the shade, then hit the button. Akhman was pedaling back for deeper cover in the office when it seemed as if the entire front wall was sheared away in a gale-force blast of fire and scorching wind.

"STRIKER! STRIKER!"

The rare miscalculation on the suicidal tenacity of the enemy nearly cost Bolan the ultimate price. He was bouncing off the roof, slammed down as the vehicle rolled over again, the crumpling steel can shooting through the air, propelled by hurricane-strength shock waves. Glass slashing off his jaw, a fierce heat blasting through the interior, he could only hold on, ride out the invisible concussive tidal wave. The roof caved next as the crushed hull hammered solid turf, rocketed on. Bolan had a blurred, upside-down view of the oncoming impact with the motor pool. The voice of Schwarz, still yelling over the com link that was cocked halfway off his head, sounded a hundred miles away. Hands braced up against the mauled dash, Bolan readied himself as the battered shell rammed into the solid wall of the motor pool.

He strained his hearing, focused seconds later through the chiming in his ears on the explosions thundering away outside. Bolan kicked out the hanging fangs of what was left of the driver's window.

Assault rifle in hand, he squeezed through the opening, adjusted his com link.

"I'm in one piece, Gadgets."

The Executioner was rising, the assault rifle combo up and trying to pick out any targets in the demolished front of the office building, when Schwarz patched back, hollered, "Striker, run to your left!"

Bolan sprinted to his nine. He was ten yards out and still pumping his legs, when he looked back over his shoulder. The sky was raining fire and steel, a fifty-five-gallon drum thudding off the area he'd just vacated, bouncing high, its flaming liquid puked out in all directions.

THE TERRORISTS, maybe three or four left, were reeling somewhere, hacking out their guts, beyond the plumes of smoke. They had retreated right before Blancanales blew down the wall, but Bolan needed this wrapped and the four of them little more than a bad mystery for NOPD to solve. Already he made out the faraway wail of cruisers en route.

And there were still armed combatants left in play.

The Executioner stepped away from the motor pool, scanned the drifting smoke, shadows tipping into splintered sections of wood and concrete slabs, clinging to their final bitter breaths. He checked on the troops, sight lasered on the staggering silhouettes, M-16 leading the way. "Everyone still with me?" Three affirmatives, then Bolan, marching forward, handed out the orders. "Gadgets, keep us covered until you think the area is clear of any runners, then come on down. Time to bail. Carl…''

"Right. I got hung up for a second, but I'll take the back."

"Find a way in, but watch yourself. I don't think the place was mined, or they would have blown it by now. I'll take the front."

"Roger, Striker."

"Pol, go get the van."

The shock factor had kept the enemy upright, immobilized, as Bolan watched them, but now they were coming back to the reality check of murderous intent. Rolling, the Executioner held back on the M-16's trigger. Long dousings of autofire, left to right and back, and they were spinning, dark streaks of gore cutting the smoke before they toppled.

Down and martyred.

The usual odors of death slammed Bolan's senses, his boots crunching glass, wallboard, wood as he waded into the smoke. A few cautious steps farther into the ruins and he spotted movement in the deep corner. The dying hardman had to have sensed him coming, rolling onto his side, his face a bloody gargoyle's mask, eyes white with the fires of hate. Another fanatic, Bolan knew, who wouldn't give up the ghost until he got the final word in.

"Your country, American, cannot defeat us…you will not win…"

"I keep hearing that."

Bolan lifted the M-16, saw the terrorist's hand

delving into his coat pocket, his finger taking up slack on the trigger. A quick burst of autofire, and the Executioner told the terrorist exactly what he thought about that losing mantra.

CHAPTER TWELVE

Sometimes doing nothing worked best when the search for solutions hit a wall. To still and quiet the inner self, especially at the height of crisis, was a rare treat Hal Brognola could indulge. There were times, like now, when he and the other key personnel at the Farm had done all they could for the present. Naming and tracking key players on the opposition. Steering the Stony Man warriors in the right direction. Monitoring the action in the field from outer space, while retasking satellites in search of compounds where this new technology of mass death might be produced. Then tapping contacts and sources for intelligence, clues, and those always seemingly elusive magic answers as to who, where and how something as monstrous as the Angels of Islam could have ever become humankind's darkest reality.

If nothing else, sitting alone in his office, not thinking, not worrying, then a short nap on the couch had recharged his battery to go back into the Computer Room where the cyberteam was waiting with the latest round-up of intel.

Brognola took one look at Barbara Price, wheeling

around in her chair from Kurtzman's work station, clicker in hand, and he knew it wasn't good news. Each member of the cyberteam had been performing his or her own duties pertaining to the mission almost nonstop since the big Fed arrived at the Farm. The way it would work now everyone could share the floor. Interruptions, as Brognola had earlier stated, were acceptable when necessary for brainstorming in their quest to find solutions to help the warriors out there abort the crisis ASAP. He was looking for anything they had to offer, no matter how trivial they might find it.

"The latest report," Price said, "is in from my source in USAMRIID at Detrick. I've put together a short package with the facts as we know them. I think all of us need to have a better understanding of what it is we're dealing with."

She let it hang for a second, Brognola veering for the coffeepot.

"Hal, it's worse than even USAMRIID originally suspected."

"I surmised as much when I walked in."

Cup in hand, Brognola grabbed a seat at a table close to the wall monitor. "Let's have it."

"This is what an Ebola virus particle looks like," she said, snapping on a frame of what looked to Brognola like a contorted viper, the big Fed noting 120,000 scale in the bottom corner of the screen. "A filovirus, Latin for thread virus, bears no resemblance to any other virus. The filoviruses have been compared to looking like snakes or spaghetti. Note the shepherd's crook, or eyebolt, which gives the Ebola thread virus its own unique signature. Named after the Ebola River in Zaire, its exact origins are as mysterious as—one—how it spreads—and two—as mysterious as its seven different proteins, four of which to this day cannot have their RNA gene identified. Science believes Ebola could be as old as the planet itself.''

"Okay, so you're telling me it's been here since long before man, sort of lying in wait,'' Brognola said. "Plague on tap.''

"A good—or bad—way to put it,'' Kurtzman said, picking up the ball. "Consider what we learned. Six weeks is how long Ebola Zaire would take to make a trip around the earth and infect every human being. That's the good news.''

Good news? the big Fed thought, groaning inside. "Well, we've known the horror stories for some time, Bear,'' he said. "Such as how the CIA has dreaded Ebola could hop a plane from central Africa to any country in the world and start the end of the human race. We know that plague has caused more death than war or any other catastrophe.''

"Germ warfare, or the spreading of pestilence isn't something that was created in the twentieth century, as you might know. The Romans used to poison well water to kill off their enemies,'' Kurtzman said.

"The British would infect blankets with smallpox and give them to the Indians during the French and Indian wars,'' Tokaido said. "Stalin used tularemia on the Germans, killed tens and tens of thousands of them, including his own soldiers, during the siege of Stalingrad, which some historians say, is what broke the Germans back and turned the war around.''

Brognola frowned. ''All this virology and the history of germ warfare 101 aside, what I'm waiting to hear, folks, is for the other shoe to drop.''

''This bioengineered strain is worse than Ebola Zaire,'' Price said, ''which in known cases has proved fatal nine times out of ten.''

Brognola felt his stomach churn over the bad news. ''And this one has gone where no virus has gone before. One hundred percent success ratio. And it's invincible, meaning incurable, which we already know Ebola is.''

''Viruses,'' Tokaido said, ''are neither alive nor dead. I guess you could say they float in a state of limbo, waiting to latch on to a host. They never go away, only hide.''

''So, essentially all viruses are what?'' Brognola said. ''Immortal?''

''That they are,'' Kurtzman said. ''Only this engineered version of Ebola is the god—or the devil—of all known strains from Ebola Sudan to Ebola Reston. One eyedrop full of this stuff contains three hundred million particles of the virus. Detrick says it dropped it into a virus flask of water with living cells. In twenty-four hours two viruses replicated into over a billion.''

Brognola knew the case reports of humans who had died from Ebola. First the headaches, then nausea, fever, vomiting. Flulike symptoms, only Ebola, was a relentless, unstoppable molecular eating machine, the Great White Shark of viruses. A day or two tops, the infected person quickly discovered he or she had been stricken with something far worse than a bad cold. The brain fried with fever reported as high as 107 to 110 degrees Fahrenheit, the victim screaming in a petrified state of dementia. Ebola spread like a wildfire throughout the entire body, ravaging to the point of internal meltdown every organ and tissue except skeletal muscle and bone. Tiny white blisters popped out all over the face, maculopapular rash, he believed it was called. The rash then ripped the skin open, internal organs burned to goo, literally sloughing off like a snake's skin, gushing out every orifice. Then there was the black vomit of hemorrhage, choked with virus, and which, he had heard, smelled like a room stacked full of slaughtered disemboweled animals. The virus clotted and jammed and swelled the liver, kidneys, spleen, lungs, what USAMRIID termed "extreme amplification." Even cadavers carried the virus. Even...

He was having those visions again of a dying, shrieking planet when he heard his named called.

"Earth's population would be wiped out inside of a month if this strain of Ebola raced around the globe," Price said. "The United States would cease to exist in a matter of days."

"I don't want to get sidetracked," Brognola said, "but it's always been my understanding that aerosol bioweapons are extremely difficult, but not impossible, to manufacture, and germ aerosols are far more susceptible to losing their virulence when dispersed than chemical weapons.''

"Right," Tokaido said. "The bioweaponeer, or the end user, has to factor in temperature and weather conditions, for one. You want to be upwind, but the attacker will need to know his success rate is much higher when he unleashes the spray at dusk.''

"Why's that?"

"Inversion," Tokaido said. "A blanket of cool air over a warmer layer over the ground to keep the particles from getting blown away by wind.''

"So, we're assuming they have this knowledge," Brognola said.

"That, and their bioweaponeers," Kurtzman said, "will have worked out the problem that sunlight or ultraviolet light can kill viruses.''

"But not this strain of Ebola?"

"No," Kurtzman said.

Brognola felt himself growing more tense and agitated the more he heard. "Who, how and where, folks? The terrorists have either bought these Angels of Islam on the black market, or they have a clandestine lab somewhere. But for that to happen they still need help, the sale of the component parts and the technical skills for openers. Hell, to even jumpstart a primitive operational lab, you still need, what? Special filtration systems…''

"Among steel dryers and centrifuges," Tokaido said.

"And a boatload of Bunsen burners…"

"Special hermetically sealed static chambers," Tokaido added, "to control air flow to test the distribution of a small, contained explosion. Plus, we're thinking test monkeys were shipped from Africa to try out this aerosol Ebola on."

"Near impossible to track down, if you think you can plow through every ship manifest from Africa to the Middle East," Brognola said. "Not to mention those manifests would be doctored to hide the contents of the ship. And why monkeys? Why not mice or rats?"

"They use monkeys," Tokaido answered, "because their respiratory systems are nearly identical to humans. Russian microbiologists once worked up what they call the Q50. Simply put it's the measure of how much of the nasty stuff is needed to infect fifty percent of the population in one square kilometer."

"What Akira's saying," Price interjected when Brognola's scowl set in stone, "is that the CIA is actively looking at certain countries where there might be a sudden outbreak of Ebola in a remote village."

"Good God," Brognola said, "you're telling me these bastards would try this hellish nightmare out on live subjects?"

Price nodded. "A distinct and sickening possibility. The CIA is also using informants, buying contacts in the merchant marine underworld to try to find out what ships repeatedly keep docking where with monkeys from central Africa, or Asia even."

"My money's on Iraq," Brognola said.

"They haven't been ruled out," Kurtzman told him. "Along with about ten other known countries that sponsor terrorism. So far we've hit a dead end on the shipping of monkeys angle."

"All of this is both interesting and damn frightening, but someone kindly tell me they have found out more on the Russian microbiologist angle? Since you alluded earlier that's who's believed to have developed this Ebola strain."

"Hunt? Katz?" Price said.

Wethers nodded at Katz to go first. "I had a long talk with some old comrades of mine in Mossad. They have a division that specializes in tracking and hunting down chem, bio and weapons' grade nuclear matériel or component parts for the building of reprocessing plants, getting a jump on the bad guys before they can break out of the gate with weapons of mass destruction for sale to terrorists. Unfortunately, this time they came up way short." With the new computers, each member of the team was able to click in the data or graphics on their computers to the wall monitor. "Those are being called by Mossad the Fearsome Five of the Russian bioweapons program."

Brognola looked at the five faces on the monitor, as Katz recited their names. Haggard, grizzled, weary faces on two, gaunt, bearded, mean-eyed mugs on the other three, they all looked beaten and angry, but game, Brognola suspected, for anything. "They look more like KGB killers than scientists who would stand around a viral flask of Ebola all day."

"They sold out, specifically to the Kykov Family

in Moscow. My friends in Mossad have an extensive file on Russian organized crime. Of the twenty-six main Russian crime gangs, all of whom operate in forty-five countries and are interconnected with drug cartels and international terrorist organizations—which, by the way, imposes a nightmare obstacle for law enforcement just by the sheer numbers of Russian gangsters and how many countries they have scarfed up—the Kykov Family is ranked number three. Now, the Soviet bioweapons program," Katz said, "called Biopreparat, or the System, is a little over a generation old, and the sale and export of germ and chemical warfare seems to be something of a hot commodity for the Kykov gang. By the end of the late eighties, there was something in the neighborhood of thirty-two thousand scientists, and key staff with technical expertise in the field of bioweaponeering. Kykov, former KGB, has been smuggling both the technology for NBC weapons and trading in the skills of the wayward and the unemployed for years. Some of these microbiologists or virologists have been known to sell out for a case of vodka. Anyway, after the fall of communism, when many of these scientists were wondering where their next meal or drink was coming from, he made deep inroads into Vector Zhigul X4 in Siberia. The four is because it's a complete Biosafety Level Four facility, the X because of the viruses they handle. This was the top-secret bioweapons facility where these five worked."

When Katz paused, Wethers picked up the ball. "They vanished about two years ago. Along with, according to the CIA and the FSK, documents, shells and enough Ebola in their back pockets to exterminate humankind. Savva Girmil, senior member of the team, was believed sighted by the CIA and Mossad in Lebanon, but before they could confirm it he vanished once more. We know the Soviets were working with the Marburg virus, a cousin to Ebola. Girmil headed up Project Black Death, was the man who perfected weaponized Marburg as an airborne powder agent. We've learned this particular strain was so virulent test monkeys died after inhaling a single particle. Now, there was thirty tons of freeze-dried Marburg and smallpox powder lying around after the Russians proclaimed they were going democratic. Despite the treaties between Russia and our country banning the production of offensive biological weapons, the Russians went ahead and kept packing warheads, ICBMs and MIRVs, with bio agents.''

"You're telling me it wouldn't be a stretch for the Fearsome Five to take Marburg home to meet and have a tryst with its Ebola kin? And that this Girmil is still nowhere to be found?''

"Yes, and yes,'' Wethers said. "Russian intelligence operatives, working now with David, Rafael and Calvin, traced the AWOL microbiologists and contraband to a train ride from Vector Zhigul X4 all the way to another bioweapons complex in Kazakhstan where they and said contraband were believed smuggled out of the former Soviet Union by al-Amin operatives working in collusion with the Chechen Mafia.''

"Hence Chechnya," Katz said, "where al-Amin is still hard at work. If all goes according to the surgical strike against Fortress Holy War, I'm told by my senior paramilitary operative contact in the CIA that Phoenix and company will either bag top al-Amin operatives or lay waste to their operation in Chechnya. Either way al-Amin will be sanitized in that part of the world."

"There's something else you need to know about the Angels of Islam, Hal," Price interjected.

The cigar froze midway to Brognola's lips.

"Plastic explosive," the mission controller went on, "was found inside the shells. They could be set off by radio remote or satellite."

"Or it becomes a fuel-air explosive," Brognola finished, "if it's shot out of the sky."

"Exactly," Price said. "They covered all the bases."

Brognola shook his head. "So much for Homeland Security and one of our fighter jets blowing one of these things out of the sky."

"We have made a definitive link," Price said, "to the money-laundering operation of the United Front in Houston and connected the dots to the same shells and OBUs that the Kykov Family uses. Carmen?"

From her workstation, Delahunt clicked on two maps of the world, side by side. Already, even before she began framing the countries in question, Brognola saw the dots connected from Moscow to the U.S. and back to a triangulated grid of the Middle East.

"The Kykov Family deposits cash in dummy companies in Moscow, transfers funds to Saudi Arabia and Oman OBUs. Dollars or Euros are converted back to rubles, slide through interbank loan markets, where chunks are siphoned off for more OBUs.''

Brognola watched both frames as Delahunt clicked the trail, began overlaying the graphics where lines shot a course from Houston to Mexico City to the Caribbean and Venezuela to Belgium, France, then Moscow and finally halting in the triangulated Mideast quad. Other lines reached all the way from North Korea and the Philippines, touching down at the same red flags in Oman and Saudi.

''It's complicated,'' Delahunt said, ''but by the time dirty tens of millions are cleaned up and bounced all over the globe they land in Mideast banks under the guise of, what the Russian newspaper *Novaya Gazeta* coined as pseudo-import contracts.''

Brognola searched their faces, then said, ''One of you is going to tell me, I bet, there's a bunch of North Korean operatives attached to al-Amin.''

Price nodded. ''Our intercepts of CIA reports and my sources in the NSA have confirmed the basic technology for the Angels of Islam was delivered by North Korean operatives believed to have bought some of the component parts from the Kykov organization.''

''And who were paid,'' Kurtzman said, ''by funny money. Word is Kim Jong put down the brandy long enough to march out teams of special forces operatives to have a few choice words with al-Amin counterfeiters.''

If he had come in looking for the magic bullet, Brognola had just been informed the mission had only begun to become more insidious, complicated and deadly.

"So now," Brognola growled, "we've got hit squads of angry North Koreans gunning for the same bad guys as our people. Do Striker, Gary and T.J. and David know this? That our hunters could damn well become the hunted?"

"We only just found this out," Price answered. "But we'll get right on it."

"Do it," Brognola said. "Any more good news to report?"

The grim-faced mission controller shook her head.

THE BOWELS of Fort Pavel looked, smelled and sounded, David McCarter thought, just like what they were.

A torture chamber.

The Briton was tired and edgy enough after the long Herc flight to the Russian-CIA black ops compound at the eastern edge of Georgia, and the prospects of smooth sailing on this surgical strike were looking dimmer with each passing hour. Following their initial brief by General Pavel Mytkin and Chino of the CIA, the four Phoenix Force warriors had been told to return to their aboveground bunker, rest, check their weapons and gear and be ready for wheels-up as the flying armada was slated to go at dusk.

The so-called New Covert War on Terrorism, the media buzz phrase of the year, McCarter thought, meant that more often than not these days, the Stony Mar warriors were forced to share the stage with various law enforcement and intelligence agencies. In his mind, it wasn't the best way to conduct black-bag business, allied with and having to trust unknowns to watch their backs when the bullets started flying. It made matters worse when some media clown, he thought, could jet all over the world on ludicrous expense accounts and mug for the cameras in flashpoints, wanting to know the scorecard and the players, when the guys doing the real fighting—and sometimes dying—needed to operate in secret. If nothing else to save their own skin. Could be he was wrong, he decided, that Chino and the general had it worked out, were going for the gusto and not the glory. Either way, before the final brief was over, McCarter intended to pull Chino aside to get a few particulars ironed out.

With James on his left flank, Encizo and Grimaldi marching behind, all of them armed only with shouldered Berettas, McCarter followed the Russian with the AK-74 across his shoulder. They were moving down another set of steps, heading for a steel door at the end of another long narrow corridor when the Briton spotted a large rat as it scurried under the light from a naked overhead bulb, squeezed its furry girth through a crack in the base of the wall. A shrill wail tore down the hall from an open doorway, the screams trapped, echoing off the grimy concrete walls. If he wasn't accustomed to the stench of blood and guts from countless battles, the smells of fried flesh, running blood and emptied bowels would have bowled him down.

Another scream, nearly right in McCarter's ear, and he stopped, looked inside the doorway to what he could only think of as a dungeon straight from Hell. A naked figure was bolted down, wired to an electric chair, his feet in a bucket of water to give the two ghouls at the torture panel a little more jolt for their viewing pleasure. Another emaciated naked man was hung up on the black brick wall in irons. In the far corner four bodies were stacked, blood and gore running off into a drainage pipe where three or four good-sized rats were helping themselves to dinner. They were Chechen rebels, he had been informed by Chino, grabbed by Spetsnaz on earlier recons of Dhujar.

"Move, if you please. The general is waiting."

The blacksuited Russian had swiped his card on the keypad, scowling in the doorway.

"Well, I don't think any of us were expecting the Holiday Inn," James said, then the Phoenix Force commandos fell in behind McCarter, who led them into the command and control nerve center.

Compared to the Farm, this war room was low-tech. Metal tables were strewn with photos and maps. A few computers stood in the far corner, Russians and CIA ops doing some last minute intelligence gathering. No high-tech frills he could see, it looked a seat of the pants endeavor, with torture and murder pretty much the sole means of learning about the enemy.

McCarter found Chino, a lean, grizzled, dark-haired version of the late and unlamented Colonel Joe, hunched over some maps. Mytkin, beefy and balding, was standing ramrod straight next to the CIA operative.

"We've learned a few things in your absence," Chino began, glancing at the new arrivals. "Our Chechen friends in the other room have informed us," he said, stabbing areas of Dhujar that were circled, "that Wahjihab and Jack Arnold rarely leave the main compound these days, suspecting an attack is imminent. Top floor is the rebel quarters, below is the main heroin and counterfeiting lab. Eighty-plus fanatics are holed up around the clock, with pockets of rebels scattered in the hills and the village proper. The compound, after it's softened up by your ace there and my crew—all of whom are Air Force combat veterans in case there's any doubt about their abilities—will be our puppy to take down."

"The armor division will be in place in one hour," Mytkin announced. "They will encircle the village and begin shelling it before the air strike."

McCarter already knew some of the details, and under the circumstances a full encircling assault by tanks and gunships first before they bulled into the smoke was probably best.

"I just want to be clear on a few things, gents," McCarter said. "One, I'm not big on torture, nor do I like the idea of blowing up a bunch of innocent women and children, this collateral damage, General, you so glibly spoke of earlier."

Mytkin waved a hand. "Understand something, Mr. D. First, this joint effort has seen me already make many concessions. Were it up to me we would have flown in and used VX nerve gas. These people, even these innocent women and children you so nobly wish to concern yourself with, are animals. They are dirt, scum, filth, terrorists all, and I have seen with my own eyes they will arm themselves and shoot Russian soldiers in the back. I have seen them walk toward Russian soldiers with their arms up only to blow themselves up with hidden explosives."

"We'll try not to let that happen on our watch," James said.

"Since you will bear the brunt of the assault on the main compound," Mytkin said, "it will be your concern if you have qualms about shooting some ten-year-old suicide bomber."

"Two," McCarter said, "Wahjihab is ours to take."

"I thought we already hashed that over," Chino said.

"And I agreed you could have Jihad Jack," McCarter said. "Also, I want to see the results of DNA analysis if Wahjihab goes down. Bottom line, I just don't want to hear a change of tune after the smoke clears."

"Hey, Mr. D., you're not looking at a Colonel Joe operation here."

"Just so we understand each other."

"This operation has been in the works for months," Chino said. "I'm not going to stand here and tell you guys you're onboard as some courtesy, but if there's any doubts about bad intentions, duplicity and me or the general mucking up your own mission you can stow them.''

McCarter nodded. Good enough, he decided. When the shooting started if there were shadow games being played, it would all come out in the bloody wash.

"Now, can we finish hammering out a few more details?" Chino asked.

"It's your party, mate.''

CHAPTER THIRTEEN

Jack Arnold, a veteran of two overt and at least ten times that many covert wars, could honestly say there was no more deadly, more horrifying, more vicious place on the planet than Chechnya. Consider, he reflected, a few of the basic demonic tidbits about the number one hell on Earth, a quagmire of murder and mayhem so rampant, unrelenting and abominable Dante would have created a new circle just for the hordes of sinners here. The infant mortality rate, thanks to Russian tank shelling, SCUDs, Grad rockets, nine thousand pound bombs and lately nerve gas showers from Hind 24s, and Chechnya equaled the worst day of reported deaths under the age of six in either Somalia or Ethiopia, or so claimed the UN, and about the only thing he knew they ever got right were the stats. Then the countryside was awash in land mines dropped by flying armadas of Russian transport planes, part of the daily genocide ritual coming out of Moscow. Life expectancy for adult males landed around the midtwenties, and the favorite saying of a Chechen rebel was, "If we die, we win." Go figure that kind of insane thinking. Then there was kidnapping, the country's number two cash crop for its GNP, second in line, of course to narcotics trafficking. In the past six years he'd been working for the Chechens as arms merchant and intelligence broker, some days being enough that he survived and was still accepted among the al-Amin and Chechen ranks as a token jihad soldier, there had been a reported two thousand kidnappings, the various warlords raking in something like twenty million dollars U.S. in ransom. Collections came due, usually after they videotaped torture and mutilation and mailed back body parts to the families to let them know they were serious about getting their money.

Russian troops, little more than kids, underpaid, underfed, undereverything, made this hell even more miserable and lethal. They were often under orders to raze whole cities with indiscriminate shelling, indifferent to the fact they were blasting apart their own true red-blooded fellow Russian citizens, just so they could "maybe" bag a few terrorists, show Moscow a decent day's body count. Journalists were considered mad or simply fools for even thinking to dare set foot in a country where Red Cross workers were frequently kidnapped then decapitated, and even after the ransom was paid. During the day, the Russians bombed whole villages off the map in total blitzkrieg that left nothing but smoking crates and running rivers of blood and goo behind. At night the Chechen rebels headed out, cloaked in darkness, wild eyed and angered by the day's slaughter of usually their own kin, to hunt down Russian soldiers. And God pity the ones they decided to have some fun and games with before they sent them on their shrieking way with various and sundry body parts missing, prisoners often forced to cannibalize their own dismembered appendages.

So why did he stay? he wondered. He couldn't say, he really couldn't, but it was just about time to pack it up, seek out that retirement on some beach in the South Pacific. Unfortunately, big plans and lofty dreams often had a way of unraveling at the last minute.

Like right frigging now.

He wondered how it had all come this nightmare, an American ex-CIA paramilitary operative in Chechnya, part of the terrorist operation that had grown as a malignant offshoot of al-Qaeda and the Taliban. Hell, he could hear the snippy, sniveling, chickenshit media kicking around his grizzled war dog's name now, calling him Jihad Jack, al-Amin Arnold and so on, but there would be no Camp X-Ray in his future, no sir. He would die in battle, charge the guns first.

It had to have been, he thought, that humble stint in Afghanistan, while training and arming mujahadeen to kill Russians, many of those turbaned mountain fighters later comprising al-Qaeda and the hated Taliban and who were, for all intents and purposes created by the CIA, where his view of life and how he saw himself in the future changed forever. Up to then, he had believed he was fighting for freedom and justice for all, a naive myopic vision, to say the least, that had been altered permanently after he got his first taste of real money and promptly received a Dear Jack letter from his fourth wife who would clean his legal clock when he landed back in the States for R and R.

It got old, in a hurry, forever being dealt a losing hand.

So he had seen the light, praise good old Ben Franklin on all those crispy hundreds, aware that both the Company and Uncle Sam were always on the sidelines anyway, more often than not carving up the profits from war booty while spoon-feeding the lies to the American public at large how they were the good guys, soaring on the wings of angels to slay evildoers. Well, there had been so much money to make in delivering heroin for the mujahadeen to help finance their war, buy weapons, clothing and such, that he just couldn't resist getting some for himself while the getting was good. With a few fellow operatives smoothing and securing drug routes through Uzbekistan and dumping off the goodies to either the Chechen *mafiya* or the bad boys from Moscow, it wasn't long before he was drowning in seas of numbered accounts.

The problem now, he knew, would be living long enough to spend a little of that hard-earned cash. He had once heard it said that no one left Chechnya, they escaped. If what he knew was on the way, he might not ever get the chance to put that to the test.

The rebels were spread out on the ridgeline, he saw, dark bearded shadows in their camo jackets, armed with AKM Automats with a few RPGs here and there. He had already alerted Commander Khattab Rhatal he was coming up for a look. The Russian spotter planes had been making flyovers all day, leaving little doubt it was all just preparation for a massive assault. Right now the mountain-walled world around Dhujar and beyond to the Ardun River was too damn quiet. It was a silence he was all too familiar with, the onslaught on the verge of rumbling from all directions, hitting them in one spontaneous instant eruption next with the blitz.

"There," he heard Rhatal say, pointing across the valley beyond the Marjuk Gorge, holding out the infrared field glasses. "Soon, the Russians will make their telephone call."

Another Chechen favorite, he knew, letting him know the shelling was about to begin.

Arnold looked through the field glasses. Sure enough, he counted dozens of T-72s, APCs with 12.7 mm guns and cannons, towed rocket batteries, a few hundred infantry at least. One or two land mines flared off down there, but the dead were left where they fell, tanks rolling on. Typical Russian advance, no room for pity, tough luck for the mortally wounded. The life of a Russian grunt wasn't even worth the price of a cheap bottle of vodka. Rhatal informed him there were just as many soldiers and armor to the north, west and east.

A complete siege was up and coming, and he had seen in the past how the Russians treated Chechens when the guns started blasting. Did somebody, he thought, want to talk about no mercy?

They had no defenses against that kind of martial

strength, he knew, beyond a few ZSU-23-4 antiair-craft batteries. And if those ZSUs became painted on gunship screens, blown to trash by MiGs and Hinds, there would be no holding back a floodtide of Russian soldiers who were forever under fight-or-die orders from vodka-swilling brass behind the lines. It was a typical Russian military operation, he thought, a mas-sive show of force by overwhelming numbers, victory earned in spilled blood by the yard, triumph by attri-tion.

"I will leave a few snipers here," the commander said. "We bunker in the compound, ride out the shell-ing. When they come, we will be waiting. There is a plan."

"Really?" It was news to Arnold. "You care to clue me in, Commander? Since my nuts are likewise going to be in the ringer."

"In time, you will see. I am thinking bad thoughts at the moment, my American friend. Your name, I hear, has been kicked around by CIA operatives in the regions across our borders."

"Hey, look, I doubt it's just me they're coming to have a chat with. You haven't exactly endeared your-self up north with those waves of martyrs you've been busing out to Moscow lately. Don't forget, the CIA wants the head of one Wahjihab, and maybe it's him who'd better start thinking about shagging his rear out of these parts. I've been straight with you from day one, or I figure I'd have been dead a long time ago. I'm in this for the money, it's real simple."

"Wahjihab stays, you stay and fight. We all stay. Let's go."

It didn't look good for any of them, but Arnold knew he was stuck, left to only hope that if the Chechens resisted long and fierce enough, as they had in the past, the Russians would retreat.

If not…

Well, he might escape Chechnya, after all, but feared it wouldn't be on his terms. All he could do was hold on, ride it out and hope fate didn't deal him another losing hand. He still had a future, such as it was, and dying in this shithole was the last thing he wanted to contemplate.

THE HILLS WERE ALIVE, McCarter found, with the steady thunder of explosions and flying bodies of Chechens, snipers presumably, in pockets far down the ridgeline. This engagement—or fiasco—hadn't even begun to get messy, the Briton knew.

Bounding off the Hip gunship, field glasses in hand, his M-16/M-203 combo across his shoulder, the ex-SAS commando wanted a look first at the bombardment supposedly softening up their march in, assess what he already knew were long odds before storming the main compound of Fortress Holy War. Striding away from the rotor wash, flanked by Encizo, James, Chino and three other CIA operatives, McCarter took it in, began weighing their chances. Where Burjuc and Dimitak streets met, a walled courtyard—packed with APCs, Toyotas with machine guns in the beds, and one ZSU battery near the compound—circled Fortress Holy War. A double wooden door on the south end would have to be blown. Once inside there would be volatile precursor chemicals for processing raw opium into heroin, booby traps, armed and crazed suicide fanatics, top to bottom, maybe the whole damn place rigged to blow like the factory in Croatia. Not good at all.

A look over his shoulder, and McCarter glanced at the CIA ops who were carrying small but bulging "mine detecting" bags. The Chechen prisoners had been dismembered, arms and legs and heads shoved into burlap sacks that would get tossed down stairwells, around corners, down halls in some attempt, vain and perhaps a long shot it would even worked, McCarter thought, to set off any mines if the real high-tech detectors turned up such problems on the way in.

Even as their chopper ride had touched down on a stretch of ridgeline to the far southwest, clean of bogeys on their Russian flyboys' IR screens, McCarter saw the tanks were still lobbing wave after wave of shells into the sprawling village from all points of the compass. In Chechnya, electricity, like running clean water, was considered a rich man's luxury. Only the main compound had electricity, pumped in by several generators. The rest of Dhujar, where it wasn't being lit up by explosions or already on fire, was an imposing maze of dark buildings, narrow alleys, courtyards.

Scanning the village, he saw armed shadows scurrying past the overturned, flaming hulls of Volgas, minivans, Toyotas. It was nothing but chaos down there, the crunching din of endless explosions rocking and lighting up the valley. Most of the runners were heading for the back entrance of the counterfeiting-drug lab complex, which was tucked near the base of the mountains. Russian infantry and tanks were already breaching the northern perimeter, even as the air assault began in earnest. First the MiGs screamed down, unloading on apartment buildings, whole sections of structures vaporized in rising fireballs, then the Hinds began swarming in behind the fighter jets, pounding away at anything and everything, giving it all the minigun and rocket gusto they could dish out in a few heartbeats. McCarter gnashed his teeth. This wasn't what he wanted, to be part of indiscriminate slaughter of innocent civilians. The claim by the good Russian general, though, was that entire nests of Chechen terrorists would shield themselves inside clusters of women, children, the elderly and infirm inside apartments. If they hid behind the shawls and skirts of women, Mytkin said they were fair game.

Still, that piece of sadistic logic didn't cut it with McCarter. This wasn't war, he knew, this was a massacre of innocents, genocide to be exact. Even if he was ordered by Stony Man in the future, he would refuse to attach himself to some horror show of slaughter like this ever again. Chances were the Farm didn't know, nor had he even had an inkling it was going to be some extermination campaign by rolling armed Russian Gestapo storm troopers laying waste to anything that moved. Small comfort, he thought, that his side of the attack was going in against armed opposition. This, though, wasn't a night for nobility or virtue. This was hell on Earth, times twenty, plain and simple.

"Nothing we can do, Mr. D.," Chino shouted over the rotor wash, "but sit tight for about fifteen minutes and watch the show. I know you find the wholesale massacre of Chechen noncombatants distasteful, but this is Chechnya, what can I say? It's how they do business here."

McCarter said nothing, as Grimaldi patched through over the com link. "Eagle One to Phoenix One, come in."

Tapping his com link, McCarter said, "Phoenix One. Go."

"We've got you painted on our screens. Looks like the Russian transponders they gave you are holding up. Look alive, we're going to unload on the main compound on our first flyover. The hills are jumping about a thousand meters due east of your position with bogeys."

McCarter laid out the score of artillery around the compound.

"Roger. We'll make a sweep, then I'll call in some Hind mop-up, then, we hope, they'll watch your backs. Work to do, Phoenix One, over and out."

McCarter looked up, heard the thunder of the flying battleship as it sailed in from the west. It grew quickly, a winged leviathan, maybe coming in for its first hammerdown at five or six hundred feet.

The Spectre went to grim work, eating up the earth,

savaging any poor combatants down there who were unfortunate enough to get painted and locked on by a Bofors 40 mm cannon, twin 20 mm Vulcans and a 105 mm howitzer.

One last look at the main compound, shadows scrambling for the machine-gun emplacements, two more going for the ZSU and Grimaldi and killing crew dumped a payload from hell on a flyover that was all thunder and fire.

"Any chance," McCarter growled at Chino, "you can raise Mytkin and have him call off the tanks while we hit the back door?"

"It's already done. Just say the word."

"Do it! What the hell are you waiting for?"

LEAPING OUT of the cab of the transport truck, Jong Din, fisting his AK-47, led a team of twenty North Korean special forces commandos down into a narrow gully where the land was broken up in craters he assumed scarred the plain from past shelling. He could hardly feel grateful the gangster had safely infiltrated them into the country, working out the details on the fly, since it was Jong Din's money that had greased certain skids. What he found waiting might just skew, even abort what had been in its earlier conception a shaky plan to begin with.

The targeted village, due north where the conniving Arabs were hiding, was taking an aerial drubbing and tank bombardment the likes of which he had never seen, nor could even begin to imagine. It left him wondering which way, and how to proceed. The noise alone slammed his senses, one rolling peal of deafening thunder after another. But the hellish din would prove the least of his concerns, if and when he advanced.

Settling into a crevice, rising up over the lip of the ridge, he looked at the destruction raining on the Chechen stronghold village. He choked down bitter rage, the Russian gangster not giving him the first hint the village was a prime and massive terror target for what looked like half the Russian military. If he survived this, he would have more than a few choice words for the gangster.

It was a miracle of sorts, he thought, he and his commandos had made it this far, encroaching on the blind side edges of the armor sweeping down the streets, infantry already going house to house, kicking down doors, autofire rattling from everywhere, it seemed, screams of victims swept away in the distance by blasts and bullets. And with the gunships scissoring over apartment buildings, the minarets of a few mosques blown away by missiles as if to add insult to murderous injury, the Russians, both on the ground and in the air, shooting and blowing up everything standing, moving, or crawling...

It could well prove suicide to attempt to infiltrate this large village, but he wouldn't shirk his orders. To go back and report to his superiors in-country, sitting in tense waiting with the gangster, that he hadn't even attempted...

He cursed the gangster, whom, he knew, was in a dacha hundreds of miles away in the Ukraine, safe with his vodka and whores, assuring the general everything would turn out as he hoped. Even though the Russian had gotten him safe passage down through Chechnya, with help from his connections to a corrupt arm in Spetsnaz and the FSK, this wasn't what Jong Din had bargained for.

There was nothing he could do except carry out his duty.

He had a mental picture from recon and purchased sat photos of the village layout. According to the gangster's inside source, the bulk of Chechen and al-Amin rebels and thieves was at the far southern edge of the village. In some respects, he began thinking the besieged village, with all the pandemonium, burning vehicles and combatants locked into death duels in hand-to-hand, might just work to his advantage.

There was only one way to find out.

He gave it a few moments, searching out holes in the advancing armor, aware the streets were laid out in quasi-circles, a haphazard pattern created, he suspected, by some drunken Chechen engineer. That was if he could even call this abysmal hellhole anything remotely close to civilization.

Jong Din stood and addressed his shock troops. In no uncertain terms, he told them they would move in, shoot anyone and everybody they came across while fighting their way to the main complex.

He only hoped they had enough bullets.

CHAPTER FOURTEEN

The enemy would never know the truth.

As he ran down the steps to the second level, trailing the Chechen commander, the armed contingent of Rhatal's soldiers, his own al-Amin comrades and the American former CIA operative, he had been prepared for this moment for more than three years. The truth was, he had craved even before then to do something spectacular for the jihad, something that would immortalize him on the earth, as well as in heaven.

It had been quite the calling, he briefly reflected, the Successor himself had his operatives seek him out eventually in Saudi Arabia, as he had been told would someday happen. He had been a mere foot soldier in the jihad, training in the Mawar Dhalibab camps before he was shipped back to Riyadh. One morning the sheikh had told him to go home to his wife and family of fourteen. There would be money enough to provide for them the rest of their lives. What was the meaning of this abrupt dismissal? he had wondered. He recalled his bitter disappointment, about to protest, wondering if he had been deemed unworthy to be marched out and used by God as a tool to further jihad. Then the sheikh stated he had a divine plan for him, and he was to be patient, wait for the appointed hour, do exactly as he was told when the Successor or one of his operatives finally arrived at his home. There had been some fine-tuning on his face, of course, the nose and chin altered with implants, liposuction around the jaw and cheekbones to blend in the correct and perfect angular hawkish features. Beyond the face, he was the exact same height and weight, a dead ringer for the new holy leader the infidels were coming to kill.

He was about to martyr himself, and he felt honored, no fear, no hesitation, he told himself, when it came time to act.

Now, in less than two minutes after entering the lab downstairs, former al-Qaeda warriors he had trained with in Afghanistan had him prepared to do his holy part. The packets of wired-up C-4 were wrapped around his torso, bulking out his camo jacket as he shrugged it back on. He was ready to rush the invaders when they were drawn in by the forces upstairs. One small depression of the radio remote's button and, whether they were Russian or American intelligence operatives, he wouldn't only take them out, as he soared to God on the fireball, but there wouldn't be enough left of him to scrape up on a pinhead for DNA analysis under a microscope. The beauty of the deceit, he thought, was that only he and Commander Rhatal knew his true identity.

The string of bare overhead lights flickered, threatened to wink out as their bombs rained and the building shook under the constant thunderous barrage. Small groups of Chechen fighters and al-Amin warriors, he saw, were splitting up down the corridor that would lead to a secret passage that would take the others into a tunnel. From there, whoever the commander selected to go aboveground and fight the enemy would escape the coming martyr stand in the complex. They would die in the streets of the village, of course, but the idea, as always, was to take more of the enemy with them in death than the other way around. It was all but lost here anyway, and he had suspected the worst for days, since they, too, like the enemy, had informants within the Russian military and intelligence.

Behind and above, he heard a ferocious series of explosions nearly on top his head, dust showering, lights blinking. Rhatal was on his handheld radio, taking the report. He heard it was his time next. "They are here," Rhatal told him. "Go with God."

He smiled. He would have liked to check a mirror one last time before marching up top, but it would be enough to know the enemy—or whoever was left behind to tell the tale—would proclaim that Nawir Wahjihab had been killed, a suicide bomber, in the ruins of a bloody battle in a remote Chechen village only a handful of human beings had ever heard about.

Ali Fawzi felt as light as air as he began his march back up the steps. He had but one regret, as he felt the sheer force of explosions blowing shock waves back in his face: the sheikh, if he was even still alive, wouldn't be there to witness this glorious moment.

THE T-72, CALLED IN by Chino, bulldozed a gaping hole in the courtyard wall, about midway down, on the southside. McCarter led the charge into hell, Encizo and James on his flanks, M-16/M-203 combos all around, with the Cuban warrior lugging Little Bulldozer across his shoulder. Chino and his shooters spilled out of the gunship on their heels, peeling off behind the Phoenix Force warriors, as planned, rushing through another maw in the wall where a Hind 24 had just punched a missile through it to get them going. Once inside the courtyard, all bets were off, McCarter thought.

It was the worst of all possible commando worlds, McCarter knew, visions of the Croatian factory leaping to mind, the whole complex possibly mined and ready to blast them all to hell. Not only that, there were too many players doing too much their own way, with Mytkin somewhere in the air, calling the shots from the safety of some distant chopper. With what high-tech gear they had at their disposal, their experience together in combat, the ex-SAS commando could do little else but keep rolling, start shooting and take his chances.

Standard operating procedure.

The guts of Fortress Holy War, at least, belonged to them. Everywhere beyond the complex, McCarter heard the fierce shelling, small-arms fire and gunship bombardments rage on. To the east, he spotted the flaming shell of a Hind as some rebel just scored with either a ZSU burst or maybe a Stinger before half of another apartment building was demolished by T-72s and swarming Hind wrecking balls. The stricken gunship quickly floated out of sight beyond the black wreath of oily smoke billowing over the courtyard. McCarter had his own problems right then, and the Russians, he hoped, wouldn't add to an already heaped plate of potential fiascos, foul-ups and quicksand pits.

On orders from Chino, who was in contact with the Russians over their frequency, McCarter forged ahead even as the T-72's big gun thundered a round and blew in the back doors, his ears chiming with the cannon shot. One more massive punch erupted from the tank's gun, a shell exploding in the bowels of the complex beyond the boiling smoke. McCarter was past the killing Goliath, the T-72 backing out, grinding away as tracks chewed up rubble and a strewed corpse or two, gone to help the Russians in their extermination quest.

McCarter, Encizo and James came under fire from dark-clad fanatics, ten yards in and running. The courtyard was a choking miasma of death, a graveyard of flaming wreckage, a sea of littered corpses. McCarter knew the wounded could rise from anywhere in this mess, but his combat senses were already way off the instinct monitor, assault rifle searching out the enemy, finger holding back the trigger. Chino and company were on their own for the time being, in the corner of McCarter's eye for a millisecond, the CIA hitters grabbing a firepoint near a line of battered fiery hulls while the Hind came down from the west and began blasting entry points in the compound's facade.

On the fly, the Phoenix Force warriors unloaded their M-16s, shooting from the hip. There were eight fanatics, running toward them from the twisted scrap of the ZSU battery. Firelight framed their thousand-mile-stares. Shell shock waited on no man to clear the cobwebs in this hell.

Eight up, eight down, and Phoenix Force was surging for its entry point.

McCarter threw himself up against the wall on the other side of jagged fangs, his senses swimming in smoke and blood and thunder. The noise of battle was so loud he had to shout over his com link as James took a reading on his handheld thermal imaging unit.

"Eleven left standing on the top floor," James shouted back. "Thirty-two yards in, spread out from ten to three o'clock."

"Phoenix One to C-Man, come in," McCarter said, tapping the second button on his com link. When Chino patched back, McCarter told them the score and their intent.

"Do it! We'll meet you on the flip side for link-up!"

"On a count of three, mates! One…"

On three, McCarter went in low, veered to his right and loosed his M-203 charge on a line of impact for roughly two o'clock. Return fire lit up the bevy of fanatic snarls behind the muzzle-flashes downrange. Sizzling lead snapped the air over McCarter's head, lasting all of two heartbeats, then a triple combo from the Phoenix Force commandos of flesh-grinding razor steel bits, a white phosphorous furnace blast and the frag detonation ripped through the enemy ranks. Shadows were already wending their way to McCarter's left flank, Chino and boys squeezing through rubble.

McCarter put them out of mind as he went in, dumping another 40 mm frag bomb down the M-203's gullet, the shrieking of the mangled and the torched-up damned flaying his ears. It was nearly impossible to tell what the upstairs had once been, since every piece of furniture was now nothing but smoking matchsticks and metallic scrap, glinting orange and white sheens where fires had broken out in small pockets across the sprawling trash heap. No need for NVD headgear; the glow of fire would have to lead the way down.

McCarter focused on the hideous wailing across the room, a flaming scarecrow staggering out of the smoke. A triburst from the Phoenix Force threesome and they were kicked back, flopping over slabs of debris.

From there on, McCarter knew it wouldn't get any easier.

He was searching the thick drifts of smoke for more targets, Encizo and James on his left flank, the ex-SEAL reading the heat-seeking monitor when it happened.

The figure materialized out of the smoke wreath, wobbly, more shell shock, no doubt, but McCarter saw two things in the next instant. One—he recognized the face of Nawir Wahjihab, set in the stone of memory from his intel packet. Two—the Sword of Islam was lifting a radio remote box in his hand, his frame clearly beefed up, a walking mummy of high explosive.

It was incredible, and McCarter almost balked, glimpsing the strange smile on that infamous face.

"Hit the deck!" McCarter bellowed, and tapped the trigger on his M-203.

WHERE IT WAS ALL HEADED was simply a madman's guess. They were trapped, damned and screwed, running through a tunnel ripe with sewage, an entire army of black-op headhunters out there, waiting to cut them to ribbons. Jack Arnold was thinking how much life sucked right then, but kept pace with Rhatal, AK-74 in hand, an RPG rocket launcher across his shoulder. Four spare clips and two extra missiles wouldn't cut it, he knew, not with a division of armor and a fleet of gunships on the prowl. Tack on roughly twenty-five rebels and terrorists, and he had to believe they wouldn't make it twenty feet out of town. It occurred to him he could throw himself at the mercy of the Russians, claim he was a double agent. The problem was he knew Rhatal was right about his sullied rep. Even his own people, he knew, had his mug plastered on a wanted poster as a terrorist conspirator.

"Care to tell me what the plan is, Commander?" Arnold shouted as a wave of screams and the thunder of still more explosions blasted down the tunnel.

"My cousin, Hamuk, his house."

"Yeah? And?"

"From there we walk to the mountains. Caves."

Simple.

And stuck.

It sucked.

Arnold was second in line as they reached a set of steel rungs and began climbing. He was through the opening when he heard the sounds of crashing from somewhere in the dark. He focused on the hanging kerosene lamp, recognized the machine-gun babble of Russians, then it all went to hell.

No time for Rhatal and Hamuk to kiss and embrace, all that Chechen touchy-feelie routine. Arnold saw three, then four men near the foyer gunned down. The RPG was off his shoulder, no sense in jacking around with close-quarters combat, and he cut the warhead loose.

"IT WAS HIM!"

Rafael Encizo was on his back, the voices floating through his ringing head from miles away.

"Rafe!"

McCarter and James were shaking him.

"He's okay, just dinged up!"

Chino growled that it was no big deal that one of their own was down. All Encizo could figure was that flying rubble had smashed off his head, punched out the lights. He remembered McCarter's shouted warning, then he was dropping as the 40 mm blast vaporized Wahjihab, blew him out of sight.

"If you don't mind, we'll see for ourselves," James barked. "Rafe?"

Encizo climbed to his feet, revived by adrenaline and the pulsing thunder of battle raging in the village. He checked himself, touched the gash on his scalp where blood ran free. "I'll live."

"Beeline and Smart-ass!" Chino yelled. "Grab ten and hit the back!"

"What's the plan?" Encizo asked, shaking some more of the cobwebs out of his chiming skull.

"You know what planet you're on?" Chino asked.

"Mars," Encizo shot back.

"Then let's blast the rat bastards out of the cellar!"

Little Bulldozer off his shoulder, Encizo fell in with McCarter and James.

"That's the bastard's arm," Chino snarled at one of his commandos. "Bag it!"

"If you don't mind," James shouted, flanking the rubble by the wide opening that led down to the next as autofire roared from below, "DNA tests can wait!"

In sync with James's and McCarter's M-203 barrage, Encizo began pumping out one 40 mm charge after another.

CHAPTER FIFTEEN

Even though Jong Din knew it was a suicide march, he was still there to kill Chechens and other assorted Arab terrorists who had fleeced Pyongyang with counterfeit money. If the slaughter included Russian soldiers and whoever else turned up before his AK-47, that was fine, too. Not even women and children were exempt, since he'd heard the stories how the smallest child, weighted down with explosives, would charge Russian soldiers in this sordid part of the world, gladly blowing themselves up as long they took with them at least a full squad or better of their hated enemies.

There was no turning back, no retreat, he knew, forging ahead into the stink of burning gasoline from the bonfires of tossed and turned vehicles, but there was never any other way except a bull charge into this hell. Whatever would happen in the next coming minutes—and he assumed the worst—he didn't expect to live long enough to lay eyes on Nawir Wahjihab. Small comfort, the Arab was a major target for the Russian army, wouldn't live out the night, but he, too, would die here, standing and shooting, no return to his superiors, dishonored in defeat.

The North Korean contingent had barely hit the first line of stone hovels when the slaughter began. Din had hoped to find a break somewhere to slip by armor and infantry, as the house-to-house fighting appeared confined to the east, west and north, or so he thought. A straight run up the middle of the village, then get to the main compound, attempt to hunt down the treacherous Arab. Only they were met by two to three squads of Russian soldiers as soon as they hit the street. There was a ferocious battle raging inside the large stone house, an explosion at the doorway launching stick figures back into the street. The new platoon of Russians on the scene was attempting to encircle the house, shooting out windows, lobbing in hand grenades, windows blasting out in saffron flashes. Their attention was torn between savaging the enemy inside the house, and surprise over the new foreign arrivals.

Jong Din marched ahead, gave the order to his commandos this was, essentially, the end of the line, then cut loose with his AK-47.

WAVE AFTER WAVE of Russian soldiers surged into the house, the next batch firing AK-74s over the still twitching bodies of downed comrades. All was utter madness, sound and fury, flying bodies and gouting blood. But this, he knew, was Chechnya, and it was time to get out of Dodge.

Jack Arnold was backpedaling, sweeping his autofire over the snarling, cursing crush of Russians, Chechens and al-Amin shooters blasting away at point-blank range. He was so splashed in blood and gore that he wasn't sure if he was hit, but there was no time to feel pain or worry about bleeding.

Hell, no, it was time to find the nearest window and bail.

The grenades began popping off next, a crunching din that seemed to burn the air with scorching shrapnel and superheated wind. Bodies were spinning, falling all over the room, screams and curses lancing the air, the endless howl of a rage from hell. He was running for a window that looked clear of Russian shooters when he saw three almond-skinned Asian faces framed in firelight. At first he thought he was seeing things, then he recalled the deal that had gone down here not that long ago.

North Koreans, he knew. And they had come back, he was sure, to let Wahjihab know they weren't pleased about getting the shaft with bad paper.

Jack Arnold was holding back on the trigger, turning those faces to crimson pulp when he saw it, and knew it was over.

He damn near laughed at the horrible injustice of the moment. All the work to get it this far, the blood and sweat, and now a lousy grenade had bounced up, right between his legs, gonads about to be blown off the least of his concerns.

Goodbye retirement. Forget about beachfront property and island girls and all the rum he could drink in a South Pacific paradise. Well, he had to try, at least, but he was all of one step running when the steel egg blew and sent him flying across the room.

THE BODIES of Chechen rebels and al-Amin terrorists, or what was left of them, were stacked up two to three high in spots as McCarter led the descent to the underground lab and found a maze of halls, doors and dark corridors waiting with potential combatants lying in ambush. Each corridor, he knew, had to be swept clean of any enemy still on the loose, but the Briton was beginning to think the heavy demolition job had pretty much nailed it down.

Still...

Autofire erupted from a doorway to McCarter's right. He threw himself against the wall, James and Encizo darting to the other side. In the dim light of the single overhead bulb, he had seen enough of the room to know it was the heroin lab: vats, and tables littered with vials, tubes and scales. Fat white bricks were piled up in the far corner.

Time to burn down the factory of poison.

McCarter armed a thermite grenade, counted off the numbers, then gave it a sideways whip through the door. The shooting stopped abruptly as the shadows attempted to outrun the blast.

No such luck.

They were torched up, screaming and flailing about when the Phoenix Force warriors went in, shooting from the hip, raking the lab, nine to four, where the flaming scarecrows danced.

One more white phosphorous bomb dumped into

the lab, and McCarter could be sure of its total obliteration.

Back out in the corridor, he found Chino striding toward him from a dark opening at the far north end.

"I'm told by Mytkin some of those North Koreans just hit town."

McCarter briefly recalled how Stony Man Farm had informed him he could expect some North Korean operatives, angry over getting stiffed with funny money, and looking for revenge, turning up on the mission. Just what he needed now, more complications. The Farm promised more to come on the DPRK score, as they tracked and sifted through the North Korean connection to al-Amin and the Russian Mob. Where it was headed next was speculation, but McCarter had an idea they might be packing up for a visit with the Kykov *mafiya*.

"The other rat bastards took a back door out through a tunnel. This way, if you want to go join the party," Chino said.

McCarter looked around the maze of corridors as Chino's ops swept each room. Sporadic autofire, a grenade blast, but the Briton knew it was all but over here.

"I guess we can pick up the pieces here later," McCarter said.

"What's left. We shot our wad before we came down. Did a hell of a number with that multiround launcher there, Mars," Chino told Encizo.

"I guess that's his way of congratulating me for me not getting myself killed upstairs," Encizo said, falling in behind McCarter and James as they followed Chino into the tunnel.

CHINO HAD TO CALL IN to whoever was in charge of what was a massacre above them, inform the Russians they were coming up, and try not to shoot them to hell on sight.

Cautious, McCarter was the first one through the trapdoor, his assault rifle cutting loose on two bearded figures whirling his way as he popped out of the hole. Bodies were heaped everywhere, the blood running thick in teeming pools. The smell of cordite and death clawed his senses, and he found they couldn't hang around the abattoir long, since a fire had broken out in the corner of this butcher's shop.

Chino keyed his com link. "C-Man to Commander Six. We're coming out. What's the story out there?"

McCarter heard autofire beyond the doorway, then it withered, stopped, Chino barking out to the Russians packed in the hall they were on the same team.

"They're clear," Chino told McCarter. "Unfortunately, all of the North Koreans went down. No prisoners, but I'm sure there's still a few Chechen or al-Amin assholes hiding somewhere in town."

"Don't count on it," McCarter said.

"What's that mean?"

"Means we almost did what we came here to do," McCarter said.

"Means we won a battle but not the war," James added, stepping over corpses. "With Wahjihab dead and the North Koreans snuffed, any intel we might have gotten they took with them to hell.''

"Yeah, well, take a look at this. I got problems myself.''

McCarter watched as Chino rolled over a crimson sack, kicked at the head, spit.

"Jihad Jack Arnold,'' Chino said. "You guys weren't the only ones who came up short. I needed him alive and singing. This thing goes a lot further than just Chechnya. Maybe Mytkin's troops got lucky and bagged a few head honchos to take back to the fort.''

McCarter looked at Encizo and James, Chino cursing his own bad luck. They had survived, wiped out a few platoons of bad guys, but as far as getting answers, leads to keep the campaign going, the Briton felt they had come up short.

"Let's get the hell out of here,'' McCarter growled.

COLONEL YIN YSOON of the North Korean special forces had once heard during a briefing and while viewing an American cowboy movie with the great leader that Texas was so big, it was larger than most nations in the world. Big cowboy hats. Big cities. Big oil. Big money. Big ranches. Big mountains. Big-breasted cowgirls.

Big.

That was all the great leader, a diminutive pudgy drunken but dangerous clown in his mind, could keep saying as he downed one shot of brandy after another, chortling as American cowboys and Indians shot each other in a gun battle where no one ever seemed to run out of bullets.

Right then, the only thing big about Houston that Colonel Yin Ysoon could see was himself, his sound-suppressed Glock 17 and this moment where one battle was about to be won.

Out of the twenty-eight employees or swarthy Mideast types who'd come to pay tribute at United Front before the sun set and the doors were closed, only three were still alive. The outer offices and cubicles, from reception area to boardroom, was littered with the bullet-riddled bodies of men and women, all gunned down by either Glocks or MAC-10s when Ysoon and his eight commandos first rolled into the building. The president of United Front, Mawli al-Hashid, and his two top executives, who were also his sons, were stretched out on the plush carpeting of their big executive suite, facedown, looking terribly small to him in their terror.

Ysoon claimed a wingback seat after pulling it up over and in front of the bound Arabs. He heard one last familiar chug, somewhere beyond the open doors, called out Yan Yik's name, waited. Moments later, the small dark-haired captain in the cashmere coat came into the suite, cracked a fresh clip into his Glock, racked the slide.

"One, sir. Hiding under her desk."

"Watch the front doors, but have your men check the building again."

"Yes, sir."

Ysoon indulged a long moment to savor the triumph, recalling the great leader's drunken tirade how they had been outwitted by Arab terrorists and the criminals were to be found and punished, or he wasn't to return alive to Pyongyang. This was what, he believed the Americans called, payback, and in more ways than one.

The wall safe, hidden behind a large poster of brown-skinned impoverished faces with the phrase Help Us Save the Children, was already opened, three of his commandos filling nylon bags with U.S. dollars. Considering how much they had been duped out of and precisely what the Arabs had stolen from them, handing off their fake currency, it was a small courtesy as far as this payback went.

And these men in suits, he thought, fronting for the terrorists, cleaning their blood money, were every bit as criminal and accountable as the killers and thieves he was seeking.

On paper, their intelligence had determined United Front was worth in excess of one hundred million dollars, reaching out to plop veritable planeloads of money into the black holes of shell companies from Mexico City to Singapore. Of course, most of that money was cash contributions, siphoned off from various terrorist organizations that needed to hide dollars, rubles, Euros earned from the sale of drugs and weapons. Then there were the Wahjihabs of the Islamic fundamentalist world, ever ready to spread their blood money through these so-called charity organizations to finance their murder machine.

"We can talk now, we are alone. It is simple. I ask

questions, you provide the answers I want. Or I start shooting. Simple.''

Flanked by his sons, the Saudi craned his head around. ''I am a legitimate businessman, and what you have done is come here and commit mass murder—''

''Please, do not insult my intelligence or my character.''

''And you are a thief,'' the eldest son, Habib, Ysoon believed, spit. ''You come here, slaughter innocent people and then steal money that is meant to feed and clothe the poor of the world!''

''Spare me the lies. First, I am only reclaiming what is rightfully mine,'' Ysoon said. ''Your people, Mr. al-Hashid, paid my operatives with counterfeit money. They have in their possession something they did not rightfully earn. Now, I know you have operatives in Mexico. I know you send funds to a certain corrupt *federale* through couriers or direct transfer of funds to a bank in Mexico City. I know your organization is linked to a major drug cartel down there, and that both these drug dealers and the *federale* are hiding your operatives. I know what was taken from my operatives under false pretenses is either somewhere in Mexico or on its way. One time. Where in Mexico are your operatives? And how can I contact them for a meeting?''

''Operatives?'' the father growled. ''We run an international charity. We are not terrorists.''

Ysoon saw he needed to make a statement. Casually he shot the eldest on in the back of the leg. "Do not move! And stop your screaming!"

"Tell him what he wants to know, Father," the other son implored.

When the father began to berate his son in Arabic, Ysoon pumped a round into Habib's other leg, bringing on another round of howling. "English, if you do not mind!"

"You murdered all of my employees," the father snarled. "Say I even know what you are talking about, what will stop you from killing us?"

"You people believe in jihad, that you are at war with anyone who is not Muslim. You believe you will go to Paradise if you defy the infidel, or die in battle, am I right?" Defiant silence, then Ysoon cored a bullet into the back of Habib's skull. "Your other son is next. Consider yourself at war. You have lost this fight, but if you truly believe in your God and your paradise, then you will be fine, even in death."

"Father, tell him!"

Ysoon, who had put enough prisoners through torture, either physical or mental, watched the Saudi squeeze his eyes shut. He had almost broken the man.

"Very well. For what you have done and are about to do, I have no problem sending you to your death."

Ysoon listened. The town was called Ciudad Zapulcha, fifty miles southwest of Laredo on the Texas-Mexico border. Ysoon heard the number for a secured sat phone, the contact whose name was simply Fouad. Quickly Ysoon took his cell phone, dialed one of his commandos who was watching the premises outside.

He gave him the information, informed him to contact their people already in place in Mexico, told them they could go ahead and move on this terrorist haven.

Ysoon stood, drawing on the other son when the father said, smiling, "There is one thing you do not know. The merchandise was seized by the Americans. I am told the ones who originally purchased it know this. They are unhappy, and they are looking to find and blame anyone who has assisted them."

"You are telling me what? That this Nawir Wahjihab and his suicide soldiers are gunning for me? I am to blame for their misfortune because the Coast Guard or the FBI captured what they essentially stolen from us?"

"Perhaps even as we speak."

It gave Ysoon pause. These Arabs, he knew, were crazy enough to somehow feel he was responsible for the lost shipment, send out a kill team, shoot or blow him up on sight.

Indeed, he had been right when telling the Arab to consider themselves at war.

Ysoon was taking no prisoners. Squeezing the trigger, as his commandos began zipping up the booty, he tunneled a small hole in the back of the other son's head. The father was muttering something, probably praying, when Ysoon heard the shooting, the voices of his men shouting outside in the office.

He was moving for the door, heart pounding, seeing that army of suicide killers in his mind, when his captain rushed in.

"Four men have entered the building."

"Arabs?"

"Americans. They have assault rifles, and they came in firing. A gut feeling, but I do not think they are from the police."

"Nor I," Colonel Ysoon said. He reached down and pulled al-Hashid to his feet. "You just may live a few minutes longer before you go to your God."

CHAPTER SIXTEEN

United Front, according to the Farm's tracking of the charity organization's main cash contributors and numerous affiliations with questionable foreign banks, reached all the way around the globe. Various terrorist groups, from Hamas, Hezbollah, al-Amin–al-Qaeda and right through to the IRA even, funneled narcotics and arms money through the organization's dozen or so shell companies. A few stops in-between on the money trail, but the big bucks eventually stopped at the doorstep of an Omani bank which, in turn, filtered even more cleaned-up cash through Saudi Arabia and Lebanon. Though they were fronted by Arabs in Houston, United Front appeared to be primarily concerned with shipping food, medicine and clothes to Latin American and Asian countries, with a smattering of African nations thrown into the boiling ruse to hide the fact that the principal state sponsors behind UF were Saudi, Omani, Syrian and Lebanese. The treachery didn't end with just feeding the hungry as a means to keep the lid sealed tight on the bubbling terror money pot. Teachers for the poor were, according to the Stony Man intel team, shipped out of *mad-*

rassas from Algeria to Pakistan where the fanatical tenets of fundamental Islam were preached and the impoverished masses, fed, clothed and sheltered by their new saviors, indoctrinated by the fires of hatred toward anything of the West, were being groomed to be later recruited as potential suicide soldiers. Neither the Red Cross, UNICEF nor the United Nations recognized UF as a legitimate charitable organization. And, for once, even a few movers and shakers in the UN had openly tagged United Front as a black hole for the swallowing, infusion and transport of terrorist money.

Bolan knew all of this, and it didn't surprise him that the enemy had devised a new way to use what was supposed to be good to plant the seeds of evil.

Which was why the Executioner had ordered the blitz on the office building, take al-Hashid and sons prisoners of the Justice Department, if possible, go in, weapons drawn, give it up without a shot being fired. The problem was, Bolan had a nagging suspicion on the walk up someone else had beaten them to the quarry and were already in the process of being the ones doing all the punching.

It wasn't long before his gut instinct panned out as hard reality.

The rolling com van parked in a vacant lot, Bolan and Schwarz were going for the front doors, already alerted by Lyons and Blancanales in the back that two targets of Asian descent looked to be packing weapons and were watching the rear.

Moving up the side of the white stuccoed, two-story complex, the soldier held the Uzi subgun out and ready, the pockets of his trench coat filled with a bevy of grenades and spare clips. The charity's main Houston office was perched at the edge of what was called the Pasadena-Baytown Industrial Corridor. With night now spreading its blanket of dark shadows, the petrochemical processing plants sprawled away from the Stony Man warriors appeared to twinkle and shine like some eerie city of the future.

Call it a fluke, good timing, divine intervention or the hand of the god of war guiding them and putting them in the new enemy's face, but Bolan heard the shrill cry, a woman in terror, then caught the muffled cough of a sound-suppressed weapon. He was closing on the double glass doors, found they were locked, when he was just in time to spot the armed Asian stepping around the receptionist carousel. The Stony Man warriors had already been apprised that a hunting expedition of North Korean operatives might be on the loose. The particulars on this new enemy in the campaign were sketchy, but Bolan had been told they were out for some al-Amin blood, since it seemed the source for the Angels of Islam was Pyongyang, and the Democratic People's Republic of Korea didn't take kindly to getting snookered with bad money for their weapons of mass destruction. No problem. Bolan and his Stony Man commandos intended to make sure they remained the hunters.

The Executioner hit the glass with a long burst of Uzi subgun fire, Schwarz sidling up and blasting away with his M-16. Twin streams of sizzling lead reached out and tore up the North Korean just as he lifted his sound-suppressed pistol toward the two invaders. No sooner was the hardman falling than Bolan reached through the shattered glass and unlatched the door. He was inside, Schwarz on his heels, when two more North Koreans came charging through the doorway that appeared to Bolan to lead to the main office bay. He and Schwarz fired, on the march, driving two more NK ops back on a spray of crimson and shredded cashmere.

The Executioner hit a crouch beside the door, looked inside and found a slaughterhouse heaped before them.

THE SPAS-12 autoshotgun was up and booming in Lyons's fists as soon as the two NK ops began digging out pistols, damn near cutting one of them in two with the blast. Blancanales hosed down the other hardman with a burst of M-16 autofire, but the two NKs had what he had coined the Bad Guy Look when he was once L.A.'s finest. It was something in the eyes, a cunning animal way, a savage predator that always betrayed them, something to hide and something worth killing for. They could piss and moan about profiling all they wanted, he thought, but more often than not gut instinct had saved the life of a cop or a soldier. Sure, he knew a few tender toes got stepped on once in a while, all in the name of civil rights, but the talking heads were never the ones whose butts were out there on the firing line, risking life and limb to protect society at large.

And these two had gone for broke as soon as Lyons and Blancanales had turned the alley corner, no hesitation, all menacing intent in the eyes and hands.

Two menaces to society were history now.

Lyons heard his com link crackle with Bolan's voice. "Striker to Able One."

Lyons and Schwarz hit the metal back door. "Able One here. What do you have?"

"North Koreans. Six maybe seven we're engaging. Heads up, they'll be coming your way."

"Roger."

Blancanales threw open the door, crouched, and Lyons heard the retort of autofire and the familiar chug-chug of suppressed pistols and the muffled burping of a MAC-10 fixed up for minimal sound.

"One more thing," Lyons heard Bolan say. "They executed everyone from the looks of it. Don't anticipate bagging a live one."

"We copy."

And Bolan was gone, Lyons and Blancanales surging into the corridor, weapons up and ready to greet the mass murderers.

SIGNALING FOR SCHWARZ to break to the left, Bolan went into the main office area, vectoring to his right. Triggering his Uzi on the fly, he caught one more NK op as the enemy began spilling out of a back office, firing as a pack on the move. It sickened Bolan to find that the North Koreans had come in here, blasting away, shooting down the women, perhaps even a few innocents as well as the guilty.

Indiscriminate slaughter, but the Executioner could play that game, too.

Bullets began blowing apart computer terminals, sparks and glass raining behind Bolan as he bolted down a wallboard partition plastered with pictures of the family of the woman slumped in her chair.

"If it's al-Hashid you want, I suggest you throw down your weapons. Let us walk out of here and you can have him!"

Holes were drilled through the partition, Bolan peering around the corner, finding a beefy NK, his arm locked around the throat of the United Front's president, a pistol jammed in his ear.

"You can keep him!" Bolan shouted back, lining them up, five in all, six if he wanted to include al-Hashid. It would have been a small coup, taking al-Hashid alive, but Bolan already knew where and to whom the dirty money went down in Mexico.

This was simply another stop in the rolling Stony Man slaughter. The mother lode of terrorists was believed to be waiting south of the border.

"Hit them, Striker?" Bolan heard Schwarz ask over his com link.

"Take them out, but spare al-Hashid if you can."

The NK had to have seen the end coming. He shoved al-Hashid ahead, pumped two rounds into his back as his operatives cut loose with a mixed bag of pistols, MAC-10s and mini-Uzis. Two more were caught in the vise of bullets and buckshot, as Lyons and Blancanales roared open on their rear, and Bolan saw them blown out of the picture.

In tandem with Schwarz's M-16 autofire, Bolan held back on the trigger of the Uzi. For some reason three NKs decided to charge Bolan's and Schwarz's guns. Two leaped over workstations, spraying subguns, tearing up more wallboard and blasting apart more computers. Bolan nailed one NK with a burst to the chest, catching him in midflight, flinging him headfirst into a computer monitor. Two NKs with large duffel bags were being riddled with autoshotgun and M-16 fire. One of them was eviscerated, stem to stern, guts, blood and a grisly blast furnace of innards taking to the air before his bag was burst apart by another SPAS pounding. The air began raining cash next, as Bolan sprinted ahead, trying to get an angle on the last two hunkered down in a row of work cubicles. The two NKs popped up, spraying the room, but Schwarz, moving in on their right flank, and Bolan, sealing them off on the opposite side, closed the steel net of flying lead on them.

The Executioner burned out his clip, helping Schwarz pound them to the carpet with a long barrage.

"We've got a live one over here, Striker," Lyons called out. "It's not al-Hashid. He's already on his way to the big stock exchange in hell."

It was the NK hostage taker, Bolan saw, as he cut the gap for the back hall.

"I'd say check them for ID, but it's doubtful they're the card-carrying kind," Bolan said.

"We'll do it anyway, if just for laughs," Lyons said.

"Pol, how about you and Gadgets grab up whatever cash you can," Bolan said. "I'm sure down the road we can put it to better use than it was meant for here."

"Ciudad Zapulcha…"

"What's he saying?" Schwarz asked.

"Where the money goes and the drones were supposed to go," Bolan said.

"If…we can't nail these terrorists…" The NK op croaked out a strangled laugh. "Perhaps…you will have better luck, no?"

Bolan cracked a fresh mag home into his Uzi, chambered a round. He lifted the Israeli subgun, as the NK op reached out for his pistol. "Yes, but this one's for the home team. Ours."

THE MOROCCAN YACHT was simply called *Heaven,* and for his purposes paradise was simply what it had been carrying the past nine months to Marseilles. As far as he knew it was set to happen, but there were arrangements still to work out, some late intelligence he'd just received that needed answers to troublesome questions. Once word had reached him by E-mail in Casablanca that the shipment had been seized he had ordered his cadre in Marseilles to go to Status Red.

There had been a contingency plan all along, just in case the deal fell through and the tracks of the shipment were traced back to the crime boss who might not hold up under interrogation. So, he was there to initiate war, clean up any messes they might have left behind—unless, of course, the crime boss could assure delivery of more merchandise somehow, and that his lips weren't loose. That was doubtful, considering what the cargo was, but too much time and expense had carried the dream this far, and he couldn't see abandoning any plans at this late stage.

This was jihad, no more, no less.

Ah, but he rather liked Marseilles, this huge waterfront city, twice the size of Paris, but lacking the City of Light's finer touches of culture. With sixteen districts, Marseilles was Europe's second largest port. There was a long history here of piracy, too, since all manner of North Africans, Arabs, Armenians and so on had set up large neighborhoods that thrived primarily on smuggling. Everything from heroin to abducted teenaged girls from all over the world was for sale here if a man had the money. A perfect town to slip contraband through, or so it had been. There was no point in dwelling on what had happened, no sense in looking back on the glory days, since the future still held the promise of "something big." Regret, he thought, was for losers. And he had been chosen, long ago, to make sure the something big happened.

He stepped onto the dock, his passport declaring him as Heinz Kessler in the pocket of his topcoat, just in case the police, jumpier than ever these days since the attacks had swept through several European countries, decided to stop and question him. He had dyed his hair blond, cut it close to his scalp, shaved before setting sail from Morocco. The blue contact lens provided the finishing touch, but when he and his men unleashed war on the crime family it wouldn't much matter what the disguise, since he intended to be right there when—or if—they began mopping up the problems.

There were six of them, all declared German nationals, businessmen, shadows coming down the dock. He took a moment to enjoy the spectacular view of Vieux Port, choked with small boats and larger pleasure craft, laughter and music sweeping over him. With its craggy mountainous backdrop and pristine beaches, a part of him regretted he hadn't come here for some much-needed R and R. In the distance he could hear the din of nightlife surging on from any number of restaurants and cafés. Marseilles, he knew, was also one of the most dangerous cities on Earth. Should some mugger attempt to relieve him of his duffel bag, stuffed with Euros, the MAC-10 in special shoulder rigging beneath his coat would take care of any predator in the night.

He looked at Abdul, and said, "It is ready."

"Yes."

"Then, I have a call to make and we will see what Monsieur Puchain is really all about. I also hope one of you has more to report about these two Westerners who suddenly show up with their most curious proposition to sell weapons grade uranium and plutonium to Monsieur Puchain."

They parted, allowing their leader to take point.

And Nawir Wahjihab marched his jihad soldiers away from *Heaven.*

CHAPTER SEVENTEEN

Cary Mann, a.k.a. Gary Manning, and Timothy Hawke, a.k.a. T. J. Hawkins had already discussed the explosive dimension of their undercover con job. If found out, the two of them alone in a city where the hardened criminal population outnumbered law-abiding citizens by at least three to one, according to Interpol stats, and where murder for hire was reputed by the FBI to be a market as viable and thriving as prostitution, Marseilles would be the last place on Earth they ever saw.

Tough job, tough sell in a hard town, but Manning knew the two of them were more than ready and willing to go the distance, up for the task, however it shook out.

Normally they worked as key cogs of the ultracovert five commando juggernaut known as Phoenix Force. This time out, as explained by Stony Man Farm, there was too much going on in too many places, too many bad guys on the prowl with too many different agendas and too many questions that needed answering. So they had split the difference with their brethren, going into Marseilles, the Batman and Robin, as they told themselves, of the underworld market as salesmen for weapons grade U-235 and Pu-239.

The trouble was, René Puchain wasn't buying the snow job, or so Manning's gut was telling him.

After their initial meeting with the number-one crime boss in all of France, and perhaps Europe, laying out their sales pitch and handing off phony résumés and references in the mercenary world—which were backed up, airtight, they hoped, by Interpol, the FBI, CIA and Justice Department—Puchain had simply told them he'd call. They were staying in a seedy drug-and-whore-infested hotel on La Canebière, the murderous heart and dark soul of all Marseilles, when Puchain called him on the cell number he'd given the crime boss. No way would Manning let the Marseilles gangster know where they were staying, since the bulk of their gear and weapons was stowed in the room. That didn't mean they hadn't been shadowed all over Marseilles since landing, and even then, as Manning walked beside Hawkins, he had the nagging suspicion any number of night denizens out trolling for a good time or with murder in their hearts was a potential enemy.

As they cut a corner, moving down the alley for Puchain's sprawling digs, some combo restaurant-night-club-gambling parlor-house of ill repute, a bleached-blond hooker came cooing up to them.

"Later," Manning told her, marching past before she launched into her own sales pitch.

"Much later," Hawkins muttered to a spate of cursing.

The big Canadian and the ex-Army Ranger beelined for the trio of armed goons waiting at the side door. Manning wanted to feel casual, dive right into his business spiel but something kept biting at combat instincts, warning him this whole scam was about to blow up in their faces.

The way it was supposed to work, if Puchain sent them packing they'd march right to the Number Two Godfather, a pimp by the name of Vincent Rousiloux who hung his hat right down the block. Even still, the two Stony Man warriors intended to pay the whoremonger a visit anyway, offer him a better deal, hoping to set the stage for a shootout between rivals. Word was Rousiloux and Puchain hated each other, had itched for years to plant each other's head on their own mantel. Some past gangland warfare had erupted between the two organizations, and both mobsters were known to have dealings with Arab terrorists who were always shopping for the best bargain to haul their contraband. Right then Puchain was still on top, but the rumor mill churned that Rousiloux was looking to carve up Number One's turf, steal his Arab clientele. It wouldn't take much, Manning knew, to light the fuse to get the crime cannibals to eat each other up. The thing was, the two of them might get caught in the cross fire.

Duty.

They were, ostensibly, there to get a lead on al-Amin thugs operating in the port city, then paint the bull's-eye on terrorist backs. If a few more snakes could get ground up as they set their gunsights eventually on al-Amin vipers, so much the better. Either way, Marseilles would be a little kinder and gentler place to live once they blew town.

Provided, of course, they could pull off the impossible without ending up as fish food.

"Inside," the one they knew as Answain told them. "Three steps, then stop and put your hands up."

They did as ordered and were relieved of their weapons inside the doorway. "This nonsense again," Hawkins growled as they were both thoroughly frisked. "You're not exactly proving to us we're headed for a long and profitable future as business partners."

"Yes, yes, I know," Answain said, and gave both Stony Man warriors a gentle shove to get them moving for the main dining room. "You already told us Marseilles is much too dangerous to be walking around without these weapons. And, my friends, 'we' do not have anything to prove to 'you.' It remains to be seen what the future is between us."

Manning threw Hawkins a look. This didn't bode well, he thought, walking into a dining room with enough tables and booths Manning figured Puchain could have packed half the city in here. He found the crime boss sitting at the same upraised booth in the far corner. He counted up the same twenty goons, spread around the room, bulges of shoulder-holstered pistols beneath a mix of sports coat and leather jackets. The place was empty now except for the main players. Not even a few whores trolled the upstairs balconies, no sounds of dice rolling, roulette wheels spinning from the back parlors. The fun and games nowhere to be found like the last time they met.

"Gentlemen," Puchain greeted them, then took a sip of red wine. "Do not bother to sit. You won't be staying long."

"Okay, fine," Manning said. "I take it we won't be doing business. Bon voyage. We can always take our offer somewhere else."

Puchain raised a hand, smiling. "Like down the street to some pimp?"

Manning and Hawkins spun on their heels.

"Hold on, if you please. Not so fast."

"Look, pal, whoever we take our offer to," Hawkins said, "isn't really any concern of yours if you're not interested. It's a buyer's market."

"So it would seem," Puchain agreed. "You come here, offer me ten kilograms of enriched uranium for a mere five million when the market rate is between seven hundred thousand U.S. dollars to one to even sixty million and per kilogram. Plutonium alone, highly enriched, goes for one million per kilogram. Then you tell me you can get Cesium 137 and 133. Radium 226, all in the million-dollar-per-kilo category. It makes me wonder about its quality or if you are mere amateurs to this game of nuclear smuggling."

"I thought we explained that," Manning said. "We need to unload it. Fast."

"Yes, yes. So I heard you explain."

"Hey, we're not looking to dump off a bunch of radioactive junk," Hawkins said. "And we didn't stroll into some dump in the Ukraine and help ourselves to discarded waste of questionable quality. You're either in or you're out, and we're gone if you're out."

"One American, one Canadian. I gather the Canadians lack as much in manners as Americans these days. And they demand instant gratification."

"Hey, we don't need this crap," Manning said. "Thanks for wasting our time. Thanks for nothing."

"Hold on, you impertinent…ah, but your references checked out. Almost too good to be true. Do not be offended. I have to be extremely careful, what with Interpol, the CIA traipsing around all over the city, putting bugs even under my pillow, agents often coming here, buying women, or asking for jobs as a waiter. Prudence and caution. I have not survived lawmen, pimps and swindlers this long by being careless. I want you to know that what you are offering to sell, also, I could get as much quantity and be assured of its quality from my Russian counterparts."

"What, you want a sample?" Manning said. "Bring your spacesuit and your Geiger counter if that's the case. It's good."

Puchain tapped a finger on the rim of his glass. "If you are such entrepreneurs, then you know that it is not only extremely risky to deal in nuclear cargo, but it is also not very profitable. The market these days demands, uh, something more complete. Ready to, uh, go, as you might say. Instant big bang for the buck."

"Sorry, but we couldn't exactly pack a thermonuclear warhead for the flight," Manning said.

Puchain chuckled. "If, as you want me to believe, you are so well connected, then surely you could bring to me something more complete than a vat of irradiated water. The people I deal with are interested in more than just a dirty bomb, though, if the need demanded it, they would probably make you a serious offer."

"Bottom line, Puchain," Manning said. "In or out?"

Puchain nodded, sipped his drink. "I need to make some calls for prospective buyers, since I don't want the stuff lying around my restaurant or one of my warehouses for the law to raid. Give me another day or so before I give you my answer."

Manning knew it was time to up the ante, and begin to attempt to set the savages at each other's throats. "Don't take too long, René. But you wouldn't mind if we went shopping down the street, would you? Time is money."

The gaze narrowed enough for Manning to know they were no longer welcome in Marseilles. Puchain shrugged, the smile phony. "Whatever you feel it is you have to do."

"If that's all," Hawkins said, and looked back over his shoulder at Answain. "Can we get…"

"Yes, of course. Antoine, give them back their toys."

Weapons retrieved and stowed, Manning and Hawkins walked away in silence.

"Be careful," Manning heard Puchain call out, and glanced back. "It is as you said. Marseilles is a very dangerous city."

And that was all Manning needed to hear. They had just become walking targets. He wondered how far they'd get down the block before the crime boss unchained the hellhounds.

WAHJIHAB WAS PLEASED with what his Marseilles operatives had accomplished. With ten of his best and most trusted men gathered in the living room of the third floor in the apartment on La Canebière, he smiled to himself. He had already checked the wiring personally, all of it set to blow, homed in to one radio frequency that he would control. It had taken the better part of nine months, but five hundred pounds of C-4 had been smuggled in, piecemeal, literally block by block, guarded nearly around the clock by these same operatives. They had all learned the art of warfare well, he knew, from their months of training and study in Afghanistan. Demolitions had become their specialty.

The plastique was also dirty.

Quite the feat, he thought, wrapping himself up in ten pound of C-4, shrugging on his topcoat to cover the bundles. Enriched uranium, plutonium, cesium and radium waste, purchased from the Russian mafia, was interspersed between the planted blocks in flimsy containers. Not only that, but two other apartments directly below, rented out months back by more of his operatives, were likewise primed with radioactive waste. Three apartments all together, strategically positioned on both sides below, and the structure, if it wasn't blown off the street, would topple. Then there would be radiation dispersed over several city blocks, a cloud of invisible doom that would float down over the infidels, see them fall ill within weeks. The panic alone over the monstrous blast would create chaos in a city that already bordered anarchy under the best of times.

And the beauty of it all, he knew, was the building was nearly right on top of the crime boss's establishment. In fact, the hydraulic aluminum folding ladder in the bedroom would reach across the alley to Puchain's rooftop. From there, a glass cutter would get them through the skylight. He knew the floor plan from memory. If Puchain played true to his self-indulgent form, he would be downstairs in the main dining room, swilling wine, chortling with guests, master of ceremony. It would have helped to have sent in a spy, know for sure who was where, but Wahjihab didn't mind a little uncertainty for the sake of drama.

"Tell me about these two men who just arrived in Marseilles."

Ali finished turning himself into a C-4 bomb, then said, "Our informant on the inside said one is American, one Canadian. They are armed. They offered to sell Puchain enriched uranium and plutonium for an incredibly cheap price."

"Did he buy?"

"No," Ali said. "He said he needed to think about it."

"The man has his own sources inside Russia for that," Wahjihab said. "The same sellers we use."

"Are you thinking they may be American agents?" Habib asked.

"I am thinking exactly that. I am thinking Puchain is going to sell us out. I am thinking we are essentially finished here in France."

"We go to war?" Ali wanted to know, his eyes lighting up with the prospect of jihad.

"Yes."

Wahjihab showed his soldiers his best winning smile. With Zabir suiting up with C-4 that made for three suicide bombers who would get their orders where to position themselves in the next few minutes. Only Wahjihab didn't intend to light himself up as any martyr. What his men didn't know would, in truth, kill them. Since he had been personally chosen as savior and avenger for the Islamic world, his legend had to live on, as well as making sure he kept on breathing, planning future operations. There would be doubt, when the dust of battle settled, that he had died, blowing himself up like one of those teenagers he and his operatives recruited in Palestine, beefing up Hamas and Hezbollah with arms and money to continue their holy struggle against the Jews.

He was the Successor, and he had to live on. The bullets were going to fly, though, the bombs blowing, this entire building riding a radioactive firecloud to the sky, but he would fight his way out of Marseilles.

Another contingency plan, his backup for flight was already in place.

Still he needed to reassure his men, harden their resolve, one of the martyrs. "I was chosen by the sheikh as the Successor. But all of us here knows the jihad is more important than any one fighter. Knowing what must be done here tonight I already chose a successor myself. If it is God's will, then we will all die here tonight in this city, at war with Puchain and his criminals. But it is a holy cause we perform, making sure this treacherous criminal, whom, I believe, had something to do with the shipment getting seized, is dead. I will take five more of us along when go to make certain God's will be done. Come. We finish arming ourselves, then we pray one last time and go out to do battle against the enemy."

LESS THAN A BLOCK OUT of Puchain's, Manning counted three familiar faces on their tail. They were angling across La Canebière, weaving through traffic where drivers hooted and howled for whores on the sidewalks, when Manning decided an abrupt change in plans was necessary.

It was time to go to war. This con job thing as sellers of contraband obviously wasn't going to cut it.

"T.J.," he said, hitting the walk, searching for an alley.

"I saw them. I take it you have some ideas?"

"Slow the pace. We hit an alley. Not quite up against the wall, give ourselves a little elbow room. Try and take one alive. With luck, we can take one of Puchain's goons to Rousiloux as a show of good faith that we have no use for the Number One crime boss who came looking to stick it to us. We'll show Rousiloux he's our boy, but how we'll convince him…we'll just wing it when the time comes.''

''Well, we came here, already knowing we were going to be targets.''

''So let the games begin.''

Manning and Hawkins slowed their strides. A quick look back revealed the trio of goons cutting the gap, two of them already reaching inside their coats as they knew they were pegged, and Manning found the ambush hole he was looking for.

''Three steps in, side by side,'' Manning said.

Mini-Uzis out and up, they waited in the shadows. The alley appeared empty behind them, whores and johns creating the ruckus pretty much out on the street. If gunfire broke out, well, this was Marseilles, Manning thought. As in any big city the world over, most folks tended to look the other way, see no evil and so on when they were suddenly thrust in the proximity of terminal encounters.

The shadows wheeled around the corner, nearly ran into the compact subguns. Manning drilled a left hook off the jaw of one goon, flattened him, but the other two weren't going to go quietly. The standing thugs already had pistols out, and the extensions of sound suppressors told Manning they had more on their minds than a simple chat about the nuclear-smuggling business.

Puchain either sent them out on the hunt, wanted

some brutal Q and A session under the threat of death, or the crime boss simply wanted them on permanent vacation in Marseilles.

Thug Two was Manning's concern. The pistol was sweeping around when the big Canadian cracked his subgun off the goon's skull. He was grabbing the gun hand next, driving a leg sweep through the gangster's knee, sending him down, when the pistol began chugging, spitting hot lead past his ear. But this was a street fight, Manning knew, where everything went and dirty tricks pulled off hard and fast usually decided who won, who lost and who died.

The thug was down on his back, Manning glimpsing Hawkins shooting a toe into Goon Three's family jewels. That kind of action generally crippled and felled a guy like a poleaxed steer, only the goon simply bent over, snarled and tried to line up Hawkins for a point-blank drilling. Manning speared a knee into the sac of his own problem, a guttural belch in his face, Hawkins just above him, banging a head butt off something that cracked open like foam and rained hot fluid on his forehead. A clawed hand was coming up, fingers looking to take out his eyes when Manning blocked the arm at the last second. They needed only one, so he shoved the muzzle of his subgun under his opponent's chin and hit the trigger. It was the next best thing to a sound suppressor, three rounds on a rocket ride up through the brain, blowing off his scalp, and Manning's problem went limp.

Number One was clambering to his feet when Manning reached over, jacked him up and thrust the mini-

Uzi under his jaw. One more head butt, and Hawkins's troubles toppled to the alley.

"We take your guy," Manning told Hawkins.

"Okay, here it is, asshole," the big Canadian told his goon. "First, you speak English?" The goon acted like he wanted to get defiant, then Manning put some pressure on the muzzle to help the guy confirm he understood. "We're taking our business to Rousiloux. After this little show of affection from your boss, I'm going to practically not only give away our store, but I'm going to make damn sure Vincent gets a major hook-up with our friends in Moscow. I'm going to see, with a lot of help and clout from certain Russians, Vincent takes the throne here. Your boss, asshole that he is, was stupid but he'll live long enough to regret marching out some flunkies to try and off us. Think you can remember all that?"

A stiff nod.

Manning whipped him around and kicked him in the ass. "So, get moving!"

Their sales pitch, Manning saw, was wobbling to his feet, groaning and spurting blood everywhere from a crushed nose. Hawkins helped him stand.

According to their earlier recon, Manning knew Rousiloux's house of games was two blocks over. Peering down the alley, he saw car lights filtering past the shroud of darkness. Their exit, and Manning indicated the direction out of there to Hawkins. A quick check of their entry point, and no one appeared concerned about the battle here that had lasted maybe all of five seconds. Time to boogie.

"Any crap from you, Pierre," Manning warned the goon, "and a broken nose will feel like a shot of morphine compared to what we'll do next. Nod, if you agree."

The grunt, then the nod flinging a few drops of blood off his chin, and Hawkins began manhandling their prisoner behind Manning as they melted into the deeper shadows down the alley.

CHAPTER EIGHTEEN

Vincent Rousiloux used to believe he did his best thinking with a head swimming in Canadian whiskey. He used to think how he should put more policemen and judges in his pockets, even something as note-worthy as buying out the entire legal system in the city, if only to rub elbows with a better class of individuals instead of wallowing in drunken misery with thieves, murderers and whores. He used to think of ways he could be climbing the ladder of success, a human rocket shooting to the top of the underworld, somehow, someway become more than a mere pimp and second-rate arms dealer and minor league white slaver and narcotics peddler. He used to think if he had more connections, specifically to Moscow, more and bigger warehouses that business would somehow flourish on its own, like some spawning virus, money alone doing all the talking, buying the best of every-thing, money alone consuming his rival, no less, as he hired the best assassins on the continent. If he had better soldiers, professional talent even, recruited out of law enforcement, intelligence agencies and the mil-itary he used to think how much his status would

grow, an empire blossoming before his very eyes simply out of fear of the hired help. And then there was
the respect, or lack of respect factor, aware how his
name was disgracefully kicked about the city by that
bastard, Puchain. He used to…

Ah, the hell with, he thought. Used to, could have
and should have, that seemed to be the mantra he had
lived by. And so he poured himself another whiskey,
fired up another cigarette, hating everyone and everything, wondering why, or when and if things would
ever get better. He told Cici he wanted to be alone,
this miserable slut, he thought, whose only real interest in him was to see how much money she could
either beg or borrow from him, or skim from the
night's take of any poor slob willing to cough up a
few bucks.

"Not tonight," he growled at her when she insisted
on making him feel better. "Get lost!"

He watched her get up, pouting, as she strutted to
the bar in high heels that made her at least four inches
taller than his diminutive five-two. That was another
thing that bugged him more and more lately, especially the talk he was catching through the grapevine
about many things, the least of which was his un-
sightly appearance, the most of which was he should
be out there shopping for Viagra instead of consuming whiskey around the clock. Short and pudgy, he
was getting older in a hurry, losing more of his curly
mop so that now he had a full and shiny moonspot
on his dome. He was getting heavier, too, so that now
he had to hoist his belly up just to…

The sight of the rabble at the bar, his soldiers, drinking, laughing, a couple of them passing a joint around, began to inflame some growing ire even more. So he drank, brooded, thought.

The angry truth was, he thought, he did nothing but seethe about his Puchain problem, dreaming—or to be more precise—fantasizing how many various ways he could torture and kill his hated rival. If he could just get rid of Puchain, wipe out his organization in some tremendous epic blaze, he might find respect and honor was suddenly owed him, the gossipers and naysayers and backstabbers changing their tune, bowing and scraping for favors on bended knee. All he could do, an all-consuming obsession, was dream about skinning the man alive, putting him on a rack, dunking him in boiling water. He would—

Sitting alone now in his corner table, the bar packed with the after-hours crowd, far too much of the clientele consisting of his soldiers, spending his hard-earned money on his whores, he was thinking he should just proceed with total gangland war. The problem was, he needed a plan of attack. Or did he? What he needed was hard and seasoned professional shooters and not a bunch of street thugs. He needed men with a big pair, who had no fear, might even march themselves into Puchain's place and just start shooting, laughing in the face of death. Maybe if he searched harder, shelled out more money, he would find his saviors.

What to do? he pondered. There were enough guns and grenades in the back room. It shouldn't take much for his own crew of nineteen to arm themselves like a bunch of Rambos, simply drive themselves over to Puchain's place and just do it, absolute obliteration or else don't come back. Just shoot and blast the place up so bad it toppled on Puchain's twitching corpse, worry about police problems later. About fifteen or so "ifs" shot through his mind. If they could sober up. If they could forget about playing grabass long enough to focus on his Puchain problem. If they could shoot straight. If they could pull it off without dragging the police to his doorstep. If there was a strong leader somewhere in this pack of cutthroats. If...

He was killing the glass of whiskey, taking long angry puffs on his cigarette when he heard some ruckus in the far corner. Voices were swirling through his raging buzz in English, demanding tones, from somewhere beyond the velvet curtain that led to the waiting "cat" room near the foyer.

"What is it?" he barked, or tried to sound tough, hating the sound of his own perpetually squeaking voice. That was another thing he hated about himself. More talk. He had heard Puchain spread the malicious slander about his voice, telling people it sounded like Vincent Rousiloux's soprano squeak made it seem as if he had a vise forever clamped to his sac.

"Americans," André called from across the room, blocking the entrance, one hand wrapped around a bottle of Scotch, the other holding on to his shoulder-holstered side arm.

"One American. I'm Canadian."

"What do they want?"

"To talk. They say they can make you the Number One boss. They killed one of Puchain's men, so they say, and beat the daylights out of two more in some ambush by Puchain. They say they have an offer for you. They claim they can make you king."

"Not quite the way I put it, Pierre. You want to let us in, or should we take our talent somewhere else?"

Could this be true? he wondered, and felt hope flare alive all of a sudden. Were they warriors, or slick scamming wannabes with more show than go? If they were con artists, he would know soon enough. If not, if they were serious, then he would put them to task, sit back, watch them work, wait and see if they could make his Puchain problem disappear. What would it hurt to hear their spiel? Worst case, he would simply have them shot.

"Let them in!"

THE INTEL PHOTO of Vincent Rousiloux, Hawkins thought, didn't do the man proper injustice. As Hawkins manhandled the prisoner into what he could only think of as a den of cutthroats, the whole barroom nothing but a Sodom and Gomorrah free-for-all of drinking, smoking and scraggly riffraff fondling the house goodies, several words jumped to mind as he looked at the creature sitting by himself at his table. Hideous. Grotesque. Cartoonish. Bald on top, a curly mop's fell to skinny shoulders, but the rest of the small frame looked amply packed with fat. Long beaked nose, black eyes, bushy brows, then there was the voice. The freak sounded like some hysterical teenaged girl every time he opened his mouth. Finishing off this parody of a human being was the fact the Number Two crime boss was whacked out of his gourd on booze, a thin line of slobber trickling down over the moles on his chin.

Hawkins slung the prisoner to the floor.

"Who are you? What is the meaning of this?"

"This is some garbage," Manning said, "that Puchain sent out to kill me and my friend here."

"And you are?"

"Mann."

"Hawke."

Rousiloux nodded, then a smile broke over his face. "This one, he doesn't look so good."

Hawkins heard a few chuckles from the bar.

"You did this to him?"

"What I thought you were just told," Manning said. "Ambush. Another one's laid out in the alley with his brains blown out, if you want to go have a look."

"What are you, besides a lot of mouth at the moment?"

"Independent contractors," Manning said.

"Troubleshooters," Hawkins added.

"And you are here to what? Fix my Puchain problem?"

"Here it is," Manning said. "We went to Puchain with a deal to get him some special merchandise for a very generous price on our part."

"Which is what, this special merchandise?"

"Never mind for now," Manning said. "Let's just say with what we have on tap, and if we do business, I can make some very big name connections from Mother Russia practically all yours. Put you over the top. I made Puchain an offer I was sure he wouldn't refuse. Puchain wasn't buying. Instead he set a wolf pack on us. I killed the one, my friend here gave this one a week's worth of intensive plastic surgery, and we sent another one back to Puchain to tell him he's finished in Marseilles. Point-blank, Vince. Without or without you, me and my friend are going back to settle up with Puchain. We don't like double-crossing SOBs or guys who aren't straight shooters."

"So, you went to him with this special deal first? Not me? Why should I have this sudden honor now? Why should I not be insulted you didn't seek me out first?"

"We heard he was the number one mover and shaker of contraband in this town," Hawkins said.

"And I am?"

"Number two," Manning said. "So we heard. You want to be number one, maybe me and my pal here can make it happen. I'm not here to listen about hurt feelings and how you feel insulted we didn't come running to your door as soon as we got off the banana boat."

"You have a big and smart mouth."

"Yeah," Manning said. "You want to see if I can back up the talk, walk the walk, cut us loose on Puchain."

"Really? You are that good?"

"I wouldn't be here if I didn't think so."

"So, how are you going to make this big thing happen?"

"Take out Puchain and his pirates," Manning said. "Full frontal assault. But we might need a little assistance from your boys here if they can put the bottle down."

Manning waited, watched as Rousiloux nodded, drank, then looked at his soldiers. The big Canadian felt the heat stir around him, some of the cutthroats muttering, one of them snarling for Rousiloux to send them on their way but with a hard lesson, as in a few broken bones.

"You hear this?" Rousiloux squeaked out. "These two are men of action. Or so they want us to believe. However, I like them already, I think, but the jury is out. Will you sit with me and share a drink first? Sort of get to know you more."

"Some other time," Manning said. "Problem is, we lit a fire under Puchain's ass. If he knows we're here, he might break out of the gate first. You want the guy taken out, I think now is the time to act."

"Yes, yes, while you are still hot, still motivated. I see. May I ask what is your price for all this generosity?"

"Employment," Manning said. "We can negotiate about money later. Right now, I think we need to remove Puchain from the picture."

"I agree. Seeing as you might have brought my Puchain hemorrhoid to my place anyway. André! Put the bottle and the joint down! Work now, play later.

It is time to do what I've been wanting to do for what has felt like an eternity. We go to war with Puchain! If these men are not as good as they want me to believe, they will either die or you can kill them as you see fit. Is that a problem, *monsieurs?*"

"Is what a problem?" Hawkins asked.

"That I set my men upon you if you are all talk."

"Fair enough," Manning agreed.

Now that they were in, Hawkins wasn't so sure how this was going to fall. It sounded like they'd pushed all the right buttons, but Rousiloux didn't strike him as any master battle strategist. A moment later he was sure of it.

"So, here it is my new friends," Rousiloux said, poured another drink. "You and my men, you drive straight to Puchain's establishment. Back door, front door, I care not. Blow the doors down. This full frontal assault you mentioned. You walk right in there and shoot him, shoot them all."

"Wait a second."

Rousiloux glowered at Manning. "No? You are all talk then?"

"Hardly, but I think a little planning might go a long way."

Rousiloux slammed his small pink fist on the table. "Now or never! The best plan is simply one of straightforward action! I have waited too long, suffered too much abuse as Puchain's organization grows and grows and I remain little more than a pimp! No more. Tonight it happens! Tonight Puchain dies and I become number one! Do it my way. Are we clear?''

Hawkins looked at Manning, shrugged. "Looks like we found a new employer."

"Okay, you're on," Manning told Rousiloux. "How many guns are going along for this joyride?"

"With you two, twenty-one. As many, I believe, as Puchain has. Even odds. Now, go arm yourselves with more than what I believe are machine pistols under those jackets. This one," he said, sneering at the prisoner. "He stays here. I can always shoot him later."

Manning nodded as Rousiloux bleated for all of them to get moving.

"Bring me back good news, or do not return," Rousiloux said, as Manning and Hawkins followed the cutthroats away from the bar.

Hawkins had a bad feeling where this was all headed, as in straight to hell. Already they were catching resentful looks from nineteen bad guys who were little more than drunken scumbag criminals, he believed. Well, they had just gotten themselves involved in a full-blown shooting war, pretty much the plan going in all along. It was going to prove nothing more than a massive bullrush into Puchain's place, shoot them all to hell, or get slaughtered in the attempt. Hawkins knew he and Manning were in it for the long bloody haul, no matter what the outcome.

If this was it...

He shoved any pessimistic thoughts out of his mind, hoping that a warrior's skill, heart and guts would carry the two of them through the night. For some reason, instinct warned him they were going to need more than a quick mean gun before this was finished.

The gates of hell, he thought, had just opened wide and angry.

At least, he knew, everyone was going to prove fair game in the killing zone.

CHAPTER NINETEEN

As soon as Puchain heard the report from Alles he knew what in all likelihood was coming next, and what had to be done to avert another humiliating disaster such as the one suffered by the three soldiers he sent to kill the mercenaries. Even before the American and the Canadian had left him he had a feeling they weren't to be trusted, and that they were far more than what they claimed. His mind, in fact, had been made up. They were operatives of some sort, perhaps CIA, coming to him with all the right answers, proper credentials at their disposal to back up their ruse as dealers of mass death. It was too pat, and he had been sure it was some sort of setup from the first moment he had laid eyes on them. He would have shot them dead in front of his booth, but the idea of cleaning up such a mess...well, it had seemed a simple task, hunting them down in the streets of Marseilles where random murder was commonplace, easily overlooked by the police as a routine occurrence in a city where crime was the main occupation. And now it had backfired.

He was incensed, even more, that one of his top

soldiers had allowed himself to get beaten like a dog in the street, Vichieux shot dead in an alley, and Valmaille whisked away by the two treacherous mercenaries, ostensibly, to be dumped at the feet of Rousiloux as some bargaining chip to curry favor from the hideous gangster. The message brought to him by Alles from the mercenaries, clearly threatening, was reason enough to brace himself for war. They would be back, alone or with the creature's gangsters, but he would be ready for battle.

"Get me a weapon now!" Puchain growled at one of his soldiers. He was out of his booth, glared at Alles, considered striking the man for his failure and apparent lack of nerve, then thought better of it. Two of his finest were no longer there to help tackle what he knew was a coming battle, and there was no point in heaping embarrassment on someone he might need to beef up his force, another gun when the shooting started. Yes, he would need everyone available, ready and willing to fight to the death. He knew how much Rousiloux despised and envied him. The talk about Marseilles, the odious creature forever railing to any and all he would listen how he would someday kill him, was near legendary in its fiery braggadocio. He should have seen this coming, wondering if he'd grown too confident, or soft as he had been riding the high life for so long, trusting that no one would dare touch him in a city he owned. "An assault rifle, plenty of spare clips!"

He needed to stay calm and in control, his men watching, but he found himself pacing the dining-room floor, wondering why he was suddenly afraid, feeling as if fate had been eager to test his mettle, power and manhood in some all-out war with a vicious rival and treacherous foreigners for some time. Moments later, he was handed a FAMAS 5.56 mm assault rifle, four clips that he snugged in his waistband.

"The outrage of this!" he rasped, cracking home a magazine.

Answain walked up to Puchain, his hands filled with an Uzi subgun. "What would you have us do? We cannot sit here, knowing the monster man has been talking about war all over the city for some time. Making all manner of threatening noise. If he thinks he can use those two, he will. He cares nothing for the lives of his own men, all desperate criminals who will do anything for money. They will come."

"I know that! We go to them and fire the first shots!"

He was about to begin issuing orders when he thought he heard a series of thumps from upstairs. The noise seemed to filter down the balcony steps from his own office. He was about to go investigate when he saw the armed shadows spilling down both sides of the balcony.

"Not so fast, Monsieur Puchain. I believe you know who I am."

He knew, yes, and it was all he could do, the muzzles of their weapons drawn down on them on the floor, to keep from erupting at yet another devious circumstance. Not only that, but he saw Kessler, a.k.a.

Nawir Wahjihab, was prepared to blow up himself and the rest of them in a suicide stand. Suddenly the odious creature down the block seemed the least of his concerns.

"SO, YOU ARE BIG MEN, big shooters. Big tough guys. You are going to save the night, make Vincent the superstar of the underworld he has always wanted to be."

The man called André was grinning, his goons chuckling, as if they were all going to the high-school prom instead of about to engage in full-blown combat. At least eighteen out of the nineteen brigands reeked of booze and pot. They were wild-eyed, hopped up on chemicals, sweating out the night's indulgences.

Thugs.

Even still, all of them were armed with an assortment of assault rifles and submachine guns, and Manning clearly sensed they were no slouches when it came to cold-blooded killing. Manning and Hawkins had been equipped with MP-5s, four French frag grenades which, when asked, André claimed they had four-second delay fuses. Manning and Hawkins had thoroughly checked their own weapons, the big Canadian wishing he had one of those M-16/M-203 combos like André was toting.

Before leaving the freakish runt, Manning recalled how four more hardmen had crawled out of the upstairs rooms, whores in tow, guns in hand. Obviously Rousiloux had more shooters on tap than he let on, but Manning intended to wax the freak before he left town. Four or forty gangsters ready to go to bat for him, it made no difference. Manning could play the game the crazy way, too. No, there would be no second-in-line gangster to step up and claim the crown from Puchain, since Manning didn't believe in unfinished missions. All this was assuming they could take care of grim business here.

They were out of the fleet of luxury vehicles, the armada parked in a dark empty lot south of Puchain's huge domain. André kept smiling, chortling, blowing whiskey fumes in Manning's face. They were insane, or stupid or both, the big Canadian decided. This was a suicide charge, no doubt about it. No plan, no scheme...

He knew they were in way too deep to show doubt about it all now. But the Phoenix Force commando had some ideas to bail himself and Hawkins out of the fire, or go down in the attempt. He glanced at Hawkins on his flank, hoped the ex-Army Ranger read the steady cold anger in his eyes. They had no chance to put together their own plan, surrounded the whole time by Rousiloux's goons, but Manning could be sure that once the fireworks began blowing around the joint, Hawkins would take his cue.

Manning planned on back-shooting these brigand SOBs. Unless, of course, that was their own plan, Rousiloux having pulled André aside for a Puchain-type encore.

"Recall what Monsieur Rousiloux said?" André laughed as the small army of shadows rolled up the alley, going right for the same side door where the two of them had been let in on previous encounters.

"I'm sure you're going to remind us," Manning said.

"One hundred thousand dollars, American, per head of Puchain's men. A quarter million for Puchain himself. A very nice payday. Buy us all many women, all the whiskey we can drink for the rest of our lives."

"Let's hope we all live long enough to collect and spend," Hawkins said. "I believe your boss also said something about work now, play later. I suggest your get your mind on more than just a good time."

"Monsieur Rousiloux said to hurry back, he is waiting for breaking news."

"Hey, we're here," Manning said. "Let's cut the crap and get to work."

They reached the door, Manning scanning the alley, the street beyond. Nightlife buzzed on, the party people oblivious to all but their own chasing of pleasure, or crime, or both.

Manning saw one of the brigands pull out a wad of plastique and det cord.

"You, my friend," André said, poking Manning in the chest with the muzzle of his M-16, "and your American counterpart, you will lead the way."

Worst-case, Manning thought, from bad to worse to downright ugly. They were being offered up as cannon fodder. While they came under fire, probably shot up off the starting line, André and his cutthroats would rush past their falling bodies.

Manning bit back a curse.

"Problems with that?"

"If we're going to be risking our butts and maybe the first ones facing the meat grinder, how about giving me and my 'American counterpart' one of those?" Manning said, nodding at the M-16/M-203.

André looked over his shoulder at his men, chuckled, shrugged. "Sure."

They exchanged their subguns for the big combo blasters.

"A few of those 40 mms?"

"You want a lot."

"I'm prepared to give a lot."

"Very well."

Manning and Hawkins took and dumped three 40 mm charges each into the combat vests they had taken back at the runt's whorehouse.

The plastique primed, the brigands fell back, hugging the wall, Manning and Hawkins taking up positions on the other side of the door. They were far enough out of earshot that Manning chanced a harsh whisper, said, "Follow my lead, T.J."

"LOWER THOSE WEAPONS and tell your men to stop moving!"

"You first!" he heard Puchain yell, the gangster shuffling back toward his booth, assault rifle held rock-steady in his hands, the boss flanked by two goons as if they would shield him from certain death. "And you and your other two mad bombers stay back! One more step we start blasting! Damn you, Wahjihab, last warning!"

Wahjihab closed on the gangster, two more steps, then stopped near the bar. He held the smaller of the two remote boxes in one hand, grasped the Uzi subgun with the other. He was prepared to die, he decided, or at least give the appearance to both sides he was ready to go to God in one moment of insanity. He took in the numbers quickly, saw most of them were packed in front of and behind the bar across the room. Maybe twenty all together. Two blasts from his warriors should take out most of the opposition. While the shattered remnants shot it out, he would escape, simply walk right out the front door, hit the street, move for the port.

"My men have been living right under your noses for months, Puchain," Wahjihab said. "You are not nearly as informed as you believed."

"What do you want?"

"My shipment was lost."

"So? It happened. What? You want your money back?"

"That would be a good start."

"No."

"No?"

"What part of 'no' do you not understand?"

He had come, half-expecting the gangster would break, at best, relent, at worst and seek to renegotiate. Something else, though, seemed to be at work to have the gangster so worked up, a look behind the eyes that told Wahjihab the man had other concerns besides getting blown up under his own roof. Wahjihab spotted Zabir and Ali across the room, gauged the distance, and figured he was maybe a few feet from the worst of the lethal touch of the blast radius.

Zabir took another step toward the French gangsters.

Wahjihab felt it ready to crack wide open, ready to hurl himself over the bar.

"I told you bastards to stop moving!"

Wahjihab cut loose with his Uzi, catching two of Puchain's gangsters with a quick burst across their chests. By the time he had Puchain lined up, the underworld boss was throwing himself behind a booth, lost to sight. Wahjihab flung himself over the bar, knowing what was next, as the room erupted with weapons' fire and the thunder of twin explosions.

MANNING HEARD the pitched battle, just around the corner, felt the heat of some tremendous blast scorching around the marble post. He could only assume Puchain had more enemies in the neighborhood than just Rousiloux. It was only a wild guess at that point, until he saw the combatants with his own eyes, but his gut told him al-Amin operatives had come here to collect, strike up a new deal or reap blood vengeance for the shipment of drones they'd lost.

"Move it!"

André barked at them to hit the dining-room floor first. They were nearly at the end of the wide service corridor, when Manning looked over his shoulder. The brigands had opted to fall back, hold up until Manning and Hawkins broke out into the open first.

They were jammed tight, and they were no longer grinning and laughing.

"Do it," Manning told Hawkins.

The big Canadian wheeled in tandem with Hawkins, both Stony Man warriors ripping free with long sweeps of autofire. The Frenchmen screamed, cursed, tried to bring their weapons up, but Manning and Hawkins had them locked in, chewed up, flailing into one another, banging off the walls, human bowling pins.

"Fall back for cover!" Manning roared at Hawkins, still firing, eating them up with a relentless lead dicing that flayed away at cloth and flesh. "Fire in the hole, T.J.!" he yelled as Hawkins pulled up and covered himself behind the wall's edge.

The 40 mm charge chugged away, Manning glimpsing a few bloody walking wounded, attempting to return fire before the blast tore through them.

Now the floor show, Manning thought, and took in the raging battle in the dining room.

"What's the plan, Gary?"

"Good question."

A groan from behind, Manning momentarily surprised that anything was still moving around in the thick pall of smoke, and he burned out his last few rounds as he spotted the possum.

"Let's grab a few spares, T.J., then…hell, then let's go find out who the new thugs on the block are."

CHAPTER TWENTY

Puchain heard his own bitter, defeated chuckle, then he tasted the blood on his lips, wondered a moment if the sour copper liquid in his mouth belonged to him or if he'd taken a gory bath from one of his soldiers. Not that it really mattered, since he was down, too, knew he was gut shot. Everything was murky and faraway in eyes tearing from blood splash, smoke and the biting hands of the fireballs that had nearly sucked the life out of him with their sheer force of thermonuclear-esque wind. He flopped down the short landing, rolling up in the crushed ruins of what used to be his favorite booth. Someone had tagged him with a lucky shot to the stomach, just as he was launching himself over the table when Wahjihab had beaten him to the draw.

All was lost, that much he was sure of. That the Arabs could have simply marched right in here, or were holed up in his own backyard, if Wahjihab was to be believed, meant he had a traitor in his own organization. With all the smoke filling the dining room, the thundering drum of weapons' fire sounding as if it would never end, and making out the strewed bodies all over the floor or dumped over tables, he had to believe he would never know who the informant was. He saw Answain, glazed stare looking him back, inches away. His top lieutenant had taken a bullet for him, for whatever damn good it now did anybody on the French side of this hell. There would be no successor, the kingdom crashing down in raging finality even as he bled out. He had to chuckle, then cut loose a bitter oath, even as the pain tore through his body. Rousiloux had won, the son of a bitch, even if someone else had done all the dirty work and all the dying for him, and by goddamn mistake of all the fickle whores of fate.

Still, there might be a chance he could either fight back, show the Arabs what going out in a blaze of glory was really all about, or simply crawl out of the building at the very least, regroup somehow, live to fight another day. The crazy Arabs had blown themselves up, taking out at least half of their own, if he had judged the close proximity of those martyrs to their fellow terrorists before the whole place went up like a supernova...

Hope? He had to know. He wasn't dead yet, and he had never backed down from a fight. And he hadn't become king of the underworld by turning the other cheek.

He saw his vision, fading, all sound, in and out, as he scrabbled through the debris, searching for a weapon. What the hell, he reasoned. Perhaps he had lived too long anyway. If the kingdom was to be obliterated on this night of murder and mayhem, it would be best if he died on his feet, and not try to slither out of there like some slug.

IT WAS A TURKEY SHOOT, no more, no less, for Manning and Hawkins. They waded into the warring factions, pretty much cutting loose on their blind side, picking off stray rats in the smoking barrel where and as they showed. Manning barely made out a few swarthy, bearded faces behind the walls of smoke, but it was enough of an al-Amin sighting to confirm his earlier speculation. It was a gift dumped in his lap by the smiling gods of war, so why not take what he could get in terms of any and all enemy kills?

Splitting off to Hawkins's left flank, the two Stony Man warriors began unloading 40 mm hellbombs, racking up a decent body count in two shakes. Whoever survived the suicide bombings were reeling about the dining room, clinging to the last shred of savage hope, firing away in all directions, basic spray and pray. Puchain's goons and the al-Amin fighters were going at it, nearly toe-to-toe, blasting away at each other in a raging in-your-face last stand. It made life that much easier for Manning and Hawkins to nail it down.

Two more big blasts rocked the dining room, bodies sailing all over the place, arms and legs and meaty chunks of human flesh flying around on all points.

One figure was up and running, Manning saw, and it looked as if he had hunkered down behind the bar. He was firing back into the mess on the main floor with an Uzi spray, then was gone to Manning's sight as some withering fire began seeking them out to claim the big Canadian's full attention.

Senses choked with smoke, blood and leaking guts, Manning rolled ahead, firing on the move. He spotted the trio of problems, staked out in front of the bar, swaying on their feet, trying in vain to hold it together, subguns shaking in bloodied hands. Manning blew them over the bar with a long hosing of autofire. French gangsters or Arab terrorists it didn't matter at that point. There was evil enough in this hell to make the Devil shout with glee.

Two wounded rats turned up in the ruins, weaving around, coming on just the same, and Manning and Hawkins finished them off with quick bursts to the chest, kicking them back through a cloud of smoke.

"T.J.! How we looking?"

"I think it's a wrap here, Gary."

"Stay alert. We had a runner."

"I saw him."

"You…"

He was parting the smoke when Manning found Puchain crawling out from under the pulverized shards of his table.

"Us, René," Manning said, filling his M-16 with a fresh mag. "Played it straight, this might not have happened."

"Wahjihab…"

Manning felt his heart rate speed up. It couldn't be, could it? he wondered. Was the rabbit the most wanted terrorist in the world?

"That's who caused this grief for you, René?"

"What's it matter…yes."

"Well, looks like your buddy, Vince Rousiloux, just became top dog in this town. Don't worry, René. You'll be seeing him in hell real soon."

Puchain looked set to curse when Manning drilled a 3-round burst into his chest, pinning him at the foot of the ruins of his favorite booth.

"Let's walk through it, Gary, see if we can find a jihad scumbag who might still give us a little insight about the Sword of Islam."

"I suggest speed, since even the police in Marseilles might not turn a deaf ear to this kind of fracas."

How HE'D CLEARED the gangster's palace, or what was left of it, hitting the streets, free and clear and heading for Vieux Port, was nothing short of divine intervention in his mind. God had willed he flee the fighting back there, leave the dying to lesser ranking jihad warriors. That much was clear to him, since he was still alive. After all, he had a future to consider, leadership to carry on, an entire Muslim world to save, in truth. Martyrdom sounded good when filling impressionable minds of young potential fighters for future battles, but in reality he didn't much think dying—at least his death—would bring the requisite vengeance against the infidels. Who wanted to die anyway? How could this war be won, total victory achieved, if those at the top and leading the legions of warriors blithely threw their lives away?

Not he. Not this night at least.

There was still a chance he could be chased down by the two mysterious shooters who had arrived late on the battle scene. It had been little more than a quick look, but he had seen them bulling into the battle, chewing up both sides with autofire and rockets, mopping up against unwitting and shell-shocked opposition. He suspected, the way the war had panned out, those two would be the only survivors. Who they were didn't matter in the final analysis, as long he didn't see them again.

It was most curious, he thought, how so far no sirens were sounding, but Puchain's place was massive, thick-walled, or maybe there were no police floating about the immediate neighborhoods. But this was Marseilles, after all, and even the police, he knew, didn't like to get their hands any dirtier than necessary unless they were taking money or feeling up a prostitute in place of a bribe. Meaning they'd rather take a few Euros, or get in some cheap kicks during their shift to look the other way if some gangster insisted they leave his turf alone, even if they heard reports of gunfire.

The streets and alleys began to clear of even skulking shadows as he saw the masts and lights of boats and pleasure craft in the distance. He wasn't going to *Heaven*. Instead he had devised an alternate way out of Marseilles that required a hike up the craggy cliff side to waiting brethren of al-Amin who would help him leave the country. Not even they knew his next destination. It was always smartest to never let even his most trusted brothers in jihad know his future plans. The infidel so-called Camp X-Ray was the best case in point of how knowledge could be turned against the cause. How many strikes against the West had been uncovered and foiled because Taliban and al-Qaeda prisoners had been let in on details of the sheikh's planned future strikes, blabbing away under interrogation, spilling out critical details that had aborted God's righteous missions? Too many, he knew. Lessons to be learned from past mistakes.

End of discussion.

Ideally he would have liked to have put more distance between himself and the doomed apartment building. But there were the two nameless warriors to consider. Say they gave chase, busting out the doors even now...

Why worry? Why wait?

Wahjihab pulled the second box, thumbed on the red light, turned so he could take in a view of the big bang.

NOTHING STIRRED in the carnage, not even a rat was twitching in the slaughterbed. It was over, but Manning had to wonder where in the hell it all went from there. Of course, there was still the runt whoremaster to deal with, and Manning was up for a quickie blast and burn before they boogied from Marseilles.

Manning and Hawkins were at the bar on the other side, the west face, the big Canadian thought, as he looked across the room where he'd seen who he believed was Wahjihab bolt the premises.

"I didn't get a good look, but he sure didn't look

like anything I've seen on some cable snippet about the world's most wanted terrorists. Or anything our people sent along, past pics, all that.''

Hawkins was searching the clinging shrouds of smoke, as if he half expected the Sword of Islam to come running at them in a suicide charge. ''Plastic surgery, that's what the Farm thought. It's the only way, with half the world's military, police and intelligence operatives hunting for his scalp, he could remain at large. Master of disguise, and with his money he could probably clone himself at some Russian Frankenstein lab in Siberia for all we know.''

''Hell, T.J., if what I saw was what I think I saw, I was looking at a guy who looked more like some Eurotrash business scoundrel than your standard sunbaked Mideast terrorist.''

Hawkins shrugged. ''We could spend three days here, Gary, scraping up blown-off fingers, figuring out which body parts belong to who, which is which. But I don't think this is the time for any lengthy forensics examination of the dead. If it was Wahjihab, he'll turn up at some point.''

''Okay, let's grab up what spare clips and 40 mm grenades we can find.''

''Rousiloux's next on the hit parade?'' Hawkins asked.

''Right. I've got some ideas on how—''

Manning was stepping away from the bar when he was sure the end of the world had just dropped on them from out of the sky. There was thunder, so loud, it seemed to split his skull, the noise alone nearly bowling him down, then the far wall blew in, a flying wave of rubble, fire and smoke swelling every inch in all directions. He wasn't sure what happened next, hoping Hawkins was in flight, going for cover behind the bar, but Manning didn't have time to shout or look for his warrior-comrade.

Gary Manning was hurling himself over the bar as a hurricane of debris, screaming fire and searing wind tore through the building like the sudden burst of the gates of hell spilling forth the damned.

THE NUMBERS, provided them by the DEA in Base Blastoff outside Nuevo Laredo, were in on Hernando Cordero. And the score sheet didn't include the two thousand head of cattle penned up to the west. Ranchero Cordero was a flimsy false front, erected by the Cordero cartel and backed by the usual parade of corrupt *federales* and politicians in Mexico City to hide the three hundred metric tons of cocaine, heroin and marijuana they smuggled across the border every year for the past five years. A chunk of that dope was also handed off to Arab terrorists to help finance their murder machine, pad their bank accounts around the world.

Al-Amin.

King Cordero and cronies were the next first logical links to sever on the hit list chain for Bolan and Able Team. The facts, gathered by a midlevel drug dealer in the Cordero organization, scooped up and playing ball now with the DEA, combined with aerial and satellite surveillance of the compound, were also in and tallied. It came complete with enemy numbers here, and the inside layout of the hacienda. This was a tear-and-torch job. But Bolan had come here, not only to bag and tag the ten hardmen guarding the roost, but to flag Cordero and the mysterious visitor he was playing host to as prisoners of war.

The nighttime desert world in this hardscrabble stretch of northeastern Mexico, fifty miles southwest of the Rio Grande, buzzed, rattled and howled with any variety of predators. It was tough going, getting it this far, their Hummer parked on the other side of some hills, but Bolan and Blancanales were almost to the low retaining wall surrounding the hacienda. Crabbing along on his elbows and knees, M-16/M-203 combo extended, Bolan watched the dark world through NVD goggles, alert for anything that might be attracted to his body heat.

The Executioner figured that by now, Pol, having taken a ten-minute crawl-crouch-jog start as planned, had made the south wall, was in position to go over the adobe barricade and start a wrecking ball-style assault. His job was to take out the motor pool of twelve vehicles, blast them through the front doors with Little Bulldozer. The backside—north—would be Bolan's point of blazing entry. Two Bell Jet-Rangers on the helipad would have to likewise go up in flaming scrap. There was a runway and small hangars farther north, but they would wait. In those hangars were two of the latest in high-tech smuggler's angels of white death. They were called Velocity, small planes, with fiberglass skin that could absorb radar, virtually invisible to ground and sky watchers. The Velocity toys did the bulk of delivering the poison across the borders these days for Cordero. Anybody making a run for those hangars…

Well, this night there would be no escape, no way out for the bad guys.

The word was King Cordero's special guest was unidentified, but believed by the DEA to be of Arab extraction. A snatch of two key components in the drug cartel-terror connection south of the border could go a long way, the soldier knew, in dismantling the whole al-Amin operation down here. A complete thrashing of the Cordero cartel would also be a major coup. It never hurt to bring along a few extra bullets, just in case.

A part of Bolan didn't like splitting up the team, having sent Lyons and Schwarz on ahead to Ciudad Zapulcha to hole up, sit tight and watch what the DEA tagged as a wild town. They were to rendezvous with a DEA informant called El Condor, who supposedly was a gold mine of intelligence, specifically keyed in to a meeting in the wings between North Korean operatives and al-Amin thugs.

The Executioner reached the wall, stood, stripped off his NVD headgear and stowed it in a small nylon pouch. He knew there would be sensors, motion detectors, cameras…

This was no stealth strike.

This was straight-on bulldozing.

He keyed his com link. "Striker to Politician, come in."

"Politician here, Striker."

The wall rounded to the south, so Bolan couldn't see Blancanales, but figured he was in place, ready to scale and start blasting.

"You set?"

"Just give the word, Striker."

"Let's rock."

The Executioner reached up, grabbed the top of the wall and hauled himself up and over, hit the ground as silent as a ghost. He had already seen the three armed shadows near the north edge of the hacienda on the way down and in. They were still milling about, so the Executioner rolled their way. Floodlights bathed the grounds, but he did his best to try to keep to the shadows as he vectored for the helipad. Even still he was swathed in some outreaching glow. The hardmen spotted him on the march, began shouting, flapping their arms, a cigarette arcing away, when the Executioner squeezed the trigger.

CHAPTER TWENTY-ONE

Hamid Furqan couldn't decide which peoples of either Mexico or the United States he despised more, but began to think it was pretty much a toss-up. North of the border the infidels wallowed in the lap of obscene wealth, flaunting it for all the world to see and envy, while their neighbors to the south lived in abject, hateful poverty. It was a glaring disparity in wealth, he supposed, that made the Mexicans view the Yankees in either awe, wanting to have what they had, live like they did, or outright hold them in jealous hatred. The latter emotion toward the Americans—without the envy part—he could understand, and he didn't suffer from the Mexican schizophrenic view of the United States. The Americans, in essence, had not only occupied his own country, but they treated Mexicans with the same contempt, he believed, they did any and all Arabs, even the ones they lied to and claimed were their friends. In both countries, however, they still worshiped money, and where there was love of money there was also crime. Love of money was something that Furqan understood, likewise the crime that came with it, though he didn't view his own need for quick, big truckloads of cash as anything other than a desire to support the altruistic vision of jihad. Love of money, though, tended to motivate men to do things they might not normally do to attain it, and when they had it they would do anything to hold on to it. In short, it more often than not brought out the worst in men, and it didn't matter if it was his own homeland of Saudi Arabia, or some drug lord's estate in the middle of a Mexican desert.

Money was the next best thing to God, he knew, the world over.

The trouble was, money was all the pig with the oily black hair, sweaty mustache and the black eyes of a vulture could think or talk about. The bigger problem facing him, however, was that Furqan needed a few quick bucks, and he was about to put his hand out to this pig for quite the sizeable loan.

How to artfully word the approach? he wondered. He was in deep trouble, the hour of doom at hand, and he began to think maybe this was no time to be tactful or even polite.

For hours on end now, though, Furqan had sat patiently in the huge gaming room, listening to the drug lord glorifying his rags to riches story, a poor fatherless thief in the streets of some tumbleweed hell in Sonora, where he was responsible for raising six brothers and five sisters, five of whom had died of starvation and disease or were the victims of murder by the time he was twelve. He had shut his ears to most of it, all the climb-to-the-top talk, how much the Mexican was worth in dollar terms, who he owned, how much he was a man of respect, watching with mounting agitation but nodding and smiling where appropriate at all this bluster and bravado.

Sickening.

He wished now he hadn't come here alone, but he couldn't spare any of his soldiers for reasons he needed to discuss with Hernando Cordero. So he was stuck, forced to play the role of the humble guest while the drug lord drank rum, smoked Havana cigars, snorted white lines, sweated it out from too much booze and cocaine, laughed like some hyena and shot pool with his top lieutenant. They were playing straight pool, a hundred dollars U.S. per made shot. The drug lord's mood began to sour the more he lost, the more cocaine he snuffed up, getting edgy, volatile. He began to shake, from either simmering violence or too much coke, spilling his drink on the green felt, flicking ashes everywhere. Once a thief and a pig, Furqan thought, always a thief and pig, even if he now wrapped himself in hundred-dollar bills, the world all his.

The Saudi, known as the Negotiator, figured it was just about time to broach the two subjects he had come here to discuss, but he wondered if there would ever be a good time to drop the bomb about money with Cordero, the man already some borderline psychotic poisoned mess.

"I came here," Furqan said, as the drug lord cursed, missing an easy shot to the side pocket, slamming his stick on the table, "because I am going to need some assistance with the North Koreans."

Cordero froze. "Aha! I have heard about your problems, amigo. I have heard the tales how you paid the North Koreans with counterfeit money. Lucky for you that you did not do the same to me, or you would be staked out in the desert sun for the ants and the scorpions to eat your eyeballs out. Yes, I know their operatives are in my country, in Acapulco, I understand from my own sources, looking for you—"

"They are closer than you think. They are en route, as we speak, to Ciudad Zapulcha to meet with my men there."

The black eyes bored into Furqan. "I hear worry in your voice, my friend. You have made them angry, you have cheated them, and now they want blood."

"I do not want a war with the North Koreans. They have something I desperately need. I lost a most valuable shipment, but I can get more of the merchandise that was seized by the Americans. I need some time, though. I can pay, I can make sufficient reparations to the North Koreans, but I need a small favor from you. Actually I need two favors."

Now he had the drug lord's full attention. Favors meant bartering, someone getting the upper hand, and Cordero surely believed he was a master at coming out on top of any negotiation.

Degenerate pig, Furqan thought, then decided the man was more like a snake.

Cordero leaned the cue stick against the table, ran a hairy, sweaty hand over the ample gut nearly sticking out of his silk robe. He smiled, but there was a dangerous glint in the Mexican drug lord's eyes.

"You are in trouble, so you come to your old friend, Hernando Cordero. Hernando Cordero, who has blessed you and your organization with enough white powder, with more phony visas and passports, connected you to more important men of power in this country to allow you to even be and stay here, unmolested by the *federales* and the American DEA and FBI. I am counting up at least twenty or more favors already owed in my mind. I ask myself, 'now what?' Am I a fool? How much more can I give before I receive?"

It galled Furqan to sit there, practically forced to beg and grovel. Had the shipment reached him safely, had he picked up all that counterfeit Mexican currency...

Too late to curse and cry now. Perhaps war was unavoidable. Perhaps he would be forced to ride back to Ciudad Zapulcha and put an ultimatum to the North Koreans. If he couldn't get his hands on the final product he needed from the Asians...

Well, any future drones would just prove big steel shells, useless junk, even if they were stuffed with the most deadly virus know to man.

"How much money, my friend? And how much interest, if I say yes, is in it for me?"

He already had the figure on the tip of his tongue, an outrageous sum that not even a greedy buzzard like Cordero could turn down when—

The series of explosions shook the walls and jolted Furqan out of his seat. Out of respect for Cordero and his home he had left his pistol and assault rifle in his

Jeep. Now they were being attacked, and he was without defense. Two of Cordero's armed guards charged into the room. They were in a panic, shooting off a stream of rapid-fire Spanish, which, having lived as long as he had in Mexico, Furqan had no trouble understanding.

"Where? How many?"

Cordero looked set to burst out of his skin.

"I do not know! They are attacking from everywhere! Perhaps twenty, or thirty men at least! It has to be!"

Cordero was hammering his second in command on the shoulders, roaring at him to go take care of the situation. As the drug lord held his ground, staring at nothing, Furqan had a sick, sinking feeling the trouble that had besieged the operatives of al-Amin in America had found him.

The sound of thunderous blasts kept rocking the walls of the hacienda, seemed to grow closer with each rolling peal. He knew they had to do something, even if that meant fleeing the premises.

"I suggest," he practically shouted at Cordero, "that we do something besides stand here!"

"Yes, yes! Hurry! My men will fight them off while we take one of the helicopters!"

Furqan fought off the sneer. The man wanted to run, instead of standing his ground, defending his empire. He began to wonder about all that blustering machismo Cordero had just been spouting off about. He began to think too much money had made him too soft, careless, and that maybe he deserved to lose all he had. Under the circumstances, since they'd been hit in a shock attack by an unknown force and who knew how many shooters, it seemed the only option.

"You can fly?"

"But of course!"

Furqan was dubious but too damn angry and afraid to question the truth behind the statement.

THE MORE THE MISSION ground on, the more the pace to get to and burn down the enemy accelerated. Or so it seemed to Blancanales.

He had his standing orders from Bolan, which was to take the drug kingpin alive, but that didn't mean the hired help was exempt from his killing touch.

As the motor pool was vaporized to flaming and flying trash before his eyes, he figured he had cut down two hardmen in the rolling wave of fireballs, Little Bulldozer was smoking in his hands now, having just bellowed volumes about rough justice for drug dealing scum who also held hands with terrorists. Figure intel had the hardforce pegged at ten to twelve, and figure the Executioner was already tagging a few goons on his own, and Blancanales could feel victory within his grasp.

He couldn't afford to get cocky yet, since he still had to breach the front door, get inside and bag himself a drug lord and a suspected al-Amin operative, a guest of Cordero's.

Blancanales had done all the damage he could to the motor pool, sheets of flaming wreckage pounding the front facade, winging off pillars.

Time to move inside.

If anybody was going to break for freedom, they would be doing it on foot.

Blancanales marched ahead, slung Little Bulldozer across his shoulder, filled his hands with the M-16/M-203 combo. He was skirting past the roaring flames, his nose choked with the stink of torched gasoline, when two hardmen came racing out the front door.

They never saw Blancanales, never knew what hit them as the Stony Man warrior mowed them down before they even got off a shot.

Two more in the bag.

Getting better all the time.

AFTER MOWING DOWN the trio at the corner, then blasting the choppers clear off the helipad with a double 40 mm launching, the Executioner patched in for a quick check with Blancanales. Sitrep in, and he had a head count of enemy down.

Three to go, if the DEA was right, so why not torque up the heat, he figured, go in blasting.

Another 40 mm hellbomb down the chute, and the Executioner blew in the bay window with a fireball that would have taken out anything in at least a thirty-yard radius beyond. With that in mind he charged into the smoke. Clearing the swirling cloud, he made out voices, tearing up the vicinity with shouting and cursing from some point down a wide hallway. Coming from the south end, he figured the living room was where any survivors were left standing.

Bolan figured he could help them decide.

He was running hard, combat senses cranked up, when he burst into the sprawling living room. One armed shadow, back turned to Bolan, seemed to be arguing with the foursome on a landing that was swathed in tropical vegetation. He had the face of Hernando Cordero branded to memory, likewise the mystery guest, but the other two he figured for hired guns.

The warrior triggered a short burst of autofire up the shouter's spine, flinging him over a white leather couch big enough to seat a hundred people.

"No shoot! No shoot! I am unarmed!"

Cordero, blubbering to be spared, thrust his arms into the air.

The standing goons were pulling their act together, swinging assault rifles toward Bolan when Blancanales mimicked the soldier's back-shooting entrance. They were kicked down the landing, all flailing arms and angry howls, when the mystery guest went berserk. Whoever he was, the man was screaming something, bending and snapping up a discarded rifle when Bolan and Blancanales scythed through him in a cross-fire hurricane.

"No!" Cordero screamed. "Don't shoot me! No gun!"

"No problem if you cooperate," the Executioner said, long strides carrying him toward the kingpin, his eyes scanning the offshooting hallways for any signs of menacing life. "How many here, Cordero?"

"Ten!"

"Including you?"

"That would make eleven."

"If you're lying…"

"I am not lying!"

"Pol, cuff him."

"You are Americans? I am under arrest?"

"No," the Executioner said, saw the dark confusion and fear shadow the drug lord's face, as Blancanales pulled his arms down and fastened the plastic cuffs. "Arrest could end up being the least of your problems."

"IT AIN'T MIAMI, is it, Carl?"

Lyons lowered the infrared field glasses, scowled at Schwarz. It wasn't any time for smart-ass, but Lyons skipped making any snappy comeback. Voices tended to carry in the desert for one thing. Second, they weren't more than fifty yards on the north end from the hellhole called Ciudad Zapulcha.

And the place where the big powwow was supposed to go down was crawling with armed shadows.

Being a former cop, Lyons knew all about stakeouts, the whole watch-and-wait game where if a man wasn't careful he could let his vigilance down, maybe even nod off while the bad guys did whatever it was they were going to do. Even sneak up and start blasting away at the watchers.

They were stretched out on their bellies on the ridgeline of a low hill, their Hummer parked in a gully behind their roost. Both Stony Man warriors were togged in blacksuit, with M-16/M-203 pieces within easy reach, side arms snugged away, grenades slotted in the pouches of their combat vests. Even at that late hour, Lyons spied more shadows than he could count, all clearly armed, milling—or patrolling the squalid town proper—most of the activity confined to what the intel pics had nailed down as the cantina.

They had been out there, the better part of an hour, waiting for their DEA informant, the guy with all the right answers, Lyons sarcastically thought, to come rolling their way out of the night. They were in the rendezvous spot the DEA special agent had told them El Condor would come to them bearing whatever the news. Striker's orders were to survey the town, watch for the alleged North Korean contingent that was supposed to meet with al-Amin terrorists. It was their call, Bolan had told them, whether they went in if and when any shooting began, muscle their way into the killing field.

Lyons checked his watch. If all fell according to plan—and these days it rarely did—Bolan and Blancanales should have wrapped up their blitz by now, en route to join the stakeout.

"We've got a visitor."

Lyons saw the dark shape of a van heading their way, vectoring slowly from the southwest, the pre-arranged direction. El Condor, or so he hoped. But it could be anybody, since the DEA had informed them all this patch of outlaw country was alive with bandits, immigrants on the move for the border, and every type of bad guy from drug smugglers to...

Badlands.

It ain't Miami, Lyons thought. Hell, it wasn't even South Central L.A., which, from what little he'd seen and heard about Ciudad Zapulcha was the choicest R and R spot between the two.

The van killed its headlights. Lyons and Schwarz took up arms, waiting as a slight figure stepped out, began walking their way.

"Hold it right there," Lyons called out as quietly as possible.

"The mothership has landed."

Lyons heaved a breath. The password business always sounded hokey, leaving him to wonder where the clowns who thought up this nonsense got their material. Still, it determined who was who, and often saved the lives of operatives in the field.

"And it's coming to take the bad guys away."

Lyons and Schwarz stood, allowing the dark shape to cut the gap until they were feet apart.

"You'd better be this El Condor," Lyons said.

"Who else would I be?"

"You can call me L."

"S."

"Señors L and S. I have good news and I have bad news. Good news—the North Koreans are less than two miles out and on the way to meet with the terrorists in the cantina."

When he hesitated, Lyons growled, "The bad news?"

El Condor hesitated, and Lyons nearly shouted, his gut rumbling telling him the bad news was monster bad news.

"I fear I have been made as an informant for the DEA. I fear that, even as we speak, some very bad hombres from town have spotted me coming to meet you, and they are on the way to punch our tickets."

Lyons corrected himself. This was the mother behemoth of bad news.

* * * * *

The heart-stopping action
concludes in ECHOES OF WAR,
Book II of THE TERROR FILE,
Available October 2003.

DEATH LANDS®

Devil Riders

JAMES AXLER

DEATH LANDS

Devil Riders

*Available in September 2003
at your favorite retail outlet.*

Stranded in the salty desert wastes of West Texas, hopes for a hot meal and clean bed in an isolated ville die fast when Ryan and his companions run into a despotic baron manipulating the lifeblood of the desert: water. But it's his fortress stockpiled with enough armaments to wage war in the dunes that interests Ryan, especially when he learns the enemy may be none other than the greatest—and long dead—Deathlands legend: the Trader.

GOLD EAGLE®

GDL63

James Axler
Outlanders®

SEA OF
PLAGUE

The loyalties that united the Cerberus warriors have become
undone, as a bizarre messenger from the future provides a look
into encroaching horror and death. Kane and his band have one
option: fix two fatal fault lines in the time continuum—and rewrite
history before it happens. But first they must restore power to the
barons who dare to defy the greater evil: the mysterious new
Imperator. Then they must wage war in the jungles of India, where
the deadly, beautiful Scorpia Prime and her horrifying bio-weapon
are about to drown the world in a sea of plague....

In the Outlands, the shocking truth is humanity's last hope.

THE Destroyer®

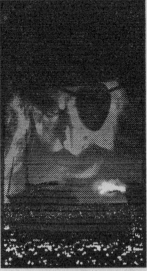

TROUBLED WATERS

Thomas "Captain" Kidd is the new scourge of the Caribbean, and when he and his crew kidnap the daughter of a senator, CURE sets out to kick some serious pirate booty. Posing as rich tourists, Remo and Chiun set a course for the tropics to tempt these freebooters into the mistake of their career. But Remo soon finds himself swimming with sharks, while Chiun senses some illicit treasure in his future. Even so, they are ready to dispatch the sea raiders to an afterlife between the devil and the deep blue sea.

Available in October 2003 at your favorite retail outlet.

James Axler
Outlanders®

AWAKENING

Cryogenically preserved before the nukes obliterated their own way of life, an elite team of battle-hardened American fighting men has now been reactivated. Their first mission in a tortured new world: move in and secure Cerberus Redoubt and the mattrans network at any cost. In a world where trust is hard won and harder kept, Kane and his fellow exiles must convince Team Phoenix that they are on the same side—for humanity, and against the hybrids and their willing human allies.

In the Outlands, the shocking truth is humanity's last hope.

GOUT27